ALL AMERICA IS READING
BAD BOY BRAWLY BROWN,
THE NATIONAL BESTSELLER ON . . .

USA Today	*San Francisco Chronicle*
Wall Street Journal	*Los Angeles Times*
Washington Post	*BookSense*
Publishers Weekly	

> A *USA Today* Book Club Selection
> Selected as One of the Best Books of the Year
> by the *Los Angeles Times*

"Vivid . . . It's good to see Mosley return in masterful style, not as a writer of marvelously drawn mysteries, but in a wider sense, as a knowing chronicler of racial experiences and aspirations. It's a heavy load to lay on a ghetto guy, but Easy does it."
— *New York Daily News*

"An excellent book, perhaps the best in the series."
— *Atlantic Monthly*

"Mosley plays it just right . . . leaves us eager for more."
— *Los Angeles Times Book Review*

more . . .

"Built around a genuine puzzle that's never gimmicky or predictable . . . With his eye-opening metaphors and tough-yet-vulnerable dialogue, Mosley is the best living stylist among action writers. But dig a bare level down and you'll find him treating serious concerns as thoughtfully as any writer of literary novels."

— *Newsday*

"Skillful . . . as always, Mosley has a flair for the times as well as the crimes." — *People*

"The racial politics (and the colorful re-creation of a vanished time) complement a first-rate detective yarn without overwhelming it." — *Time Out New York*

"Easy Rawlins makes a very welcome return . . . As always, Mosley illuminates time and place with a precision few writers can match . . . He also delivers a rousing good story and continues to captivate with characters readers have grown to love."

— *Publishers Weekly* (starred review)

"Another intricate layer to this complex character . . . Both old and new readers will enjoy this latest tale."

— *San Antonio Express-News*

"Poignant . . . a powerful human drama and a vividly re-created historical moment." — *Booklist*

more . . .

"Mosley's stripped-down, thoughtful prose is always a joy to read."
— *Seattle Times*

"Easy returns more complex and compelling than ever before, a hero for his time and ours." — *Kirkus Reviews* (starred review)

"This book's a winner . . . What keeps us turning the pages is a realistic, believable, compelling hero . . . as good as it gets."
— *Denver Rocky Mountain News*

"Mosley's sharp eye for the various nuances of race in America combines with his attention-holding plot and three-dimensional characters." — *Pittsburgh Post-Gazette*

"As usual, Mosley, a master of precise prose, makes Easy's journey a captivating read . . . While Mosley deftly explores the crevices of the soul with Easy, his protagonist's struggle illuminates our own."
— *Nashville Tennessean*

"Easy reading, great writing . . . Mosley has something many other mystery writers have never heard of — a sense of history. He uses this gift well." — *Newark Star-Ledger*

"Wonderful . . . full of suspense . . . engaging, entertaining, and enlightening from the first page to the last."
— *Hartford Courant*

WALTER MOSLEY

BAD BOY
BRAWLY BROWN

GRAND CENTRAL
PUBLISHING

NEW YORK   BOSTON

For Leroy Mosley

———

Grand Central Publishing Edition
Copyright © 2002 by Walter Mosley

This Grand Central Publishing edition is published by arrangement with Little, Brown and Company, 237 Park Avenue, New York, NY 10017.

Grand Central Publishing
Hachette Book Group USA
237 Park Avenue
New York, NY 10017

Visit our Web site at www.HachetteBookGroupUSA.com.

Printed in the United States of America

First Grand Central Publishing Trade Edition: August 2008
10 9 8 7 6 5 4 3 2 1

Grand Central Publishing is a division of Hachette Book Group USA, Inc. The Grand Central Publishing name and logo is a trademark of Hachette Book Group USA, Inc.

The Library of Congress has cataloged the hardcover edition as follows:
Mosley, Walter.
    Bad Boy Brawly Brown : an Easy Rawlins novel / by Walter Mosley — 1st ed.
        p. cm.
    ISBN 0-316-07301-6
        1. Rawlins, Easy (Fictitious character) — Fiction. 2. African American men — Fiction. 3. Los Angeles (Calif.) — Fiction. I. Title.

    PS3563.O88456 B43 2002
    813'.54 — dc21   2002016232

ISBN 978-0-446-19822-6 (pbk.)

Designed by Cassandra J. Pappas

Bad Boy
Brawly Brown

1/ MOUSE IS DEAD. Those words had gone through my mind every morning for three months. *Mouse is dead because of me.*

When I sat up, Bonnie rolled her shoulder and sighed in her sleep. The sky through our bedroom window was just beginning to brighten.

The image of Raymond, his eyes open and unseeing, lying stock-still on EttaMae's front lawn, was still in my mind. I lurched out of bed and stumbled to the bathroom. My feet hurt every morning, too, as if I had spent all night walking, searching for EttaMae, to ask her where she'd taken Ray after carrying him out of the hospital.

So he was still alive? I asked a nurse who had been on duty that evening.

No, she said flatly. *His pulse was gone. The head nurse had just called the doctor to pronounce him dead when that crazy woman hit*

Arnold in the head with a suture tray and took Mr. Alexander's body over her shoulder.

I wandered into the living room and pulled the sash to open the drapes. Red sunlight glinted through the ragged palms at the end of our block. I had never wept over Raymond's demise, but that tattered light reflected a pain deep in my mind.

*I*T TOOK ME over half an hour to get dressed. No two socks matched and every shirt seemed to be the wrong color. While I was tying my shoes Bonnie woke up.

"What are you doing, Easy?" she asked. She had been born in British Guyana but her father was from Martinique, so there was the music of the French language in her English accent.

"Gettin' dressed," I said.

"Where are you going?"

"Where you think I'ma be goin' at this time'a day? To work." I was feeling mean because of that red light in the far-off sky.

"But it's Saturday, baby."

"What?"

Bonnie climbed out of the bed and hugged me. Her naked skin was firm and warm.

I pulled away from her.

"You want some breakfast?" I asked.

"Maybe a little later," she said. "I didn't get in from Idlewild until two this morning. And I have to go back out again today."

"Then you go to bed," I said.

"You sure? I mean . . . did you need to talk?"

"Naw. Nuthin's wrong. Just stupid is all. Thinkin' Saturday's a workday. Damn."

"Are you going to be okay?" she asked.

"Yeah. Sure I am."

Bonnie had a fine figure. And she was not ashamed to be seen naked. Looking at her pulling on those covers reminded me of why I fell for her. If I hadn't been so sad, I would have followed her back under those blankets.

*F*EATHER'S LITTLE YELLOW DOG, Frenchie, was hiding somewhere, snarling at me while I made sausages and eggs. He was the love of my little girl's life, so I accepted his hatred. He blamed me for the death of Idabell Turner, his first owner; I blamed myself for the death of my best friend.

I WAS SITTING at breakfast, smoking a Chesterfield and wondering if EttaMae had moved back down to Houston. I still had friends down there in the Fifth Ward. Maybe if I wrote to Lenora Circel and just dropped a line about Etta — *say hi to Etta for me* or *give Etta my love*. Then when she wrote back I might learn something.

"Hi, Dad."

My hand twitched, flicking two inches of cigarette ash on the eggs.

Jesus was standing there in front of me.

"I told you not to sneak up on me like that, boy."

"I said hi," he explained.

The eggs were ruined but I wasn't hungry. And I couldn't stay mad at Jesus, anyway. I might have taken him in when he was a child, but the truth was that *he* had adopted *me*. Jesus worked hard at making our home run smoothly, and his love for me was stronger than blood.

"What you doin' today?" I asked him.

"Nuthin'. Messin' around."

"Sit down," I said.

Jesus didn't move the chair as he sat, because there was enough room for him to slide in under the table. He never wasted a movement — or a word.

"I wanna drop out of high school," he said.

"Say what?"

His dark eyes stared into mine. He had the smooth, eggshell-brown skin and the straight black hair of people who had lived in the Southwest for thousands of years.

"It's only a year and a half till you graduate," I said. "A diploma will help you get a job. And if you keep up with track, you could get a scholarship to UCLA."

He looked down at my hands.

"Why?" I asked.

"I don't know," he said. "I just don't wanna be there. I don't wanna be there all the time."

"You think I like goin' to work?"

"You like it enough," he said. "'Cause if you didn't like it, you'd quit."

I could see that he'd made up his mind, that he'd thought about this decision for a long time. He probably had the papers for me to sign under his bed.

I was about to tell him no, that he'd have to stick out the year at least. But then the phone rang. It was a loud ringer, especially at six-thirty in the morning.

While I limped to the counter Jesus left on silent bare feet.

"Hello?"

"Easy?" It was a man's voice.

"John? Is that you?"

"I'm in trouble and I need you to do me a favor," John said all in a rush. He'd been practicing just like Jesus.

My heart quickened. The little yellow dog stuck his nose out from under the kitchen cabinet.

I don't know if it was an old friend's voice or the worry in his tone that got to me. But all of a sudden I wasn't miserable or sad.

"What you need, John?"

"Why'ont you come over to the lots, Easy? I wanna look you in the eye when I tell ya what we want."

"Oh," I said, thinking about *we* and the fact that whatever John had to say was too serious to be discussed over the phone. "Sure. As soon as I can make it."

I hung up with a giddy feeling running around my gut. I could feel the grin on my lips.

"Who was that?" Bonnie asked. She was standing at the door to our bedroom, half wrapped in a terry-cloth robe. She was more beautiful than any man could possibly deserve.

"John."

"The bartender?"

"Do you have to leave today?" I asked.

"Sorry. But after this trip I'll have a whole week off."

"I can't wait that long," I said.

I gathered her up in my arms and carried her back into the bedroom.

"Easy, what are you doing?"

I tossed her on the bed and then closed the door to the kitchen. I took off my pants and stood over her.

"Easy, what's got into you?"

The look on my face was answer enough for any arguments she might have had about the children or her need for sleep.

I couldn't have explained my sudden passion. All I knew was the smell of that woman, her taste and texture on my skin and tongue, was something I had never known before in my life. It was as if I discovered sex for the first time that morning.

2 / *JESUS, FEATHER, BONNIE, AND I* sat down to breakfast at nine o'clock. Jesus had made the pancakes from a mix while we were still in bed, proving once more that he was a better son than I deserved.

"Those pancakes were delicious," Bonnie said to the boy.

"I'm dropping out of school," he replied.

"Do it hurt if you drop?" Feather asked, and then she giggled.

I snickered and Bonnie gave me a hard look.

"When did you decide that?" Bonnie asked.

"I 'ont know," he said. "Lately."

"Did you know about this, Easy?"

"He told me this morning."

"What do you think?"

"I think we have to talk about it."

Jesus chose that moment to stand up and walk out of the kitchen.

It was a rare show of anger on his part. I wanted to stop him, make him come back to the table and discuss his education. But I still felt feverish and giddy. I wanted to run from the room, too.

"Jesus," Bonnie called. But he pretended not to hear.

"Juice, wait up," little Feather screamed. She jumped out of her chair and ran for the door.

"Feather," I said.

She stopped and turned around. She was full-faced but not chubby, with bushy blond hair, light skin, and Negro features. She was another man's child but I was the only father that she had ever known.

"Um . . . ah . . . ," she stammered. "May I be excused?"

"Go on," I said, and she was gone.

Frenchie ran after her. The screen door was already closed but he scratched at it until it bounced open, then ran to find his little-girl master.

When I looked over at Bonnie I found her gazing at me as if I were some Martian just dropped out of the Twilight Zone.

"What's wrong with you, Easy?"

"He just sprung it on me this morning," I explained. "And I know Juice. If you tell him no straight out, he won't do any homework or he might even try to get in trouble so they have to expel him."

"So you just let him throw his life away?"

"I have to talk to him, honey. I have to see what his problem is. Maybe we can work something out."

I was no longer grinning, but there was a carefree tone in my words.

"It's not just Jesus. You're acting very strange this morning," Bonnie said.

"Strange? When's the last time I made you feel that good?"

"You never made me feel like that before," she said. Her dark eyes were large and filled with concern. The shape of Bonnie Shay's face contained the continent of Africa. Those eyes saw in me things that I could barely imagine.

"Well then, what you complainin' about?"

She reached across the table, binding my arms with hers.

"What's wrong?" The question gained a lot of weight the second time around.

"Nuthin's wrong. I just decided to come back to bed and love my woman — that's all." I tried to pull away but she was too strong. "And I know how to deal with my own boy."

"What did John want?"

"I don't know. Really. He just said that he needed a favor and that I should come on down to his lots. It's probably just a construction thing. I know a lot more about that kinda stuff than John does."

"You told me that he's hardly called you in the last year," Bonnie said.

Her grip loosened slightly. I took the advantage to pull away. "So?"

"Isn't that what you said you used to do?" she asked.

"What are you talkin' about?"

"Favors. Didn't you say that you used to trade in favors? That before you had honest work, you used to help people when they couldn't go to the authorities?"

"It ain't nuthin' like that here," I said. "John's an old friend, that's all."

"What are you doing making love to me three times this morning? Why are you just sitting there smiling while your son tells you that he's dropping out of high school?"

I heard her questions but they didn't mean anything to me. If I thought she'd've let me, I would have taken her back into the bedroom for number four.

"I guess the love kinda built up. You know, I been so tired at night."

"You've been sad, Easy. Sad because of your friend. I don't care that you need to grieve."

That was too much. I stood up, hoping that the air would be cooler above my head. In the few months since Raymond's death I had come closer to Bonnie than I ever had with a woman. She knew my dreams and property holdings, but I could not talk to her about my impotence — my failure to save Mouse's life.

"It's okay. Nuthin's wrong. I was just a little confused when I woke up. It just kinda threw me off, that's all."

Bonnie stood up and caressed my face with her fingers, then shook her head slowly and shrugged. It was her way of saying that a fool was his own worst enemy.

"I'm going to be gone for three or four days," she said. "Depending on the layovers and weather."

"Oh. Yeah."

"I told you that I'd have to be gone for days at a time now and then," she said sweetly.

Bonnie and I hadn't been together long. She moved in with me only a week after Mouse had died, but already I found myself aimless and unsatisfied when she was away.

"That's okay," I said. "Just don't forget where home is."

"Don't *you* forget who loves you," she said.

3 / I DROVE MY NEW USED PONTIAC with all the windows down and a Chesterfield cigarette between my lips. Somewhere, way in the back of my mind, there was an alarm going off. It was like the uneasy feeling after a nightmare that you can't remember. The worry had no picture, so it was more like a suspicion than fear. At the same time I was happy to be driving toward someone else's troubles. The sensation of delight on top of anxiety made me smile. It was a grin that represented a whole lifetime of laughing at pain.

*J*OHN'S LOTS were on an unpaved street that hadn't been properly named yet. There was a sign where the street name should have been that read A229-B. John was building six homes, three on either side of the street. He was part of a syndicate put together by Jew-elle MacDonald, the girlfriend of my real estate agent, Mofass.

Mofass had been dying from emphysema for the past few years. The doctors gave him three months to live about every six months or so. But Jewelle kept him going and made the few shanty houses he owned into nearly a real estate empire. Jewelle had put together six or seven colored businessmen to invest, along with a downtown real estate firm, in a couple of blocks under construction in Compton.

John was standing out in front of the first of his houses on the north side of the road. The straw hat, T-shirt, and blue jeans looked wrong on him. John was a night man, a bartender from the time he was sixteen in Texas. He was taller, stronger, and blacker than I, ugly enough to be beautiful and silent as a stone.

"Hey, John," I said from the car window. My tires had kicked up a low-riding mist of red and yellow dust.

"Easy."

I got out and nodded at him. That was all the greeting old friends like us needed.

"Nice-lookin' frame, anyway," I said waving at the unfinished wooden structure behind him.

"It sure is gonna be nice," he said. "They all comin' along good. Mercury an' Chapman workin' out just fine."

John gestured and I saw the two men across the street. Chapman was hammering at a beam near the roof of one house while Mercury pushed a wheelbarrow full of debris. Both men were ex-burglars I'd helped out in my old life of doing favors. They used to make their liv-ing by tunneling into businesses the night before payday, when the safe was sure to be full of cash.

It was a good living, and they weren't greedy — two jobs a year kept them in groceries. But one day they decided to hit a dockwork-ers' payroll in Redondo Beach. That safe had too much money for the payroll, and within a week there were white men in cheap suits canvassing Watts, looking for the whereabouts of the two black burglars who specialized in payrolls.

When they realized their situation, Mercury came to me.

"How could you be stupid enough to knock over the dockworkers?" I asked him. Chapman had been so scared that he refused to leave his mother's house.

"How we gonna know that they was mob men, Mr. Rawlins?"

"By the way they shoot you in back'a your head," I said.

Mercury moaned and I felt for him. Even if he had been a white man, there would have been little hope for his survival.

When I called the shop steward at the dockworkers' union, he laughed at me. That is, until I told him that I was coming down there with Raymond "Mouse" Alexander. Even the criminals in the white community had heard about Mouse.

I wore denim overalls the night of the meeting. Mercury's and Chapman's clothes were so nondescript that I can't even remember the colors. But Mouse wore a butter-cream gabardine suit. He was a killing man, then and always, but back then Mouse didn't question himself, didn't wonder at all.

"They made a mistake, Bob," Mouse said to the man who had introduced himself as Mr. Robert. He wore a long coat and hat and stood over Mouse, who, already a smallish man, was seated.

"That's not enough —," Mr. Robert began in his guttural, East Coast snarl.

Before he could finish, Mouse leapt to his feet, pulled out his long-nosed .41-caliber pistol, and shot the hat right off of Robert's head. The two men who stood behind him gestured toward their guns but changed their minds when they looked down the barrel of Mouse's smoking piece.

Mr. Robert was on the floor, feeling for blood under his toupee.

"So like I was sayin', Bob," Mouse continued. "They made a mistake. They didn't know that you was who you is. They didn't know that. Did you, boys?"

"No, sir!" Mercury shouted like a buck private at roll call. He was a bulky man with cheeks so fat that they made his head resemble a shiny black pear.

"Uh-uh," Chapman, the lighter-skinned, smaller, and smarter of the two, grunted.

"So . . ." Mouse smiled.

The shop steward and the three thugs, all of them white men, had their eyes on him. You could see that they wanted to kill him. Each one was thinking that they probably had the upper hand in numbers of guns. And each one knew that the first one to move would die.

I was biting my tongue because I hadn't expected a fight. I brought Raymond around for weight, not for violence. Why would those men get angry if we wanted to return their money? Along with the insurance from the legal payroll, they'd make a nice profit on the deal.

"All me an' my friends need to know is what the finder's fee is," Mouse said.

"You must be crazy, nigger," Robert said.

Mouse pulled the hammer back on his pistol as he asked, "What did you say?"

The thug was looking up into Mouse's steel-gray eyes. He saw something there.

"Ten percent," he uttered.

Mouse smiled.

We walked out of the beachside warehouse with $3,500 in our pockets. Mouse gave five hundred each to Mercury and Chapman and split the remainder with me.

The burglars gave up their life of crime that very day. I'd never seen anything like it. Usually a thief stays a thief; either that or he becomes a jailbird. But those men set down roots and started a new life. They married two sisters, Blesta and Jolie Ridgeway, and went to work in construction.

When I heard that John was building, I got them together. Jewelle had set up a traveling crew of workers who went from one site to another among her various investors. But each work site needed a couple of permanent employees to do detail work and prepare for the larger jobs.

". . . and every house gonna be different, too," John was saying. "Brick, aluminum-sided, wood and plaster. One-, two-, and three-bedroom."

"You hate it, don't you, John?"

An old hardness came into the ex-bartender's face, a look that somehow seemed happy.

"Yeah, Easy. Here I am, out in the sun every day. Damn. You know I'm black enough as it is."

"Then why you doin' it, man? You think you gonna get rich?"

"Alva Torres," he said.

I didn't know John's girlfriend all that well. She didn't approve of his old friends, so he stopped seeing most of them. He talked to me on the phone every once in a while, but we rarely saw each other.

Alva was tall and spare, her beauty was pure, flawless, and hard — the kind of beauty torn from the pain and ecstasy of what it was to be a Negro in this country.

Alva didn't like me but I accepted that because I once saw John grin when someone just mentioned her name.

"She wants me out of the nightlife and I cain't say no," John said meekly.

"So what you want from me?" I asked.

"Why'ont you take a ride with me over to our place? We can talk better over there."

"Hey, Mr. Rawlins," Mercury Hall called. He was coming across the graded dirt road, slapping his hands together like two chalky blackboard erasers.

"Mercury." I shook his hand and smiled. "I see you still playin' honest citizen."

"Oh yeah," he proclaimed. "Got to."

"Mr. Rawlins!" Kenneth Chapman shouted. He was an ochre-colored man, very thin with the broad features of our race. His smile was the biggest thing I had ever seen in a human mouth.

"Hey, Chapman. Don't you go shortchangin' them nails now."

His laugh was immense.

"Come on, Easy," John said.

It was from the tone of his voice that I knew whatever John had to ask was going to require sweat.

4 / *JOHN AND ALVA* were living in a box-shaped apartment building near Santa Barbara and Crenshaw. The
outside walls were slathered with white stucco that had glitter sprin-
kled in it. There were bullet holes here and there, but that wasn't un-
usual. That part of L.A. was full of Texans. Most Texans carry guns.
And if you carry a gun, it's bound to go off sooner or later.

The stairway and halls were all external, making the apartment
building resemble a cheap motel. John and I made it up to the third
floor. While he was fishing around for his keys, I looked out across
the street. Three floors was high in L.A. in 1964. I could see all the
way to downtown: a small cluster of granite buildings that looked like
a thousand movie backdrops I'd seen.

Across the way was a newly built and empty office building next
to a used-car lot. Even that made me smile. I have a soft spot for used

cars. They're like old friends or family members you love even though they always give you trouble.

"Right in here, Easy." John had worked his key in the lock and pulled the hollow wooden door open. He gestured for me to walk in and I did.

The room was the size of a ship's cabin, hardly wider than it was high. The furniture was cheap bamboo supporting fake blue leather, and the walls, though they had the sheen of being painted, were no color to speak of.

I sat down on a hammock-like footrest and regarded the bartender-turned-builder.

He walked into what I thought was a closet and said, "What you drinkin'?"

It was the question I'd heard most often from John. My most common reply had been *whiskey*, but my drinking days were over by then.

I got up to see what kind of bar John had carved out of a closet. But what I found was a kitchen in miniature. A tiny two-burner stove on top of a refrigerator no larger than a picnic cooler. The sink had no drain board or shelves.

"They call this a kitchen?" I asked.

"We had to sell the house an' put our stuff in storage," he said, as if that somehow answered my question. "To pay for the labor and some'a the legal expense for the buildins."

"Damn." I was amazed by the crowded little cooking closet.

"Hello, Mr. Rawlins." I didn't have to turn to know her voice.

"Alva."

I don't want to give the wrong impression of Alva Torres. She was a good woman, as far as I ever knew. She just didn't approve of my old life. What some might have called an economy of trading favors she saw as criminal activity.

She held out her hand in welcome, and maybe as a peace offering.

"How are ya?" I asked.

"Why don't you have a seat," she replied.

I went back to my footrest.

"What's up with you guys?" I asked as amiably as I could.

The reaction was discomfort and silence. Alva wore a gray pants suit that didn't hang right on her. She was a woman who needed bright colors and flowing lines. She stared at me as if I had tried to insult her with my question.

"It's a pretty long story, Easy," John said. "It's got to do with Alva and her first husband —"

"John," she said.

"What?"

"I don't know. I don't know if this is right."

"Well," John said, a glint of his old hardness coming through. "Make up your mind, then. Easy come over here to help if he can, but he cain't do a thing if you don't tell him what it is you want."

Alva clenched her long fingers into bony fists. "Can I trust you, Mr. Rawlins?"

The alarm in my head, the giddiness, the wind through the window of my car — they all came back to me with her question.

"I have no idea, honey," I said. "I don't know what it is that you need."

The tension went out of Alva's long body and she slumped back onto a blue bolster. John stared helplessly at her.

"My ex-husband," Alva began. "Aldridge A. Brown. He took care of Brawly when he was a child. I couldn't do it. A boy needs a man to guide him. That is, if the man will stay around."

I had no idea who she was talking about. But she was straining so hard just to get the words out that I decided to let it go for the moment.

"Aldridge wanted to be a good father. He might have been a good husband — for some other woman — but he was just . . . just . . . too much for us."

She stopped for a moment, and John went over to sit by her. He put his hand on her shoulder and she crumpled against his chest.

"Is this your son we're talkin' about?" I asked.

"Brawly," she said, nodding.

"He was workin' for me out at the lots up till a couple'a weeks ago," John said.

Alva shed silent tears that rolled down John's dirty T-shirt as if it were made of wax paper.

The woman's grief and her man sharing it moved me out of myself for a moment. In that instant I saw myself, fevered and mindless, reveling in these good people's pain. But the vision passed and for a long time I forgot that I'd even had it.

"Where'd he go?"

Alva's hard glare was daunting but I didn't look away.

"That's why we need your help, Easy," John said. "He moved out and she's afraid — *we're* afraid — that he might be in trouble."

"How old is Brawly?" I asked.

"Twenty-three, but he's young for his age." The tenderness in her voice was rare.

"Twenty-three! How old are you?"

"I had him when I was sixteen. Aldridge was the age Brawly is now."

"Excuse me for askin', honey, but you don't look nowhere near thirty-nine."

Even through that rock-hard perfection a little vanity found a chink. A smile flickered on her lips and then died.

"Why you think he's in trouble?" I asked. "I mean at twenty-three he could just be out havin' a good time."

"No, Easy. Not this boy," John said. "He broods. He did good in high school but then he got in trouble and dropped out. Now he's in wit' a bad crowd and Alva's worried."

"So you want me to find him?"

Alva sat up. The pain in her face almost made me turn away.

"Yes," she said. "And maybe, somehow, help us to get him back home."

"I'll do what I can. Sure."

"Oh," she uttered, and I did look away.

"What kinda crowd you talkin' about?" I asked John.

"They call themselves urban revolutionaries or somethin'."

"Say what?"

"The Urban Revolutionary Party," Alva said. She was sitting erect. Any show of weakness had been wiped away. "They also call themselves the First Men."

"Who are they?"

"They say that they're freedom fighters but all they want is trouble," she said. "Talkin' about the church and civil rights, but when it comes down to it they only want violence and revenge."

"Prob'ly communists," John added.

"He left some pamphlets they made," Alva said. "I'll get them for you."

She went through a door opposite the one John and I had entered.

"You got to do this right, Easy," he told me when she was gone.

"How you mean that?"

"Brawly got to come outta this safe."

"How I'm supposed to promise you that if he's runnin' around with thugs? You know yourself it's better not even to look for 'im. Either he's gonna outgrow it or it's gonna row him under. That's the way it is for all young black men."

He knew I was right.

Alva came in with four or five cheaply printed pamphlets clutched to her breast.

"Here they are." She made no attempt to hand them over.

"Can I take them?" I asked.

She swayed backward slightly. Finally John took them from her.

"Here," he said, handing the crumpled leaflets to me.

"What do you want from me, Alva?" I said loud and clear.

"I want you to find Brawly."

"That's all? If he's with these people here, you or John could go do that for yourselves."

"I want you to talk to him, Easy," she said. "If he saw us, he'd be even angrier. I want to know that he's okay and maybe, if he would listen to you, maybe . . ."

"Where he is is easy," I said. "But what he's doin' an' how he's doin' takes a closer look. I'll look him up, then come back here and tell you what I think. If he's willing to listen to reason, maybe I'll even bring him home."

"We gonna pay you now, Easy." John held up his hand as if he were defending himself from attack.

"Invite me an' the kids and Bonnie over for dinner and I'll be paid in full."

John laughed. "Still the same, huh, Easy?"

"If it work, don't fix it." It felt good trading words with my friend. "Alva," I said then. "I need two more things from you."

"What?"

"First I'ma need a picture of Brawly. And next I wanna know what your husband got to do with this."

"Nuthin'," she said. "Aldridge don't have nuthin' to do with this. Why?"

"I don't know. You're the one that brought him up. You and John."

"He said it." She sounded like a guilty student answering to a strict teacher. "I only meant about Brawly."

"You think he mighta gone to his father's house?"

"Never."

"I thought you said he was a good father? That he raised Brawly?"

"Brawly ran away from Aldridge when he was fourteen. He went to stay with my cousin; she was livin' up in Riverside then. Something happened between him and his father and he ran away. I don't think that they've seen each other since then."

"Brawly lived with his cousin? Why didn't he come to you?"

"That don't have nuthin' to do wit' nuthin', Easy," John said. He'd come up next to Alva and put his arms around her. "That's ancient history."

"Uh-huh. I see. Well, if Brawly didn't go to his father, how about this cousin?"

"No," Alva said.

"No what?"

"He's not with her."

"Excuse me, Miss Torres, but you don't know where Brawly is. That's why you called me."

"Back off, Easy," John warned. "You got them pamphlets. We told you where he's been hangin' out."

"Suppose he ain't there? Suppose I cain't get in there? Suppose he stayin' wit' this cousin an' sumpin's wrong? You cain't ask me to do this an' not tell me nuthin'."

Alva walked out again. She might have been angry but I didn't care.

"Easy, you don't know everything," John said. "Alva's had a hard time, and this thing with Brawly really hurts her. It's only been the last few years that they been close again."

"I can't help if you wanna tie me up from the git-go, man."

"Maybe I shouldn'ta called you then." It was a dismissal.

Alva had returned, again.

"John," she said. "He's right. If I want his help, I have to give him what he needs."

Saying that, she handed me a scrap of torn paper and an old photograph of a six- or seven-year-old child. The boy's hair was cut close to the scalp. He was burly and had heavy features, which made him seem pensive in spite of his smile.

"What's this?"

"It's a picture of Brawly and Isolda Moore's phone number and address."

"This Isolda's your cousin?"

The thought was so distasteful to Alva that she could only nod.

"I thought you said that she lived in Riverside?"

"She moved to L.A. a few years ago. She sent Brawly a card with her number, but he never called it."

"Now what about this picture?"

"What about it?" she asked.

"You said that Brawly's twenty-three."

"That's the only picture I have. But it's him. You'll see."

"She's right about that, Easy," John said. "Brawly looks exactly the same today. Only he's bigger."

"You know any place that he might hang out just for fun?" I asked.

"Brawly like to eat," John said. "All you got to do is look for the biggest feed bag. He likes Hambones quite a bit. That's right down the block from them thugs he's wit'."

"Find him for me, Mr. Rawlins," Alva said. "I know I haven't been kind to you and that you don't have any reason to want to help me. I'm sorry that I didn't treat you right before, but from now on my door will always be open to you."

That open door meant more than any money John could offer me. In country terms it was worth the host's weight in gold. If she was willing to pay such a high price, I wondered what the cost might be.

5/ *NOT TEN WORDS PASSED* between John and me on the ride back to the site. He was naturally a quiet man, but this silence was sullen and heavy. There was something else on his mind. But whatever it was, he wasn't sharing it with me.

When I was driving off I could hear him shouting orders at the ex-burglars.

The fever was still burning in me. For the first time I thought that I might have had some kind of flu. I went down three blocks of dirt road to the first paved street. There I pulled over to the curb to catch my breath. The February air was chilly and the sky was still blue. I was like a child, so excited that it was hard to concentrate on anything but sensations.

I knew that I had to calm down. I had to think. John called on me because he knew that I had been among desperate men my whole life. I could see when the blow was coming. But I couldn't see anything if I didn't relax.

I lit up a cigarette and took a deep draw. The smoke coiling around my dashboard brought on the cool resolve of the snake it resembled.

The pamphlet was mimeographed on newsprint, folded and stapled by hand. The Urban Revolutionary Party was a cultural group, it said, that sought the restitution and recognition of the builders of our world — African men and women. They didn't believe in *slave laws*, that is to say, any laws imposed on black men by whites, just as they didn't accept forced military service or white political leadership. They rejected the white man's notion of history, even the history of Europe. But mostly they seemed perturbed about taxes as they applied to social needs and services; *the distribution of wealth*, the blurred purple words explained, *as it applies to our labor, and the dreams that we hardly dare to imagine, is woefully inadequate.*

I'd read similar ideas before. I had read a lot in my time. Most of it white man's fictions and his histories, too. I was a sucker for history.

A car drove up and parked while I was remembering what I'd read about the plebes of ancient Rome. Two car doors slammed one after the other, but I was busy wondering whether that ancient oppressed people had some kind of pamphlets, or was it all word of mouth?

But when I heard "Step out of the car," I was dragged back to the present.

The policemen had flanked my Pontiac. One of them had his hand on his holster and the other actually had his pistol drawn. My hands rose quickly like the wings of a flightless bird when frightened by a sudden sound.

"No problem, Officers," I said.

"Use your left hand to open the door," the closer cop commanded. He was young — they both were, pale boys with guns among men who had been living on a diet of pamphlets and poverty.

I did what I was told, then stepped out of the car cautiously and slow. My hands stayed at shoulder level.

The difference between the cops was that one was a dark brunet and the other was black-haired. They were both about my height, just over six feet. The black-haired one looked into my open door as the other one tried to spin me around and push me up against the car. I say *tried* because even though I had reached my forty-fourth year, I was still sturdy.

But I turned anyway and put my hands on the roof. He holstered his gun and moved up close behind me, sliding his hands in my front pockets. After feeling around my thighs for a moment, he slapped my back pockets. I felt like a woman being groped. It wasn't pleasant. But the worst thing about it was his breath. It was so rank that I became nauseous. I tried to breathe through my mouth but even then I could taste the disease blowing out of his lungs.

When he stepped back I almost thanked him.

"Open the trunk," he said.

"Why?"

"What?"

"Listen, man." The fever had gripped me again. "I was just sittin' there, readin' my paper. I'm parked legally. Why you wanna roust me?"

His reply was to pull out his billy club.

A voice in my head said, "Kill 'im," and I went cold inside.

"The key is in the ignition," I explained.

The brown-haired cop slid in and took the key. It was awkward for him because he had his club out, too.

They made me watch while they opened up the trunk. All they found was a flat spare tire that I had been meaning to fix and a tool-box full of tools.

The black-haired cop slammed the trunk shut.

Then his partner said, "There's been some theft and vandalism around the construction out here. We're just keeping an eye on things."

I made a mental note to ask Jewelle what was really going on.

*W*HEN I GOT to Isolda Moore's house, I parked way down the block because of those cops. I was upset with myself for not paying attention. If I was going to be in the streets again, I had to be better prepared than that.

Alva's cousin lived on Harcourt Avenue, near Rimpau. It was one of those working-class L.A. fantasy homes. Powder blue, small and rounded. There was hardly a straight line to the place. The eaves of the roof were cut in the form of waves. Even the window frames were irregular and absent of straight lines. The front door was surrounded by a waist-high turret of white stucco.

As I pushed the whitewashed gate open I wondered if Isolda would be as beautiful as her cousin. Maybe Brawly would be sitting at her kitchen table, eating ribs and blowing off steam about some argument that he'd had with Alva or John.

Instead, I came upon a corpse that was half in and half out of the doorway.

He was a big man, especially around the middle. Black, he wore blue work pants and a blue work shirt that had been pulled almost off of his back. His head was crushed from behind and there were deep bloody marks in his back also made by the bludgeon.

He resembled the carcass of a beached sea lion left by the tide.

There were dozens of columns of tiny black ants making their way to and from the body. Given enough time, they might have consumed it.

The day's mail was sticking out from under his gut.

The company of the dead doesn't bother me much, not after the front lines of World War II. I'd seen death in all colors and sexes, in all sizes and states of decomposition. That's why I could step over that spilled life into Isolda's powder-blue oceanic home.

The fight and flight were evident in upturned furniture and bloody hand- and footprints on the walls and floor. It was a spare house with pine floors and not much furniture. The walls were white and the furniture mostly an ugly violet hue. The stuffed chair and couch were on their sides. In the sunny kitchen a cabinet had been ripped from the wall, and all the china and glass had shattered on the floor. There was a dollop of blood frozen in a spilling motion from the drain board into the sink.

I traced the fight from its beginning in the kitchen, through to the living room, and from there back to the front door, where the fat man had lost his race with Death.

In the corner of the little front patio I saw the weapon. It was a meat-tenderizing mallet. A stainless-steel hammer with a head made of a four-inch cube that had jagged teeth to mash up tough flesh. The mallet was slick with dark gore.

I went back in the house, into a woman's bedroom. Here the color scheme was white and pink. The neatly made bed was covered with a satin coverlet and piled with small quilted pillows at the head. The room seemed so innocent that, compared with the bedlam in the other parts of the house, it took on a sinister air.

There were four pictures taped to Isolda's bureau mirror. One was of a burly man — maybe the corpse, I couldn't be sure without turning him over. The next two were of Brawly somewhere in his teens and also as a grown-up. The last photo was of a good-looking woman in her late thirties wearing a bathing suit and laughing at Brawly, who was rubbing water out of his eyes. That picture had been taken near the Santa Monica Pier.

In one drawer I found a red and black envelope of photographs. Most of the pictures were of the woman modeling in a two-piece bathing suit. She looked rather inviting. The odd thing was that the pictures were taken inside, in a room that I hadn't seen in her house. In one photo she was lying on a bed with her legs splayed and her back arched. She was beaming a smile that could have made a new sire out of an eighty-year-old man.

While I was staring at those photographs a car door somewhere slammed. At first it was just a faraway sound, meaningless to me. Then, for some reason, I thought of the black-and-white photographs I had once seen in a book about ancient Rome. I wondered what could have made me think about the Colosseum. Then the cops came back into my mind. I ran to the front and peeked out from behind the violet drapes.

The sight of the four policemen deflated me for a second. The fact that two squad cars had been dispatched meant that someone had seen the body and called it in. I had that helpless give-it-up emotion that comes on me sometimes.

But it passed quickly.

Running was a fool's enterprise, but I took it up with vigor. I pocketed the pictures and ran to the door at the back of the kitchen. I used my shirttail as a glove to turn the knob. As I left out of there I heard a man's voice call, "Watch it, Drake. Man down."

I ducked low in the bare backyard and headed for the fence. Over that hurdle I made it to the next street through the back neighbor's driveway. Most people, men and women, in that neighborhood spent the day at work, so I wasn't too worried about being seen. I dropped the photographs into a trash can, set out for the weekly pickup, just in case I was stopped by the cops.

The only trouble I had left was walking to my car without being noticed. In any other city that would have been easy. But not in L.A.

I went the long way around and turned up two blocks on Henry. By the time I got to Isolda's block there were four police cars parked out front. An approaching patrol car drove past me. They slowed down to watch. I turned and glanced at them and kept on walking.

I guess the lure of real action pulled them away. A dead man in a doorway was still news back then.

I got the key in the ignition slot on the fourth try and drove well within the speed limit past the powder blue dream. The police in their dark uniforms reminded me of the ants that were swarming over the corpse at their feet.

6 / *FROM THE MOMENT* I heard John's voice I had expected trouble. I was looking for it. But the dead man had sobered me somewhat. I didn't want to get that far into somebody else's grief. I didn't want to be used, either. But I doubted that John and Alva would have lied to me — not about murder, anyway.

I decided not to call them until I had at least seen Brawly. If I were to tell Alva that I had come upon a dead man instead of her son, there's no telling where her imagination might have taken her. I would go to the headquarters of the Urban Revolutionary Party, hoping to catch a glimpse of the young man.

But first came food. I hadn't eaten since Juice's pancakes, and fear always stoked my appetite.

———

*H*AMBONES WAS A SOUL FOOD diner on Hooper, not far from the First Men's storefront address. I hadn't been there for a while because it catered to a rough clientele and I had spent the past few years (with one major slip) trying to deny that I ever traveled in those crowds.

Sam Houston, proud black son of Texas, owned the place. It was one long room with tables running down the length of the walls and a kitchen in the back. If you wanted to eat at the Hambone, you had to sit next to your honey and look at the man across the way.

Sam was standing at his waist-high counter at the back of the place. Behind him was the kitchen full of his family members, their spouses, and friends.

"Sam," I hailed as I walked toward him.

"I knew they was gonna take it, Easy," he bellowed. Sam's speaking voice would have been a shout for a normal man.

"Take what?"

"The Star of India," he said in a smug and satisfied tone. "Right outta the Museum of Natch'l History up there in New York City. I knew it."

I had come to his countertop by then. His loud pronouncement irritated me.

"You knew what?"

"I knew that they had to steal sumpin' like that. You cain't have no million-dollar jewel lyin' around for just any old motherfucker t'be lookin' at. I read it right here in the *Examiner*." Sam gestured at a rumpled pile of papers lying next to him on the counter.

"What the hell you talkin' 'bout, Sam?" I hadn't seen the man in at least two years, but the first words out of his mouth had already made me mad. "All the shit in the news and you gonna be worried 'bout some goddamned piece'a glass?"

"It's the money, man. Got to go wit' the money. I feel for them civil rights workers, but they dead. And them white men kilt 'em? They gonna see a white judge for tea and they mamas for dinner that night."

"How the hell you figure that?"

"I know what I know, Easy. I know what I know."

"Man, you don't know shit."

The tall man cocked his head and grinned at me just as if he was saying, *Got ya.*

Sam Houston always made me angry. It was the way he took everything he heard, saw, or read and made it seem that he was the expert. If you came up to him and said that you put up a new cinder-block wall, he'd start lecturing you on the way to build a foundation and the type of drainoff that you'd need. He hadn't lifted a finger, but now he's going to tell you what it was you did wrong.

And far too often he was right.

Sam was tall, as I said, but added to that, he had an extremely long neck. His skin had the texture of medium-brown leather with gray highlights and his eyes were great googly things that rolled around dramatically no matter what he was saying or, less often, listening to.

"I'm tellin' ya, Easy. All you got to do is read that newspaper and the whole world falls right into place."

"Yeah? How's that?"

"You own a car?"

"Uh-huh."

"What year?"

"'Fifty-eight Pontiac," I said.

"So if you push it over fifty, it's rattlin', right?"

How did he know that?

"Now," Sam went on, "Craig Breedlove broke five hundred miles per hour in his car, on the Salt Flats. You doin' the shimmy at fifty while he's solid-state at five hundred. That's where you are. The white man got cars fifty years in the future and you ain't hardly out the Dark Ages."

I nodded. I could have asked what kind of car he was driving. I could have asked how fast he could go. I could have broken his long neck. But instead, I nodded and got the first of the two things I wanted at Hambones.

Sam turned around and said, "Clarissa! Bring Easy some'a them braised short ribs!"

"Okay," said a taciturn young woman wearing pink shorts and a pink blouse. She had a green ribbon holding back her straightened hair.

"So, Easy," Sam said. "What you doin' here?"

Sam didn't let many people eat at his counter. You went back there and ordered for sit-down or take-home. But he didn't want you loitering around and obstructing his view. Most men who tried to start a conversation with Sam were told, "Sit your ass down, man. I ain't got time to fool with you. This here's a business."

The fact that he could stare and shout down most of his clientele was saying quite a lot. Because the men that patronized Hambones were not to be pushed.

Before answering Sam's question, I looked out along the walls. There were three men and four women. Each of the men had a girl-friend, and one of those girlfriends had brought a friend along. That extra woman had on a red dress that must've fit her when she was a size or so smaller. I think that it probably looked better, however, straining against her womanly form. She was looking at me and I felt that fever again. Her gaze didn't move me, though. I wasn't looking for any more love than Bonnie Shay could deliver.

I didn't know any of the men but I could feel their violence. Hard men in dark suits and white shirts with dirty collars and small cigarette holes down the breast. Felons, murderers, and sneak thiefs, too. I never understood why Sam surrounded himself with so much danger.

"Oh, nuthin'," I said, answering Sam's question.

"Uh-uh, Easy. You got to do better'n that now. I ain't seen you in two years. Odell done told me that you got a job workin' at the Board of Education, that you moved to West L.A. and bought a house. You got to need somethin' if you gonna cross all'a them lines to come here to me."

"Here you go," the pink-clad girl said, placing a heaping plate of short ribs in front of me.

"What's wrong wit' you, girl?" Sam asked angrily.

"What?" Clarissa complained.

"Go get him some greens an' corn. He ain't no animal just gonna tear at the meat. He needs him a balanced meal." Sam shook his head in disappointment and his waitress pouted.

"You want collard or turnip greens, Easy?" Sam asked me.

"Collard."

"Yeah, man, me too. You know them turnip greens is *bitter*." He sang the last word to accent his distaste. Sam Houston was a Texan all the way down to his socks.

"You know a young man name'a Brawly Brown?" I asked when Clarissa had slouched her way back to get my vegetables.

Sam pulled out a bottle of Tabasco sauce from under the counter. I opened it and doused my dark meat and gravy.

"Bad boy Brawly Brown," Sam said, and sighed. "Mm, mm, mm. Now that boy is trouble an' he don't even know it."

"You know him, then?"

"Oh yeah. Brawly got a chip on his shoulder, ants in his pants, eyes twice as big as his stomach, and a heart just drippin' right off his sleeve. If it could be too much, then that there's Brawly."

"So he's like a big kid?" I asked in a deferential tone.

"He's just too much, that's all, Easy. One day he come in here sayin' he's gonna sign up in the army an' be a paratrooper over in Asia somewhere. Gonna make him some good money and then go to college on the GI Bill. Next week he wandered the wrong way down the street, now he's a revolutionary. He wanna tell me that I'm just a slave workin' for my white master. Can you imagine? Boy look like a butterball come in here, eat my food, and insult me."

Clarissa brought up a big plate full of greens with bits of salt pork in them. The collards gave off a sharp vegetable odor laced with a hint of vinegar.

"No, I don't get it, Sam. This here is the best damn food I've eaten in many a day. Many a day."

I wasn't lying, either. When you get soul food right, it feeds the spirit. And my spirit was flying with those greens and ribs.

"Okay, Easy. You done et for free and I answered your questions. Now what you here for?"

"Brawly's mom wants to see him. She called on me and I come here to you." I saw no reason or profit in lying to Sam.

"So you know about the First Men?" he asked.

I nodded because my mouth was busy chewing.

"I don't have much patience for all this vigilante communist bullshit," Sam said. "If they come in here after me, I got a shotgun blow 'em all away."

"Why'd they come after you, Sam? I thought it was white people they couldn't stand."

"They like all the other ignorant people down here, Ease. They hate colored more'n they hate white. They see a black cop or school principal, they say that that man's a traitor to the race and deserves to die. They come around askin' for donations, an' some people out here is scared enough to cough it up. But you know they only askin' black people."

"Protection?" I was surprised.

"Not really. I told 'em no an' they just grumbled. But you know they on the edge of organized crime, they on the edge."

"How do you mean?" I asked.

"One or two of 'em come in here," Sam said. "Sometimes with Brawly and sometimes not. I can tell by the way they lean close and whisper that they plannin' things. Not lunches for chirren like they say. No. They got plans that go by the dark'a night."

"I see," I said.

I had enough of food and talk for a while. I wanted to think about it all, and Sam wasn't the kind of man to let you stand there quietly.

"Thank you, Mr. Houston," I said, straightening up. I saw Clarissa in the back, past Sam. She was looking at me.

"They got meetins every evenin' 'bout six," Sam said.

"Say what?"

"The First Men. They give talks just about every night."

"Uh-huh." I gave Clarissa a glance and she looked down, pretending to be doing something. "Thanks for your help, man."

7 / *I DECIDED TO GO DOWN* to the First Men's store-front and see what it was that they were about. Sam had his point of view and I was sure that he had told me the truth as far as he saw it; but truth, as my uncle Roger used to say, is just one man's explanation for what he thinks he understands.

The Urban Revolutionary Party was flanked by a beauty shop and a general-supplies five-and-dime. The front wall was just a big window but it was covered over by a large black curtain. In the center of the curtain was a yellow circle that had the silhouettes of a book and a spear stitched into it. The front door was locked and there wasn't anyone moving around inside, so I went to get gas at the Tunney station a few blocks away. While they were washing my windows and adding a pint of oil, I made a call on their pay phone.

"Hello?" a tiny voice answered.

"Hi, Feather."

"Hi, Daddy. Where you?"

"Down over near John's house, baby. I have to go to this meeting, so I probably won't get home till after you're in the bed."

"How come?" There was so much pain in her plea that I almost gave up on Brawly and went home.

"I'll come in and kiss you when I get in, baby. Don't worry."

"Can I have hamburgers?"

"Sure. Just tell Juice."

"Okay," she said, forgiving me all my mistakes and flaws.

"Did Bonnie leave for the airport?" I asked.

"Uh-huh."

"But Juice is there taking care of you?"

"Yes."

"Good. I love you, honey," I said.

"I love you too, Daddy."

"Bye."

She hung up and I felt loss that went all the way back to my childhood.

I DIDN'T WASTE THE TIME while waiting for the First Men to get going. I went to a small diner on San Pedro and studied for the classified building supervisor's exam. That was the next step up the ladder for me. Studying made me feel as though I still had a foot in the workaday world that Feather needed me to be a part of. She needed every day to be the same as the day before and needed something to say when her friends and teachers asked what her daddy did for a living. I became that man for a couple of hours while waiting for night to come on.

Somewhere in the middle of my third cup of coffee I remembered the dead man. That hump of skin and bones straddling the threshold of Isolda Moore's home. His form jumped into my mind and I held it there, looking to see if I should be thinking something about it.

I didn't feel a thing. Not concern for my fellow man who was murdered or fear for my own safety. I didn't kill him and I doubted if anybody saw me, so it was as if I were never there.

*T*HE GLASS DOOR to the Urban Revolutionaries' storefront was open and people were milling around inside. The sun was gone but it wasn't yet night.

The meeting room gave off a slight odor of varnish. Naked fluorescent lights glared overhead. The floor was pine and the walls were composed of cheap plasterboard paneling. There was an iron music stand against the back wall. The thirty folding chairs with reinforced cardboard seats were half filled but most of the forty-odd people in the room were too excited to sit.

The young black men and women wore dark clothes, talked and listened, posed and watched. Their voices might have seemed angry to someone who didn't know the gruff bark of the American Negro's soul. Those men and women were far beyond anger, though. They were expressing a desire for love and revenge and for something that didn't exist — had never existed. That's why they were there. They were going to create freedom out of the sow's ear called America. They believed in the spirit of the Constitution and not the direction of the cash register.

Maybe, if I stayed there long enough, I might have believed it, too.

"You a cop?" someone asked. It took me a moment to realize that he was talking to me.

It was a skinny young cork-colored man. He wore wire-rimmed glasses and a black turtleneck shirt that wasn't much wider in the body than it was in those extra long sleeves.

I almost laughed. "What?"

"I said, Are you a cop?"

"No." I looked around the room, noticing that a few heads had turned toward me.

"It's okay," the bespectacled boy said.

"What's okay?"

"It's okay if you're a cop," he explained. "We welcome those brothers who have been brainwashed. What you're going to find here tonight is truth. If you're looking for bombs and guns, you're in the wrong place. What you're going to find are the real weapons of the revolution: education and love. That's the revolution of the mind." He pointed at his own skull in a gesture that reminded me of suicide.

He was nowhere near handsome, but some girl would fall in love with his eyes. He was absolutely sure of, and in love with, his own ideas.

"I'm not no cop, brother. I heard about this place down at Hambones. They said you guys do a lotta talkin' and I decided to come on down and hear you out." My diction and grammar slid into the form I wanted Junior to hear.

He nodded and shook my hand.

"Then welcome," he said. His smile was uneven but brilliant like an old but well-cared-for blade. "My name's Xavier [he pronounced it "*ex*-avier"] Bodan. I'm the Party director."

He moved away from me then, greeting his fellow members as he made his way to the front of the room. There was a bounce to his gait that accented his youth.

I wondered if he had a mother somewhere looking for him.

"What's your name, man?" someone else asked.

This one was somewhat bigger and darker but was dressed almost the same.

"Rawlins."

"What you doin' here?"

"Is ev'rybody in this room gonna ask me that?" I sounded unfriendly enough to make myself clear. "'Cause you know I could just as well go up to that music stand and make a public announcement."

This guy was about thirty, with a perfectly round head and a belly just about the same size and shape. He sneered and chewed on a large wad of gum. I think he wanted me to be scared, but he didn't know anything outside of church or family or clubs like the Urban Party. I could tell by the way he garnered his courage that he expected to be backed up.

"Rawlins, you say?" Yet another man came from behind the gum chewer.

His skin was golden brown but everything else about him said white man. Large frame and a big square jaw that stuck straight out. His nose was slender and the only color that I could call his eyes was *not exactly brown*. The wavy hair had no oil in it. But he was still a black man, at least by American standards.

"Yeah," I said.

"This ain't no party," the white-looking black man informed me.

"You askin' me to leave?"

"Leave him alone, Conrad," a woman said. She wore a black cotton dress that might have been a slip ten years earlier.

"Look at him, Tina," the matinee idol complained.

"I am," Tina replied. "What I see is a brother."

Half the room was looking at me by then. Not exactly the way I liked to do business.

Conrad looked me up and down, contempt snarling in his white man's lips and nose. But finally he shrugged his shoulders and turned away. People started talking again, giving me only quick, wondering glances.

"Hi," the young woman that Conrad called Tina said in greeting.

"All right," I said.

"Everybody's worried that the police are going to send in some kind of black spy to take us down."

"They're right."

Tina was suddenly wary. I didn't want her to think badly of me. She was only pretty because of her youth, but that dress looked good on her and she had just put herself between me and a room full of potentially violent men and women.

"I don't mean me," I said. "I'm just sayin' that the cops work through black spies down here. That's the only way to find out what's goin' on."

Tina hadn't fully regained her composure. She brought her hands to her shoulders.

"I ain't no cop," I said. "I just wanted to take a look-see, hear what you folks got to say."

Over Tina's head I saw Clarissa, the waitress from Hambones, enter the room in her pink top and shorts. She saw me and frowned. Behind her came a beefy brown man who had once been the boy in a photograph I had in my pocket. They were across the room from me. Before I could decide whether to cross over to them, everybody faced the music stand. Some people clapped.

Xavier Bodan had taken his place at the makeshift podium. Behind him stood a large dignified-looking man with half straight, mostly gray hair that he combed back like a groomed lion's mane.

"Time to begin," Xavier chanted. "Time to begin. This is the two hundred thirty-third meeting of the Urban Revolutionary Party. For those of you who are new, I am Xavier Bodan, secretary to the executive council, and a full-fledged believer in the black man and his struggle against the slave master and his dogs."

There was applause then.

"The woman struggles just as hard, Xavier," a voice called.

The young man grinned and ducked his head, flashing lights from the flat surfaces of his glasses. "You right, Sister Em," he said. "Without the sisters, we're nothing at all."

I caught a glimpse of Brawly. He was glowering, looking around the room with the air of a bodyguard or a sergeant at arms.

"There will be a meeting of the executive committee after the general meeting. That's Tina, Conrad, Belton, and Swan. See you after. There's business for us to discuss, fund-raising and our education program, but I don't want to spend any extra time tonight arguing or planning. We all know why we're here: to spread the word and feed the children, to stand up straight and love each other."

"Preach." Someone thought we were in a church.

"We represent an island of civilization in a sea of barbarians. We bring the key to unlock eighteen million chains." Xavier smiled again and I worried for him; he seemed so frail up there.

"Tonight," he continued, "it is my honor to present a lion, a master. This is one of the men who made it possible for an organization like the First Men to come into being. He is our shelter and our conscience. He was taking blows for us before many of us were born. He was sweating in the white man's cages when we were on tricycles and playin' hopscotch. He is our beacon" — the audience started making a noise. It was like an expectant chatter. Not words exactly but pure emotions making their way into sound. "He marched in Selma in 1955" — the volume from the audience went up a notch — "he marched shoulder to shoulder with Martin Luther King" — the murmur grew into recognizable words of praise — "he is what we once were and what we strive to become" — the applause started then, softly, as if it had been rehearsed — "he is Henry Strong."

Xavier stood aside, allowing Strong to take the podium.

"Henry Strong," Xavier said again.

The applause began to thunder. They yelled and whistled. They chanted the elder man's name. They called out until he had to smile and hold up his big hands. I expected the leader to compliment the respect shown by the crowd and their mouthpiece, but he knew his audience better than I did.

"I was a Garveyite," he proclaimed.

The applause grew even stronger.

"I was with the first of the first men."

"That's the words!" a man exclaimed.

"I have seen the red sun of Dahomey and I have bathed in the African sea."

"Teach."

"I," Strong said, pausing a moment for effect, "have tasted the sweet nectar of the homeland and I am here to tell you that we are sown from the sweetest flowers in the world."

"Watch it!" someone yelled. I think it was Brawly Brown because when I looked he was plowing through the audience toward a door in back marked by an exit sign.

At that moment the glass door flew open. It shattered but I couldn't hear it, because at the same time the picture-window wall also crashed. Policemen wearing riot helmets and wielding truncheons forced their way in.

There must have been thirty of them.

The assembled crowd balked for a moment, turning to see what the problem was.

I grabbed Tina and bulled my way toward the rear exit. Just as I reached the door the blows began to fall. Blood was spilling and I knew that there would be a few more chains for Xavier to unlock that night.

8 / *"COME ON, TINA! QUICK!"* Conrad, the matinee idol, shouted.

He was seated in the driver's seat of a lime green '62 Cadillac. Next to him was Xavier, and in the backseat Henry Strong crouched down against the window. There was screaming coming from behind us, the sounds of scuffling and the occasional heavy thud and grunt.

I pressed Tina toward the automobile.

Conrad yelled, "Not you!"

"He took me out of there," Tina hissed.

I just kept on pushing until I was in the backseat. Conrad took off down the alley in spite of his unwanted passenger. He sideswiped two wooden fences and knocked over a whole family of garbage cans. I could tell by his driving that Conrad would never make the grade on the military side of the revolution; I hoped that Xavier and Strong saw that, too.

Conrad took side streets. He made so many turns, it seemed to me that we were going in circles. But at some point he pulled out onto Central. We cruised that boulevard toward Florence.

Nobody spoke for a long time.

The younger people were in a funk. Maybe it was their first taste of what the world thought of their idealism, their truth.

Strong was just scared. His eyes were still wide with fear, and his fists were clenched on the hem of Tina's dress. She didn't seem to mind. She laid three fingers on the big knuckle of his right hand. There was a great deal of tenderness in the gesture.

I stayed quiet because there was nothing I could learn from hearing my words. A police raid meant nothing to me. I'd been in whorehouses, speakeasies, barber shops, and alley craps games when the police came down. Sometimes I got away and sometimes I lied about my name. There was nothing spectacular about being rousted for being black.

After a while Conrad pulled over to the curb. He fumbled around in the front of his pants for a moment and then turned around, leveling a pistol at my head.

"Hey, Con, what's wrong wit' you?" Xavier cried.

"Conrad!" Tina added.

"Who are you, man?" Conrad demanded.

I gazed into his eyes, wondering why I felt no fear. For a moment I thought that I had gone crazy, that Mouse's death had robbed me of my own survival instinct. But then I thought that it was probably the adrenaline from the escape that kept me unafraid.

"Easy," I said.

"Say what?"

"Easy. Easy Rawlins."

"Put the gun down, Conrad," Strong demanded in a commanding baritone.

"We don't know who he is. Maybe he's the one called the pigs on us."

"They didn't need him, Conrad," Tina said. "We were right there in our own place."

"Yeah, man," Xavier complained. "Talk sense."

"Put the gun down," Strong said again.

Conrad finally did as he was told. It made no difference to me. By then I was thinking about Jesus wanting to drop out of school. Suddenly I felt that I understood my son's desire. Life was too short and too sweet to be spent in the company of fools.

"Well, Mr. Rawlins?" Strong asked.

"I was lookin' for Brawly Brown. His mother wanted to make sure that he wasn't in trouble."

"What's that supposed to mean?" Conrad wouldn't have been happy with anything I said.

"It means that she's a mother and she's worried over her son. For all she knows, he's with a gang. So I told her that I'd find him and ask him to give her a call."

Sometimes the truth is just as good as a lie.

"You're not welcome among us, Mr. Rawlins," Strong said at last. "There's no time for Good Samaritans and mother's tears while the police brutalize our souls and break our bodies."

"That's okay with me, man. You know, I don't want my body broken, neither. But could you take me back to Hambones? My ride is out in front'a there." I didn't lie but I talked in a way that hid the nature of my mind.

"No," Conrad said. "Get out here and find your own way back."

Xavier and Tina wouldn't meet my gaze.

"I think I must agree," Strong said.

"Okay. All right then." I opened the door and got out. As soon as I was on the curb the lime Caddy took off.

There I was, at least three miles from my car, but I wasn't unhappy. I walked four blocks to a small diner and called the Ajax Cab Company. They sent a red and white car straight off to pick me up. A friendly driver named Arnold Beard from North Carolina took me to my car.

He didn't ask me why I was out and so far away from my car, and I felt no need to explain.

I WAS AT MY HOUSE by eight-thirty. The volume on the TV was turned up high; I could hear it from the front porch. I knew what I would find when I got inside. Feather would be sitting almost on top of our console TV while Jesus slept behind her, sprawled out on the couch.

Frenchie, the little yellow dog, growled at me from under the TV set. I was so happy to be home that even that foul mutt's snarling felt like a welcome.

"Shhh, Daddy. Juice sleepin'." She wore her pale blue pajamas with decals of Roy Rogers and Dale Evans pasted all over them.

"Hey there, cowgirl."

"Shhh," she said, and then she giggled as I picked her up.

"Are you baby-sitting for Juice?"

"Uh-huh."

Feather put her soft arms around my neck and laid her head just below my chin. She always fell asleep in my arms at night when I came home late. She would try her best to stay awake until I got there, but the moment I picked her up she was on her way to dreamland.

By the time I had her under the covers she was in a deep sleep.

I left Jesus on the couch. It was hard to wake him up, and it had been years since I could carry him to bed. After all, he was almost seventeen years old. He'd wake up at some point and look in to check on Feather and then me before going to bed.

I put away the dishes that Jesus and Feather had washed and left in the rack to dry. Then I went to my bedroom. Frenchie followed me, snarling and crouching as if he were about to pounce. But he was no larger than a big rat. He knew that he couldn't do the kind of damage he wanted.

I stripped off my T-shirt and looked at him in the doorway.

"What you want?"

Confusion replaced hatred for a moment and then he snarled again. I threw my T-shirt on his head, causing him to yelp and run from the room.

It gave me a kind of perverse pleasure to know that there was someone close to me who was always planning my demise. Frenchie hated me, that much was sure. He blamed me for the death of his mistress, and forgiveness was not a part of his nature. Every time I saw him he reminded me that there's always somebody out to get you, that you better keep your guard up because there's no such a thing as *safe*.

I WENT TO BED feeling lonely. That's what Bonnie had brought into my life — loneliness. Before her, my company was the best company. I loved my kids but they were children; they were going to grow up and go away, and I felt that I could let them. But now my bed felt as though it were missing something when Bonnie was gone. When she was off on her flights to Europe and Africa, I never got a satisfying sleep. And when she was home, even though I was miserable over the death of Raymond, I found an island in my dreams that was the closest thing to home that I had ever known.

No one had ever really been there for me before. I never talked to my first wife. Back then I thought that a man was supposed to be strong and silent; he was supposed to make her safe and warm while paying the bills and siring children.

But Bonnie changed all that. She was on my wavelength. And she was an independent thinker. She could take an action for herself without anybody else's approval. I knew that because she'd once killed a man who attacked her and then went on with her life. Sometimes I'd wake up at night and look at her, knowing that she had crossed the same line I had. But I was never afraid. I felt like some ancient nomad who could depend on his woman to fight at his side, tooth and nail, against the wild.

That night had me wide-eyed but it wasn't just missing Bonnie. Neither was my insomnia due to the police raid or the pistol in my face. All that was just a small part of the obstacle course that had been my life. I was an orphan at eight years old in the Deep South. I had fought, and won, against men when I didn't even have hair in my armpits.

No, neither the Urban Revolutionary Party nor their cop enemies bothered me. But dead men were different.

In the cool darkness of my room I wondered about the dead man and Alva's plea to find her son. It would have been easy enough for me to go to John and tell him that murder was more than I had signed up for. I didn't even have to tell him, because it was bound to get around about the death in Alva's cousin's home. John would know that I couldn't get involved with that kind of trouble. He knew what trying to make a normal life meant.

I decided to call him and say that I'd gone to the First Men, that

I saw Brawly and he looked fine. He would have heard about the murder by then. He'd understand.

I breathed a deep sigh, relieved that my insanity was only a twelve-hour bug. But when I dozed off I found myself in the middle of a very real dream. I walked into a room where Mouse was seated at a small round table. He was wearing a dark suit and a short-brimmed hat. I remained on my feet and told him the story of my day. He was looking down while I spoke, listening to my words with gravity. When I finished he looked up with his gray eyes glittering. He shrugged as if to say, *Hey, man, what's to worry?*

I felt that giddiness in my gut again. I woke up in the middle of the night realizing that I was trying to stifle a laugh.

9/ "*MOUSE! HEY, RAYMOND,* wait up!"

He was walking down the street a block ahead of me. I increased my pace but couldn't manage to gain on him.

"Wait up, man!" I cried.

And then, suddenly, he turned around. His pistol was in his hand and he opened fire. I froze in place, knowing the deadly accuracy of his marksmanship. He let off five or six rounds and I was still standing. I looked around behind me and saw three dead men on the ground. When I looked back in Mouse's direction he smiled and tipped his hat to me. Then he turned and walked away quickly. I wanted to follow but was so frightened that I couldn't make my legs move.

"Daddy."

I felt a slight nudge at my arm.

"Daddy, wake up," Jesus said. He was kneeling over me.

I was on the floor next to the bed, partly wrapped in sheets and covers. I wondered how I got there. I didn't think I could have fallen. Maybe I was trying to hide from those killers under the bed.

"Uncle John's here," the boy said.

"What time is it?"

"About eight o'clock."

"Go out and tell him I'll be there in a few minutes."

*F*IFTEEN MINUTES LATER I strode on cramped feet into our small living room. John was standing there looking like a fish out of water in his overalls and work boots.

"Easy."

"What can I do for you, John?"

"I need your help."

"Didn't we already have this talk yesterday?" I asked.

John shifted his shoulders, looking all the more uncomfortable.

"You want some coffee or something to eat?" I asked him.

"I got to get down to the lots."

"Come on in the kitchen anyway. I just woke up."

"I ain't got time to fool around, Easy. I need your help and I need it now."

I turned my back on him and went into the kitchen.

I always liked the kitchen in the morning because that's when the sun flooded the windows. While I was filling the percolator with tap water, John walked in.

"Hey, man," he said. "I'm sorry. I know you just woke up, but things got worse overnight."

He slumped down on one of the kitchen chairs as I measured out four level tablespoons of MJB.

"What happened?"

"It's Brawly. I think he might'a killed somebody."

"Who?"

"You remember Alva told you about her ex-husband?"

"Yeah."

"He was killed yesterday at her cousin Isolda's house."

"How you know that Brawly did it?" I asked.

"I don't know. It's Isolda. She called Alva last night, only Alva wouldn't talk to her, so instead I got on the line."

"Yeah?"

"She said that Brawly and his father had had a big fight and that she was tryin' to keep 'em apart but she had to go away and she thinks that they run into each other at her house."

"So she didn't actually see Brawly kill Aldridge," I said.

"I don't know," John said. "I don't know what that woman saw and what she didn't. All I know is that Alva's takin' it bad and I'm worried about her. I'm real worried."

"About what exactly?"

A shadow moved over John's already dark visage. I got the feeling that he was about to say something and then decided against it.

"Easy, just go talk to Isolda. Okay? She's holed up in a place down off Alameda. Just go talk to her. And if you can shake Brawly loose someplace, call me and tell me where he is. I'll take care of the rest."

"All right. Gimme the address and I'll see what she has to say." When it came down to it, I couldn't send John away. I'd been in a few tight spots in my time and he had never turned his back on me.

"You want me to go with you?"

"No. You go back to your lots. Put up some timber for me. I'll talk to Isolda and I'll find Brawly, too."

There was a powerful emotion on John's strong face. If I hadn't known him better, I would have thought that he wanted to kill me. That's how hard love was for all black men at one time.

———

*H*ELLO?" HE SAID, answering the phone on the seventeenth ring.

"Jackson?"

"Easy?" I could hear his fear through the line. "Easy, how'd you get my number?"

"I always got your number, Jackson. I always got it."

He was looking around, I was sure, worried that I might be at some window or at his front door.

"Don't worry, Jackson. I ain't hidin' outside your front door." I paused. "I ain't at the back door, neither."

"I was lookin' out the window, man," he said. "You cain't fool me."

"Where's Jesus's money, Jackson?"

"Say what?"

"You heard me, man. Where's the two hundred forty-two dollars you took out from under his bed?"

"Wasn't no two hundred dollars up under there," Jackson whined. "Shit. Not even one-forty."

Jackson Blue was by far the most intelligent person I had ever known but if he was rattled, he could be fooled by a child.

"I want the boy's money," I said.

Jackson had been our houseguest for a few days when he was on the run from some Westside gangsters. He was playing a numbers game in their territory and they wanted a few ounces of flesh. I thought I was doing him a favor until he disappeared with Jesus's savings can.

"All right. Okay, man," Jackson said. "I just borrowed it, anyway. You know them men was out after me. They still are."

"I could come by and pick it up," I said.

Jackson sputtered. His fearfulness made me laugh. He was always in trouble, always around the hardest of hard men. But still, he was afraid of his own shadow.

"Where you get my number, Easy?"

Jackson was a brilliant thinker and as well read as many a university professor, but when it came to reading people, he hadn't made it through the first grade.

He had a girl who he bragged on, name of Charlene Lorraine. Charlene liked the cowardly Jackson for some crazy reason and let him share her bed now and then. She liked him but didn't respect or fear or care about him in any way. I gave her twenty dollars only two weeks after the day Raymond Alexander and John F. Kennedy were shot. She gave me Jackson's number without even asking why.

"I ain't seen him but one time, Easy," the buxom Miss Lorraine told me. "I think he must have some other girlfriend somewhere."

"So you're jealous?" I asked her.

"Jealous?" she exclaimed. "That'd be like bein' jealous if somebody else petted your little dog. He's cute and all, but it ain't like he no real man or nuthin'."

Charlene let her arms hang back making her bosom protrude even farther. She looked me up and down but I didn't bite. Not that I wouldn't have minded being reeled up into her bed, but I had Bonnie by that time and other women were not a main concern on my mind.

"John gimme your number," I lied.

"Where he get it?"

"I didn't need to know that, Jackson. What I need is a line on a few people you might have come across in your petty crimes."

"What people?"

"I want you to ask around about Aldridge Brown, Brawly Brown, and dude name of Strong run with a group called the Urban Revolutionary Party or the First Men."

"Which one?" Jackson asked. "Urban Party or First Men?"

"They go by both names."

"If I do that, you gonna let me slide on the piggy-bank money?"

"If you do that, I'll connect you with an honest job so you can pay Jesus back from your first month's salary."

"What was them names again?" he asked.

I told him.

"Okay. I could do that. Yeah. Why'ont you call me tomorrow afternoon. I should have whatever I can get by then."

"Why don't you call me, Blue?"

"Well, you know . . ."

"No. What?"

"Jesus might answer."

That was Jackson. He lived his whole life among murderers, muggers, and thieves but he was afraid of a sixteen-year-old boy who was even smaller than him.

"All right, Jackson. I'll call you tomorrow at two. You better be there."

"I ain't got nowhere else to be, Easy," he said. "Nowhere at all."

10/ THE TENEMENT ISOLDA MOORE was staying in was nothing like her house. The unpainted wooden stairs that led to her third-floor hideaway felt soggy under my weight. The hallway was misshapen. The floor was warped and sagging, the ceiling slumped. The hallway started out wide but it narrowed as I neared Isolda's door.

The photographs of her on the bureau mirror, even the secret ones of her in the bikini, had not done Miss Moore justice. She was lovely at first sight even though she was off balance from having yanked the wedged door free. She was a light brown woman in a polka-dot blue and white dress. The hemline reached just below her knees, revealing shapely legs. Isolda wore no bra and didn't seem to be missing it. Her big eyes were close together and almond shaped. Her lips were poised in the permanent expectation of a kiss.

"Yes?" she asked nervously.

"Isolda Moore?" I said. She hesitated, so I went on. "My name is Easy Rawlins. John and Alva wanted me to come over and ask you a few things about Brawly."

While I spoke, my eyes cataloged her attributes.

The worry in her face melted away when she saw the way I looked at her.

"Come on in."

The room could have been a hotel flop in a frontier town in the Old West. The walls had never felt a coat of paint and a splinter from that rough floor could have sent you to the hospital with lockjaw. But Isolda had moved whatever furniture there was next to the window and covered it all with white and pastel-colored sheets. There were fresh-picked flowering weeds in a milk bottle on the sill. The arrangement would have put a downtown florist to shame.

"Do you drink tea, Mr. Rawlins?" she asked.

"Whatever you got," I said.

She smiled and led me toward the cloth-covered furniture.

It was a medium-sized room and mostly unfinished, as I said. But Isolda's design had created a small island of style there by the window. The tea she poured was ice-cold even though there was no evidence of a refrigerator in the room.

"I keep the pitcher in a bucket full'a ice I got from the liquor store," she said, seeing the question on my face.

"You should be an interior designer," I said.

"Thank you."

Isolda swiveled on the chair she was in, and I felt my heart catch. She had all the skill and beauty of a woman who hooks up with a big-time minister or gangster, the kind of woman who needs a powerful man for her own skills to flower.

She had positioned herself so that the sun came down on her head, making her eyes glisten. I must have been staring a little too hard because she shifted again and asked, "Alva and John send you to find Brawly?"

"That they did. But really I think Alva wants me to find him."

I mentioned Alva to see if Isolda had hard feelings about her cousin.

"She must be worried sick," Isolda said, leaving me with no clue.

"John told me that Alva's ex-husband was found murdered at your house."

Isolda nodded, looking down at my hands.

"Who killed him?" I asked, again trying to shake her up.

"I really wouldn't know, Mr. Rawlins."

"John said that you thought it was Brawly."

The sun on her face made her pained expression seem unbearable.

"Brawly and Aldridge had been quarreling for years ever since . . . ever since Brawly ran away from home. I was trying to get them back together but . . . but there was never gonna be any peace between them."

"What did they fall out over originally?"

"I never knew," she said, but I didn't believe it. "That was years ago. When I went to pick him up after the fight, his jaw was all swole up and he begged me to let him come stay at my house. When I asked him about his father he showed me a bloody tooth that Aldridge had knocked out of his head."

"Why didn't he go to his mother?" I asked.

"Didn't John tell you?"

"We were with Alva. She was kind of emotional at the time."

"She is . . . very emotional. That was back around the time that her brother Leonard was killed. She took it so hard that she had a nervous breakdown and they had to put her in Camarillo."

Isolda turned her lips toward me and I had to concentrate to hear what she was saying. Her eyes looked deeply into mine, and I thought that if she wasn't a good person in her heart, many a man would have hit some jagged rocks while being distracted by her charms.

Maybe that was why Alva disliked her so much.

"That's why Brawly had to come to you?" I asked. "Because his mother was hospitalized?"

Isolda nodded. "She was really gone. When Brawly went to see her, before his fight with Aldridge, she told him that she couldn't love him and that he shouldn't come to see her anymore."

"Why did you call Alva, Miss Moore?"

"Call me Issy," she said. "That's what I go by, mainly."

"Why aren't you at your own house, Issy?"

"I haven't been back there for a few days. I went up to Riverside and when I came back, Brawly had — I mean, Aldridge was dead. I didn't go back because I was afraid for Brawly." She looked away. Maybe that meant she was taking it hard, or maybe she was going through the motions — practicing for a more serious interrogation.

"Why do you think it was Brawly?" I asked. "And why didn't you go to the cops?"

"Aldridge had come into town a few weeks ago. He came to see me."

"He was your boyfriend?"

Isolda shifted her eyes toward the window. Again they glittered in the light. I doubt if she was looking at anything. Her gaze was definitely of the internal variety.

"We were close. I mean, Aldridge kept his own schedule. If he come to town and I was with a man, he let me alone. But if I was free, he'd stay with me awhile."

"Did Alva know about you two?" I asked, looking for some kind of thread.

"I haven't spoke to Alva in ten years."

"Did Brawly know that his father was shacked up with you?"

I had hoped the rough language would get under her skin, but Isolda wasn't worried about me or what I thought.

"He came by when Aldridge was there, about two weeks ago. They were eyein' each other like wild animals in the entryway, but I had them sit down at the table like two normal human beings. I made tea and brought out some bread and butter. I told them that they was father and son and that they had to start actin' like it."

Isolda turned her gaze on me again. I didn't mind the attention. I wondered how those men felt.

"It went okay at first," she said as if I had asked my question. "They talked and asked each other 'bout what they been doin'. Brawly even laughed once."

Isolda had the wistful tones of love in her voice. I wonder if it was love for Brawly or for his father.

"But then Aldridge had to come out with that damn flask," Isolda said. "Said he wanted to make a toast to their seein' each other after so long."

"He was a bad drunk?" I asked.

"Both of 'em," she said with a sneer. "Both of 'em. That's why I give 'em tea. They drank to their reunion. They drank to me. They drank to a long life and who knows what else. Then Aldridge made the mistake of toastin' Brawly's mother. Brawly told his father that he never wanted to hear her name outta his mouth again."

She said these last words in the tone Brawly must have used. It made me cringe. I'd seen drunken men kill over just that tone of voice.

"The only reason one or the other wasn't killed right then was that I put my body in between 'em." Isolda put a hand in the air, swearing.

She pulled down the left shoulder sleeve of her polka-dot dress, revealing an ugly green bruise just above the curve of her breast. It was one of those deep marks that last for months.

"That's what I had to get before they stopped," she said. "I pushed Brawly out the door and told him not to come back until he learned how to be civil."

"So where were you when Aldridge was killed?" I asked.

"In Riverside, like I said," she said. "I heard about a man gettin' killed on my block on the radio and I called a neighbor to find out what happened. As soon as I knew, I came back down — in case Brawly needed me."

"And why didn't you go to the cops? If you didn't do it, then there's no reason to be scared."

"You ever been questioned by the cops?" Isolda asked me.

For the first time our eyes really met. It was no man-and-woman gaze, but a real understanding.

I had been "questioned" a hundred times and more. And every time my life and liberty had been on the line. It hadn't mattered that I was innocent or that they had no proof of my guilt. There was no Emancipation Proclamation posted on the jailhouse bulletin board. No Bill of Rights, either.

The sleeve of Isolda's dress was still hanging off her shoulder. My fingertips got itchy with the closeness of her flesh.

"Do you think Brawly could overpower a man Aldridge's size?" I asked.

"How you know about his size?"

"Alva told me," I said, hoping he was a fat man when she had known him.

"Brawly look like a kid," she said. "He might be a kid in his mind. But he's strong, scary strong. At a high school picnic once, when Brawly was livin' with me, some kids bet him that he couldn't pull a big stone out the ground. That rock was big. Big. Brawly yanked it up like it was made'a cardboard instead'a granite. You know he was with a couple'a heavyset footballers. I could see the fear in them boys' eyes."

"Did Brawly make that bruise on you?"

"I don't remember. It was a whole mess. Them pushin' and shovin' all over the place. But even if he did do it, it was only 'cause I got in the way."

"Where is he now?"

"I don't know."

"He have any friends you know about?"

"Why are you askin' me all these questions? Are you some kinda policeman or sumpin'?"

"Just a friend'a John and Alva's, like I said. They asked me to look for Brawly, and that's what I'm doin'."

"Well, I ain't seen 'im since he left outta my house two weeks ago."

"Did he say where he was goin'?"

"He said he was gonna kill Aldridge if he didn't watch out."

"You didn't tell me if he had any friends."

"There was this one white girl. BobbiAnne Terrell was her name, I think. They went to high school together."

"Up in Riverside?"

"Uh-huh."

"Would you know her number?"

"No. Maybe it's in the book."

Somewhere during our conversation a coldness set in between me and Isolda. Maybe it was because I represented Alva. Or maybe she saw no use in me.

"Why'd you call Alva, Issy?"

"To tell her about Aldridge and Brawly. And to find out if she knew where he was."

"Why'd you want to know that?"

"I was like a mother to that boy, Mr. Rawlins. And that's somethin' that don't just wear off."

11 / *I GOT TO JOHN'S* lots somewhere about noon. There were other houses under construction on that block but nobody was out there on Sunday, nobody but John's crew.

Mercury and Chapman were sitting on the skeleton of a front-porch-to-be, drinking from small paper cups.

"Wanna snort, Mr. Rawlins?" Mercury asked as I approached.

"What's John gonna say if he see you out here throwin' back liquor on the job?" I asked.

Since I'd recommended them, I felt somewhat responsible for their actions.

"John's a bartender, ain't he?" Chapman whined. "An' anyway, he left for home a hour ago. He said that he'd see us tomorrow."

"You want us to tell 'im you come by, Mr. Rawlins?" Mercury asked.

I picked a newspaper out of a big trash bin, unfolded it, and set it out on the unfinished porch. Then I sat down.

"Actually it's good that John's gone, because I wanted to talk to you boys when he wasn't around."

Mercury and Chapman exchanged glances. I was glad to see that they were bothered. It meant that they wanted to protect my friend.

"Don't worry, boys," I said. "It ain't nuthin' against John. Really it's to help him out."

"What is it?" Mercury asked.

Chapman clenched his hands together and stared off toward his right.

They were a good team. Chapman was the smart one but Mercury had the personality. He'd asked the questions while Chapman contemplated the answers.

"It's about Brawly," I said.

"What about him?"

"What do you boys think?"

"Think about what?" Mercury asked.

"About him quittin' this job and cuttin' it off with his mother."

"We don't know nuthin' about their family life, Easy," Chapman said. "I mean, not no more than might come up in normal conversation while workin' around here."

"Like what?" I asked.

Mercury looked to Chapman, who stuck out his lips and nodded almost imperceptibly.

"Brawly's a good kid," Mercury said. "Strong as a motherfucker but not no bully. He got temper, though. When Brawly blow his stack you better stand back. One day he got mad at John an' almost —"

Chapman brushed his hand against his lips, and Mercury switched gears.

". . . anyway . . . Brawly's a good kid. He just young and stupid."

"Stupid how?"

"For about a couple'a months now he been talkin' that Revolutionary Party bullshit. John didn't like it and Alva didn't, either, to hear Brawly tell it —"

"Brawly said that they told him he had to quit goin' to those meetins, or he was gonna be out the house," Chapman threw in.

That reminded me of something.

"Kicked outta where?" I asked. "You couldn't squeeze three people in that place they live in."

"They paid the rent on a studio in that buildin' they lived in. Brawly stayed down there," Mercury said, "on the first floor."

"Studio?" I said. "What in the hell is it that John got?"

"That's a one-bedroom," Chapman said. "A deluxe one-bedroom, if you believe what the manager say."

Chapman and Mercury laughed. I joined in with them. It was only the tip of the iceberg of what was to come in L.A., but right then it was rare enough to be funny.

"What did Brawly say about that political group?"

"Not much," Mercury mused. "Not too much. He liked it that they were so mad and that they wanted to do somethin'. You know that's just youth, Mr. Rawlins."

"He ever talk about his father?" I asked.

"Now and then," Chapman said. "Not too much."

"Yeah," Mercury said while staring down at his work boots. "He only said that him and his old man had a, whatyoumacallit, a disagreement. But that was a long time ago."

"They have a fight?" I asked.

"Somethin' like that," Mercury said. "The boy said somethin' that they had a fight over his mother or somethin' like that a long time ago and his old man hit him so hard that he knocked out one'a his teeth. That was when he was still a teenager. Then he tramped on down to his cousin Issy. Now her I done seen. You know that there's the kinda cousin your orphan boys dream about."

Chapman let out one of his big laughs. I didn't find it funny, but I knew what he was saying.

"Where'd you see Isolda?" I asked.

"She drop by now and then to pick up Brawly," Mercury said. "You know, family stuff, I guess. She'd take him for burgers. It was always on the sly, like. I don't think her and Alva got along too well."

Chapman looked at me then. He held out his hands halfheartedly asking, *Is that it?*

"Well," I said. "I guess you boys better be gettin' back to work."

"I guess so," Chapman said.

*O*N THE RIDE HOME I wondered about the complex weave of John's problem. His wife, her murdered ex-husband and brother, her son living with her cousin while she was suffering from a nervous breakdown, and the black revolutionaries with their hopeful anger, and the cops breathing down their necks.

By the time I got home I was ready to talk to my son.

He was in the backyard setting up three sawhorses, each one spaced about four feet from the next. He also had out a few planks of wood about ten feet long and four feet wide. They were between one and a half and two inches thick.

"What you doin'?" I asked him.

"I'm gonna build a boat," he said.

"Where'd you get the wood?"

"Bought it from Mr. Galway at the lumberyard."

"He deliver it?"

Jesus nodded.

This was a new phase in his life. Jesus had never before spent money on himself. Ever since he was quite young he saved his money, for fear that I'd lose my job or be put in jail. He worked four afternoons a week at a local market, bagging groceries and making deliveries for old women. Every cent went into a coffee can in his closet. In his mind everything would always be fine because if I fell down, he would be there to take up the slack.

I tried to convince him that he didn't have to worry, that he could buy himself toys or clothes or anything he wanted. But Jesus had spent his younger years with my friend Primo. In Primo's world a boy was just a smaller version of a man; he might not have been able to do as much as his larger counterpart but he was expected to do all that he could manage.

"What kinda boat?" I asked.

"Sail," Jesus said.

"You know how to build a sailboat?"

"There's a book." Jesus pointed at a large paperback that he'd gotten from the library. It was lying on the back porch, open to a page that showed three sawhorses spaced four feet apart. "It says that there's one hundred and sixty-one steps to build a sailboat."

"Come here and sit down with me," I said.

We sat together on the concrete porch. I was looking at Jesus as he stared at the grass beneath his bare feet.

"What's this about droppin' out of school?"

"I don't like it there," he said.

"Why not?"

"I don't like the kids or the teachers," he said.

"You got to say more if you want me to understand you, Juice. I mean, did somebody do something to make you mad?"

"Uh-uh. They're just stupid."

"Stupid how?"

"I don't know."

"You must have some kind of example. Did somebody do something stupid last week?"

Jesus nodded. "Mr. Andrews."

"What did he do?" I was used to asking Jesus questions. Though he had been speaking since he was twelve, words were still a rare commodity for him.

"Felicity Dorn was crying. She was sad because her cat died. Mr. Andrews told her that she had to be quiet or he was going to send her to the vice principal's office and she would miss a big test. And if she didn't take the test, she'd probably fail out."

"He was just trying to keep her from distracting the class."

"But her mother died just last year," Jesus said, looking up at me. "She couldn't help how bad she felt."

"I'm sure he didn't know that."

"But he should know. He's the teacher. All he knows is the states and their capitals and what year the presidents died."

"Are you gonna let somebody like that keep you from going to college and bein' something?"

"He went to college," Jesus said, "and it didn't help him."

I managed to keep the smile off my face. Inside I was proud of the man my son was becoming.

"You can't decide to leave school because one teacher's a fool," I said.

"That's not all. They think I'm stupid."

"No."

"Yes, they do. They don't wanna teach me. They give me homework but they don't care if I turn it in. They like it that I run fast but they don't care."

"What do you mean?" I asked.

"I don't know."

Jesus got up and moved toward his sawhorses. I touched his elbow and he stopped.

"We need to talk about this more, Juice. We need to talk about it until we can both decide. You hear me?"

"Uh-huh."

"What?"

"Yes, sir."

"All right. Go work on your boat."

12 / *I PULLED UP* in front of the restaurant at about nine.

Hambones didn't have an exit to speak of. They had a back door leading into a crevice that Sam called the alley. But that was just for the fire code, nobody could really get out that way. So I sat in my green Pontiac, which rattled whenever I pushed it over fifty miles per hour, and waited.

Hambones was a dive by 1964, but in the old days only the flashiest men and women went in there at night. That was the way it was for blacks. We couldn't frequent the fancy clubs in Hollywood and Beverly Hills. And we didn't have that class of joint in our working-class neighborhoods. So men would put on their glad rags and women would don their costume jewelry and furs and go down to some local hangout where there was a jukebox and the pretense of luxury. After a few months of notoriety musicians would begin to frequent the place. Sam Houston had Jelly Roll Morton and Lips McGee as regulars in his joint in the fifties. Louis Armstrong even made an appearance once.

Of course, musicians bring their own crowd: men who want to play like them and women who want to be played. These men and women come in all colors. And once you have a few whites down there, they start coming down in droves. Because as fancy as the Brown Derby might have been, it wasn't going to give you the kind of freedom that a black club offered. Black people know how to be free. People who had been denied for as many centuries as we had knew how to let their hair down and dance like there was no tomorrow.

MOUSE WAS THE FIRST PERSON to take me to Hambones. He hadn't been in L.A. three months when he nosed it out.

"Yeah, Ease," he said to me. "The women down there make you cry, they so fine. They don't have no liquor but you know it's cheaper in a paper bag anyways."

It was the early fifties and I was unattached. One thing good about Mouse being so dangerous was that women just loved being around him. You knew that if you were around Raymond, something unexpected was bound to happen.

We went down there looking for a woman named Millie. Millie Perette from East St. Louis. She always wore a string of real pink pearls and carried a nacre-handled pistol in a handbag hardly big enough for a cigarette case.

"Millie do you so bad that you wanna cry when you wake up in the mornin'," Mouse told me. "Because the next night is so far away."

We got there at about midnight. When all the white clubs were winding down, Sam's place was just getting a second wind. I remember a trumpet player blowing at his table, surrounded by women. People were dancing to the music, drinking and kissing to it, too. When we walked in everybody greeted Mouse as if he were the mayor of Watts rather than a recent transplant from the Fifth Ward, Houston, Texas.

He had a fifth of rye whiskey in his left hand and a terrible .41-caliber pistol under his zoot suit jacket. Mouse loved that pistol more than any woman. He once told me that the barrel could be unscrewed from the chamber and that he had twelve barrels so that if he killed somebody, he could switch. That way they couldn't ever prove that it was his gun used in the crime.

*M*ILLIE WAS AT THE BAR with a big bruiser, a dusky bronze-colored man with gold-capped teeth, a diamond ring, and a pistol tucked in the belt of his woolen suit pants. His hand was half the way down Millie's blouse and she was laughing happily, drinking from a hammered silver shot glass.

When Raymond and I walked up to the pair, I was less than pleased. The most you could hope for in Mouse's company was a bloodless evening — and you could never bank on that if there was love or money involved. The people sitting near the couple moved away as we approached. The conversation died down but the bruiser might not have noticed, because the horn still blew.

"Millie," Raymond said.

She opened up her lips in a loose fashion, showing her teeth and smiling but with an edge that said she knew the stakes had just been raised.

"I thought you said that you was gonna be up north, Ray baby," she said. And even though I was girding for fatal violence, I saw the attraction of a woman so brazen.

"Thought I'd stick around and see if you wanted to dance," Raymond said pleasantly.

"Delmont Williams," the bruiser said to Mouse, holding out his hand.

Ray looked at the hand but he didn't take it.

I fought the urge to back out the way I'd come.

"Where you from, Del?" Mouse asked.

"Chi-town's my home," he said proudly. "Three generation outta Mississippi but I still eat hog maws and call my mother 'ma'am.'"

"How long you been in town?" Mouse asked.

"What's it to ya, little man?"

"Oh. I just wondered."

Millie was beginning to understand the seriousness of the conversation. But she was more amused than she was worried. Men fighting over her charms was like a box of chocolate creams to her.

"'Bout a week or two," Delmont said. "Long enough to meet the most beautiful woman in Los Angeles."

He let his big hand rub over Millie's breast. She didn't even feel it, though, entranced as she was by the spectacle promising to unfold.

"I see," Raymond said politely. "It's Delmont — right?"

"Yeah."

"Delmont, would you step outside with me?"

"What for?"

"'Cause I don't wanna get no blood on my woman."

A little sound came out of Millie's throat then. Whether it was fear or humor, surprise or just a burp, I did not know.

Delmont looked at Millie and asked, "Are you his woman?"

"What do you think?" was her reply.

Delmont turned back to Mouse and said, "Get away from here 'fore I hurt you, boy."

"Come on outside," Mouse said. "And we'll see just what kinda man yo' ma'am made."

Delmont was high on liquor and he was intoxicated by the wild and beautiful Millie Perette, but I think at the last minute there he got an inkling of the iron core of my friend. It wasn't enough to stop him from getting to his feet, though. It wasn't enough to keep him from going out the door.

Nobody followed them out there, because no one wanted to be witness to Mouse's rage. Less than a minute after they'd gone outside, a shot was heard. Two minutes after that, Raymond returned to the restaurant. The horn had stopped playing by then.

Mouse walked up to Millie and whispered a few words into her ear. She hopped off her stool and walked out with him. I remember that she kept her thighs close together as she walked, making her posterior sway in the most intoxicating way.

Silence trailed in their wake.

A minute or two later a few of us went out to see what remained of the big man from Chicago. He wasn't in the street, so we went down two doorways and turned into the alley there. Under a weak lamp I saw Delmont, a small puddle of blood next to his head.

When he moved and moaned I jumped. Then I leaned closer and saw that he'd only been wounded in the ear.

*N*AW, MAN," Mouse said to me a few days later, when we'd finally caught up with each other. "I didn't intend to kill 'im. He was from Chi, didn't know shit. I wouldn'ta even shot 'im but he had to go callin' me names in there like I was some kinda chile. But you know, baby, Millie really liked that shit. She give it up all night long. I just touch her and she start to call on the Holy Spirit."

SITTING OUT THERE in front of Hambones, I found myself smiling. Ray had a short life but just one day out of it was a year or more to most other men. I could never feel sorry for him — only guilty that in the final moments I had let him down.

13 / *CLARISSA WALKED OUT* of Hambones at about eleven-thirty. It was a Sunday night and Hambones wasn't the hot spot that it had once been. She turned left and walked down the street. I let her go about a block or so before turning the engine over. I drove a block past her and then pulled over to the curb on the opposite side of the street.

When she walked past me again, I turned off the engine. After she was a block away I got out. She was walking swiftly, clacking her wooden heels. My shoes were rubber soled, however, so I could keep up without being heard.

She wasn't nervous, but like any woman with some sense she cast a glance backward now and then. I avoided detection by keeping to the shadows across the street. We went like that for six or seven blocks. Then Clarissa turned right on Byron. She went a block and a half before coming to a squat three-story building that looked like an oversized incinerator. It was covered with kumquat-colored plaster and seemed to sag under its own weight. Clarissa went into a door on the ground floor. A light came on in a tiny window.

I went over to her door and strained to listen. The building was so cheap that I could hear her footsteps. She opened a door, put down something metal, probably a pot. Something like a chair or couch sagged and then a radio went on in the middle of the song "The Duke of Earl."

She was cooking or brewing tea and listening to music. I figured that I'd wait around until she decided to go to bed.

Clarissa's building had a sister structure across the street. On its north side was a small entryway where the garbage cans were stored until trash day. I climbed in behind the lidded metal cans, lit up a Chesterfield, and breathed through my mouth.

The desert quiet of southern California nights was always a pleasure to me. In the South around Texas and Louisiana there were loud bugs and night birds, wind in the trees, and less identifiable noises from the wetlands and its inhabitants. But in L.A. the night was wrapped in silence as if there were always a predator near, waiting to pounce on some hushed victim.

That night, I suppose, the predator was me.

*A*LMOST NOTHING HAPPENED for the next hour or so. A family of spiders had set up a system of webs above my head, so even the rare moth didn't stay around long.

The entrance to Clarissa's apartment was illuminated by a concrete lamp that was set in the lawn in front of her door. The light in her window stayed on, so I kept to my post.

My copper-faced Gruen watch said 12:48 when a lime green

Cadillac drove up and stopped in front of Clarissa's building. I could see the damage done by the wooden fence he'd hit broadside the night before. Handsome Conrad was still in the driver's seat. He was still edgy, looking around nervously. He even glanced in my direction, but I was too deep in shadow to be seen.

Brawly hopped out of the passenger's side and said something into the back window. Conrad squealed off down the street, as if he thought the police were still chasing him. Maybe they were.

Brawly knocked on Clarissa's door. She answered with a kiss and an embrace. Brawly was a bulky kid, but Clarissa managed to get her arms around him. She was whispering something in his ear, holding on hard.

They retreated into the house, leaving me to wonder about my next move.

It didn't take me long. I crossed the street and walked up to her door. There was some kind of argument going on.

"You didn't answer my question!" Clarissa was saying in a loud tone.

I rapped on the hollow door much harder than was necessary. What followed was a sudden silence. I knocked again.

"Who is it?" came the voice that had sounded the alarm at the revolutionary headquarters the night before.

"Easy Rawlins," I said out loud. "Open up."

"Who are you?"

"Open up, Brawly, Clarissa."

That did the trick. Brawly pulled the door wide so he could see the man who knew his name.

As the door was coming open, I felt the flush of victory. But when I saw his size up close, and the anger knit into his brow, I feared that my triumph could turn into defeat.

"Who the fuck are you?" he asked.

"A man who's been to Isolda's front doorway," I said.

The words didn't seem to cause him any discomfort or fear.

"What she got to do with you?" he asked.

"Let me in, Brawly. We shouldn't be talkin' murder out where any ear could hear."

"Let him in, honey," Clarissa said. She was standing at his shoulder.

He backed up and I entered the apartment.

It was even smaller than John and Alva's place, more like a playhouse than an adult's home. If I had laid down and stretched out my arms, I could have touched one wall with the flat of my feet and the opposite one with my fingertips.

"Who is he?" Brawly asked his girlfriend.

"He's a friend'a Sam's," Clarissa said. "Easy Rawlins, like he said."

"Your mama sent me," I said.

There was a big yellow chair in a corner of the sad little room. I'd been on my feet for over an hour, so I took the opportunity to sit.

Brawly remained upright while Clarissa hovered close to him, fearful, I imagined, that he might lose control.

"What you doin' bangin' on my woman's door in the middle'a the night?"

"Lookin' for you," I said.

That was a good time to light up a cigarette. It made me feel confident while relaxing my nerves in the presence of the behemoth John asked me not to harm.

"Don't fuck with me, niggah," he said. But the words didn't sound genuine. He was big but he was still playacting, not yet a man in his own right.

"Are you the one slaughtered Aldridge Brown?" I asked him.

"What? . . ."

"Aldridge Brown," I said. "Was it you who killed him?"

Brawly grabbed me by my arms and picked me up out of the chair. He lifted me high enough that the ceiling was no more than an inch from my head.

The sense of weightlessness reminded me of when I was a defenseless child in the grip of some rough adult, yearning for the ground beneath my feet.

"What the fuck you talkin' 'bout?" he said, his voice a full octave higher.

"Put me down," I said without tripping over a single syllable.

"Put him down, baby!" Clarissa yelled.

"He was killed at Isolda's house," I said. "Beat to death at the front door yesterday morning. Ain't you read the papers?"

Brawly let me down gently enough but when he slumped onto that cotton brown couch, it felt as if the floor might collapse. As it was, the whole house shook. I imagined that people were jumping out of their beds, worried that another L.A. earthquake was shaking down the building.

"Beat to death?"

"Yeah," I said. "And when I went to talk to Isolda the only story she had was that you and Aldridge had a fight and you left sayin' that you'd kill him if he ever said your mother's name again."

"That bitch," Clarissa hissed.

"It's not true," Brawly said. "I was with . . . I wasn't even in town yesterday morning."

He shot a guilty glance at Clarissa, but she was too upset to notice.

"You didn't see Aldridge at Isolda's house?"

"Not yesterday."

"Did you two get drunk and argue a couple'a weeks ago at her house?" I asked.

"Couple'a months, yeah. We had a drink or two. The conversation got a little hot but we ain't had no fight. If we did, he'd be . . ."

Brawly didn't need to finish that sentence. "I didn't kill 'im, man. I swear."

"Somebody did," I said.

Brawly sat back, looking more than ever like the child in his mother's photograph.

"He's dead?" Brawly asked again. "Dead?"

"That's right."

"My father?" he asked of no one in particular.

Clarissa perched herself on the armrest of the sofa. She put her arm around his head.

"My father, my dad . . ."

It was a moving performance. It might have even been real remorse, but I had seen people cry over loved ones they had murdered just hours before. The feelings of pain were there whether or not their hand had delivered the final stroke.

I lit up another cigarette.

"You don't know anything about it?" I asked when the tears had passed. "I mean, you didn't even read about it or hear it on the news?"

"Brawly's been busy," Clarissa told me.

"Shut your mouth," Brawly warned.

I wouldn't have been suspicious if he followed his own advice.

"Busy doin' what?"

"Who are you, man?" Brawly asked me.

"Friend'a Alva Torres doin' a good deed by her boy."

"I ain't got nuthin' to do with her," Brawly told me.

"That's your mother, honey," Clarissa said. "That's blood."

"And just about the only drop left," I added. "She's concerned about you. When she asked me to find you, I told her she probably didn't need to worry. But now that I seen the mess your life is in, I understand why she wants you to come home."

"I don't have no home. They kicked me out."

"I don't believe that for one second, son. Your mama loves you even if you don't care for yourself."

"He's right, baby," Clarissa said.

"You don't know shit, Clarissa. So don't be tryin' to tell me nuthin'."

"The cops gonna look hard at you if they think you were fighting with him," I said.

"That was almost two months ago," Brawly said. "We made up since then."

"Where were you Saturday morning?" I asked.

"Up north," Brawly said. "I left Friday night."

"Can you prove that?"

A guilty look flashed on the boy's face. He seemed to hold himself back from looking at Clarissa.

"People saw me," he said evasively.

"Who?"

"Why I got to answer to you? Who the fuck are you to come in here in the middle'a the night and question me?" Brawly said.

When he rose up from the couch my heart did a double thump to get enough blood into action in case I needed to fight.

"I don't have to talk to you."

"I'm just tryin' to help you, boy," I said.

I made the mistake of putting my hand on his shoulder.

Brawly shoved both arms out at me and I went backward. My feet actually left the ground. I felt the wall hit my back and my left ankle twist as my foot touched down.

Clarissa said, "Baby."

The front door slammed open.

When I looked up I saw Brawly storming out into the street, leaving his girlfriend with a strange man in the middle of the night.

14 / *CLARISSA RAN TO THE DOOR* but she didn't try to stop Brawly. She must have gone through this with him before, his childish anger overruling his common sense, even his common decency.

I considered going after the boy but doubted that either my words or my fists would have made much of an impression. I could have shot him but didn't think that John or Alva would have taken kindly to that.

"I'm sorry," I said, wanting to somehow make up for the boy.

"It's okay. Brawly don't mean it. It's just that he get so mad sometimes. It ain't his fault."

"I told Alva that I'd make sure that he was okay. I guess he is. I mean, you say this is normal for him, right?"

I was at a loss with Clarissa. She didn't have anything to do with my job but there I was, intruding on her private life in the middle of the night. I took a step toward the door.

"Is that stuff about Brawly's father true?" she asked me.

"Yeah. Somebody killed him right there in Isolda's house. She thinks it must have been Brawly."

"Is that what she told the police?"

"I don't think she's seen the cops yet. She was out of town when he was killed, at least that's what she said. She never went back to her house."

"Damn," Clarissa said. "Brawly got the worst luck in blood. If they alive or dead, with him or not with him, they still bring him grief."

"His mother, too, you think?" I asked.

"She love him and all, but she don't understand him. She wanna be tellin' him what to do and don't wanna hear 'bout the ideas he got for himself."

"Like what?" I asked.

"Like what he believe in," she said. "Like what he think people oughtta be doin'."

"Like with the Urban Revolutionary Party?"

"Maybe."

Clarissa was a slight girl with knotty features. Her hair was frosted gold. Her eyes were so light a brown that you might have called them gold, too. She was at an age when the clothes accented rather than covered her figure, and her skin seemed to glow. I felt a flush of embarrassment just looking at her.

"John and Alva think that the First Men is just a gang," I said. "That's why they got me lookin' for Brawly."

"Older black folks is just scared'a what groups like the First Men stand for. They're scared to stand up and demand what the white man owes them. They just don't understand that the only way to get somethin' is to fight for it."

"They plannin' a war?" I asked.

"Only if there's no other way. What they want is better schools and jobs, history books that tell the truth, and people who look like us in government."

"Sounds like a tall order."

"It's only fair. And Xavier knows that we got to take it slow. He wanted us to turn that storefront into a place where the community could come and talk about our problems. But now the cops busted in, the people will be too scared to trust in it."

"So now what?" I really wanted to know.

"We got to find another way. That's all."

There was something that she wasn't saying, something that lurked behind her resolute words.

"So they're into the revolution and not protection?" I asked.

"Protection from what?" she replied.

I laughed then. Maybe I was getting old.

"You got a pencil, Clarissa?"

"Uh-huh, why?"

"Because I'm going to write down my phone numbers — day and night. I don't wanna mess with Brawly. If he's happy with what he's doin', then that's okay with me. But if he gets in trouble or if you see that the Party's not what they say — then you call on me. All right?"

She didn't answer the question but she did give me pencil and paper. I put down my numbers at work and at home.

Before I left I asked her, "Why do you sound so mad at Isolda? Do you know her?"

"I know what she did to Brawly," Clarissa said with a sneer.

"What?"

"That ain't for me to say."

*I*T WAS AFTER one in the morning. If I were living the life that I had promised myself, I would have gone home and tucked the kids into their beds. But the fever was still in me and there was someone I needed to talk to who I knew never went to sleep before sunrise.

He lived in a rented house on a street called Ozone Court, only half a block from the beach. It was just a tiny tar-roofed structure, but he was the only black man I knew who had managed to get a place in that neighborhood. While pressing the buzzer I planned to ask him how he got away with living in an exclusively white neighborhood. But the way he answered the door threw that question right out of my head.

"Who's there?" he asked in a gruff voice that he tried to make sound deep. "What the fuck you want this time'a night?"

Instead of answering, I pressed the buzzer again.

"What?" he said, giving up the deep voice. If that tone were in his hands, they would have been up over his head.

"Jackson Blue?" I said in a commanding voice that was not exactly my own.

"Who is it?"

I laughed then. Cowardly Jackson Blue certainly deserved a prank or two. Ever since he'd stolen Jesus's money I figured that I had the right to needle him.

He flung the door open and glared at me.

I laughed even harder. Jackson was short and slight, almost as dark as the sky above our heads, with eyes that were both bright and brilliant. Those shining, perpetually bloodshot orbs glared at me.

"What the fuck you think is so funny, niggah?"

"Lemme in, Jackson," I said. "It's cold out here."

He looked around to see if I had anyone with me and then leaned away from the door, allowing me to enter.

Jackson's house was wedged in between two larger but equally nondescript homes. From the outside his place looked small but it was much more spacious on the inside. That was because the single room that made it up was half a flight of stairs below the front door. The ceiling was at least twenty feet high.

Jackson had a big bed, a table that doubled as a hot-plate kitchen, a table desk like high school kids use, and three walls of bookshelves that ran the full height of the wall. Every inch of shelf space was packed with books. The room smelled of moldering paper. There was a wooden painter's ladder set up so that little Jackson could reach the higher shelves.

The back door was a sliding glass window that looked out on a vegetable garden.

"Where'd you get all those books, Jackson?"

"Bought 'em, mostly. A lot of 'em I been havin' for years stored in different people's garages. When I got this place I brought 'em here."

I sat at the table. Jackson snaked into his schoolboy's desk.

"You got what I wanted?" I asked him.

"That depends."

"On what?"

"You know the rent ovah here in the white world ain't cheap."

"Listen here, Jackson. I ain't playin' wit' you. You try'n get over on me an' you will end up bein' the one payin'."

Jackson wasn't worried. He'd known me for more than twenty years. I'd never laid a hand on him in that time and wasn't likely to start.

"I need to know a few things before I tell you what's what," he said.

"Yeah, all right. What is it?"

"First, how did you find where I live at? I thought about what you told me on the phone and I just don't believe John would'a had my address."

"Charlene Lorraine told me."

"How much you have to give her for that?"

"Twenty dollars."

"That's all?"

"Yeah. I gave her twenty and asked her had she seen you, and she said not much lately but the last she knew you were livin' down on Ozone."

"Prob'ly just jealous 'cause I let her ride," Jackson said, trying to shore up his pride.

"What else?" I asked.

"How much you gettin' paid to get what I know?"

"A family dinner for me and Bonnie and the kids."

"You cain't kid a kidder, man," Jackson whined. "Naw, brother. You cain't fool me."

"Jackson, why would I lie to you?"

"To keep all the loot for yourself, that's why."

"What loot?"

"You askin' 'bout the First Men, right?"

"Yeah."

Jackson was a man in his forties but he had the body of a boy. He shifted sideways in the constrictive desk and pulled his right knee up to his chin and smiled. He was the Cheshire Cat.

"They plannin' a revolution," Jackson said.

"So? What else is new? Must be half a dozen groups talkin' that shit. But even if it was real, guns and bullets not your kinda loot."

"But the money to buy 'em is," Jackson said with a grin.

All the information I'd brought together since meeting with John floated through my head: the dead man, his girlfriend, Brawly and Alva and Clarissa, even the police breaking down the walls.

"What you talkin' 'bout, Jackson?"

"Bread and bullets, baby. Bread and bullets."

Jackson was a great intellect but he had a petty soul. Bread and bullets, blood and bravery — it was all just money to him.

"What are you talkin' about?" I asked.

"I don't know," Jackson said. "But I hear that them boys is plannin' somethin' big, really big. In order to do somethin' on a grand scale, they got to have some money comin' in from somewhere. That's what my information tells me."

"Who you been talkin' to?"

"Why you wanna know about these men?"

I told Jackson about John and Alva asking me to find Brawly.

"That's it?" he asked when I had finished.

"That's all, baby," I said.

"So you ain't have nuthin' to do with the money?"

"In the first place, this money is just you supposin'," I said. "And even if you were right, you know me, Blue. I'm not a robber or a thief."

"But you an' Mouse was friends," he said in way of argument.

"What the hell does Mouse have to do with anything?" It made me angry just to hear his name.

"Mouse did some robbin' in his time," Jackson said. "One time they say he took off on a Sunday, drove all the way to Kansas City, Missouri, robbed a bank, and was back down Watts by Friday night."

"Ain't you scared to be talkin' about Raymond's business like that?" I asked.

"Why should I be scared? He's dead."

"You know anybody went to the funeral?" I asked.

Jackson's smooth brow crinkled. "No."

"So why do you think he's dead?"

"You said you saw him laid out." Jackson began stuttering, "And . . . and . . . and Martha Rimes said that he was dead in the hospital bed before . . . before . . ."

"She said that he didn't have a pulse. You know she was feeling with her fingers. Sometimes a pulse is so weak that a finger cain't feel it."

It was a pleasure to see Jackson's eyes widen in fear. He knew better than to air a man's business the way he was talking about Mouse.

"I'm sorry," he said. "Don't tell nobody, okay, Ease?"

"You the one need to learn to keep his mouth shut," I said.

We had a moment of silence. Jackson was staring at our reflection in the glass door, looking for vengeful ghosts beyond the pane.

"You hear anything useful about Brawly?" I asked then.

"He got a girlfriend live on Grand."

"Byron, you mean."

"No," Jackson said. "I know what I mean, and I mean Grand Avenue up near Sunset."

"You got a number?"

"You sure you not after some fortune, Easy?"

"What got that bug up your butt?"

"Aldridge A. Brown," Jackson said. "That's what."

"What about him?"

"They say that thirteen years ago Aldridge and a partner robbed a bank downtown. The partner got killed but Aldridge got away."

My mind froze up but I kept talking to keep Jackson from getting too inquisitive.

"Aldridge is dead, man. And if he was a bank robber, he wouldn't have anything to do with some political group. People like that rob banks for profit, not democracy."

"People change."

"Not you," I said. "Now, you got a number on this girlfriend?"

He gave me the address. But he didn't have a name or an apartment number.

"I was lucky to get that," he said when I complained.

Instead of going directly to my car, I walked the short block down to the beach. Santa Monica still had the feel of a small town in '64. Wooden buildings painted in primary colors, small storefronts that specialized in trinkets made from seashells.

The moon was hidden from sight by a large cloud, but its light still fell on waters many miles from the shore. That far-off light was like a marooned sailor's hopes — faraway and nearly impossible.

15 / *I DIDN'T GET TO SLEEP* until five. I dreamt of a dead man who took turns being Mouse and Aldridge, Brawly Brown and his inhuman strength, and a revolution in the streets of Los Angeles.

I woke up at seven-thirty and called in sick to work.

"Tell Newgate that I got that bug," I said to Priscilla Howe, his sixth secretary in two and a half years.

"You bet, Mr. Rawlins," she said. "I hope you feel better."

After that I got the kids out of bed. Jesus helped Feather dress for school and I made breakfast. It was lonely without Bonnie, but the children and I had a rhythm of life that worked perfectly.

"Where'd you go last night, Daddy?" Feather asked me.

"To see Jackson Blue," I said.

"Did he give you my money?" Jesus asked.

"He said that he'd have it in a few days."

"Jackson Blue is funny," Feather exclaimed, and then she started giggling.

Before she was finished we were all laughing and spilling our juice.

Jesus walked Feather to school and I went back to bed.

In the dream I was sitting in a bar when Raymond walked in.

"What's wrong, Easy?" he asked me.

"It's John," I said. "He wants me to save his girlfriend's boy, but the kid's in too deep."

"Kill him," Mouse said.

"Kill who?"

"The boy. Shoot him. Tell John you don't know what happened. Get it over quick, so him and his woman can start to heal."

Raymond turned to walk away.

"Ray."

"Yeah?"

"I'm sorry, man. Sorry I let you down."

"You let me die," he said, correcting me. "You let me die."

The anguish I felt was like a grease burn; it started out painful enough but then it dug deep.

*T*HE DOORBELL was a relief, a lifeline thrown out to me from some unknowing stranger. I climbed out of bed and stumbled to the door in only my boxer shorts.

The white man standing there wore a suit that could have been handed out at the Salvation Army. He was on the short side with light green eyes and curly hair that defied my color sense. It could have been red or gold or brown, depending on how you looked at it.

"Mr. Rawlins?"

"Yeah?"

He produced a ratty, worn-out wallet displaying an identity card and a badge.

"Detective Knorr," he said. "Can I come in?"

There were many things wrong with Knorr showing up on my doorstep. Not only was he shabby beyond anything I'd ever seen on Chief Parker's police force, but he was also alone. The L.A. police didn't travel solo. Or if they did, it was because they were on some clandestine assignment. And even if that made sense, what could he possibly have wanted with me? I was a senior custodian at a public junior high school. I was a homeowner, a taxpayer. I had just been sleeping in my bed, innocent of any crime.

Any of these reasons would have been enough for me to have sent Officer Knorr away. But he saved me from the total despair of my dream and I was grateful for that.

"Do I have to get dressed?" I asked him.

"Not for me."

I swung the door wide and stepped back for the policeman to enter.

"Excuse me," I said. "I just got up. I got to hit the head."

I came back wearing a bathrobe and house slippers. Knorr was sitting in my reclining chair.

"Feel better?" he asked.

"What can I do for you, Officer?"

Knorr sat at the edge of the comfortable chair. He had a medium build with small hands and thick eyebrows. The eyebrows were the same color as the hair on his head, only darker.

"The police department and the city of Los Angeles need your help, Mr. Rawlins."

"You want some coffee?" I replied.

Knorr was not easily disturbed. "Sure," he said. "Two teaspoons of milk and one sugar."

I went to the kitchen and he followed me.

"Why aren't you at work today if you don't mind me asking?" he asked.

"Hard weekend," I said while filling the kettle from the faucet.

"Parties?" His smile had no warmth or humor to it.

"It's just instant," I said. "That and Cremora."

"Perfect."

"So what do want from me?" I asked.

Knorr's green eyes settled on the lawn outside my back window. He was beaming that cold smile.

"There's blood boiling under the surface of Watts," he said.

The subtle hiss of the gas jets accented his words with a sinister edge.

"What's that supposed to mean?"

"The Negroes are getting anxious for some changes," he said. "They want to end de facto segregation. They want better jobs. They want to be treated like war heroes after coming home from World War Two and Korea. Some even question going into the army and fighting for their country."

I couldn't tell if there was sarcasm or concern in his voice. Like his smile, his tone was enigmatic.

"That's outside my field of expertise, Officer Knorr. I'm a janitor. I wax floors and empty trash bins. Boiling blood is some other department. And I already did my stint in the army."

Knorr smiled.

The kettle whistled. It began with a weak chirp that quickly became a scream, like the emergency that Knorr feared.

I poured our coffees into powder blue mugs with red roses stenciled on them. Feather had picked them out at a small shop we visited on a day trip to the little Swedish town of Solvang, just inland from Santa Barbara.

Knorr sat across from me, smiling through the rising steam. He reached into his breast pocket and came out with a small stack of photographs. He handed them to me.

They were grainy black-and-white shots, slightly blurred because the subjects were unaware of the photographer and so moved unexpectedly at times. There were many different people in the snapshots, but the constant was me: me talking to Handsome Conrad and skinny Xavier Bodan, me standing outside of the Urban Revolutionary Party's front door, me running out the back, pulling Tina by the arm and rushing toward a Cadillac that I knew was green.

The fever I'd felt two days earlier returned as a chill. For a moment a dark part of my mind wanted to strangle Officer Knorr and then make a run for the state line.

"I showed those pictures around and came up with your name, Mr. Rawlins."

"Why you wanna single me out?"

"I know everybody else's name. Christina Montes, Jasper Xavier Bodan, and Anton Breland, who also goes by the name Conrad. I could lay a name and a few aliases on everybody at that meeting. Everybody but you."

I was memorizing the names I didn't already know while trying to keep my breath from driving me to violence.

"What's the problem, Officer? Is it against some law to go to a political meeting?"

"What were you doing there?"

"Why?"

"It could have some bearing on a case that I've been assigned to."

"What case?"

"We have reason to believe that these political activists are planning some kind of violent protest. Maybe even an armed attack of some kind. I mean to keep that from happening."

It was impossible to read behind that cool expression or Knorr's soft words. Did he believe what he was asking me? Or was this some complex ploy to trip me up or to somehow vilify those children?

"I went there looking for a young man named Brawly Brown," I said.

"Why?"

"Because his mother was worried about him and wanted me to make sure that he was healthy and safe."

Knorr winked at me. I didn't know if it was a nervous tic or a sign that he was happy with my answer.

"Did you find him?"

"I saw him at the opposite end of room. Then your armored guard came through the windows and started breaking heads."

"That wasn't me. That was Captain Lorne. He thinks you can beat the Negroes by dispersing them. I know better."

Slowly a picture of the internal man was coming clear.

"So you just take pictures while he abuses our rights?" I said.

"Rights," Knorr said. "Those people don't respect what America has given them. They don't deserve rights."

"That's not for you to decide, Officer. Rights are guaranteed by the Constitution, not judged by some messenger boy from city hall."

If it was possible Knorr's green eyes got even cooler.

"This boy Brown," he said, "is at the center of the trouble I'm working on. He's been in contact with the people who are planning an insurrection."

I wondered if what Knorr was saying was true. On top of that, I wondered if he believed what he said.

"Why you gonna come in here and tell me all this, Officer? You don't know me. I might be Khrushchev's man in L.A., for all you know. I could be lookin' for Brawly to sign up for the war."

"I've talked to a few people about you, Mr. Rawlins. Easy — that's what they call you, isn't it? You have a rap sheet but not for this kind of stuff. You work one-on-one. Sometimes you're on the wrong side, but you're a loyal American. I know your war record."

"The war is over," I said. "You won and I didn't."

"You don't believe that shit," Knorr said. "If you did, you wouldn't have Jesus and Feather. . . ."

When he mentioned my children's names a chilly nausea invaded my intestines.

"You wouldn't have that job at Sojourner Truth Junior High School. I heard that you even intervened when there was gang violence at your school; you called in the cops and gave them the information they needed to keep a gang war from happening."

"What do you want from me, Officer?"

Knorr took a dirty white card from his pocket and placed it on the table.

"That's my number," he said. "Call me when you got something. As an informant we can come up with probably a thousand dollars' reward. And as an American you'll be helping your people and mine."

I didn't touch the card, nor did I look at it directly.

"Is that it?"

"Yes."

"Then why don't you leave?"

He gave me a one-eighth nod and frigid grin, then got to his feet and moved toward the door. As I watched him go, my mind went back to Mouse.

"Kill him," my friend whispered from the grave.

16 / *THAT AFTERNOON FOUND ME* on Grand Avenue, just north of Sunset. The address that Jackson had given me was a big brick edifice that looked more like a factory than an apartment building. The entrance was small, but the bell board had more than three dozen tenants listed. I went up and down the list until settling on the name B. TERRELL. I thought about the letters for a minute and then remembered Brawly's high school girlfriend.

B. Terrell's apartment was on the sixth floor. I was breathing hard by the time I was through the third flight of stairs. By the time I reached her door, I had to stop and catch my breath.

I knocked four times. The hall was empty and the lock was susceptible to the three playing cards that I carried in my wallet.

B. Terrell's apartment was of a monotonous, almost penal design. It was made up of four rooms that were all of equal size. Living room, kitchen, toilet, and bedroom. Each chamber was cube-shaped, and together they formed a bigger square. Each room had two doors that led to two other rooms. The living room was too small and the bathroom too large. The kitchen would have been hard to move around in. Only the bedroom really worked as it was supposed to.

The front door led into the living room. On a small coffee table was a framed photograph of a younger Brawly arm-in-arm with a blond-haired white girl. She had the healthy look of a Scandinavian, not pretty but handsome enough. They were smiling and obviously in love, at least at that moment. There was mail on the kitchen table addressed to BobbiAnne Terrell. In the bathroom medicine cabinet there were four boxes of Trojan condoms and a jar of petroleum jelly.

Under the bed there was a heavy metal box painted drab green. In it I found three carbines, six .45-caliber pistols, and two M-1 rifles. The top shelf of the closet had stacks of ammunition for those guns and some others.

I took one of the pistols, loaded it, and put it in my windbreaker pocket. I was halfway through the living room, on my way to the door, when the lock jiggled and the front door opened.

She was surprised to see a big black man in the middle of the room, but not enough to scream or run. I was surprised, too.

"Hello," she said, sounding more curious than afraid.

She looked just as she did in the photograph. The dress was even the same, a coral-colored one-piece that buttoned down the front. She had a nice figure, if you liked your women on the beefy side. Her face was wide and freckled in the center.

"Hi," I said.

"Who are you?"

"Easy," I said. "Easy Rawlins."

"What are you doing in my apartment?"

"Looking for Brawly Brown. The door was unlocked and I didn't have anywhere else to be, so I walked in and called his name. I was just about to leave when you came in."

"Why are you looking for Brawly?"

"Lotta people looking for him," I said. "But I'm representing Alva, his mother."

BobbiAnne checked the doorknob but there was no way to tell if it had been unlocked when I got there.

"I've looked everywhere," I said, intending to calm her with conversation. "The First Men, at his cousin Isolda's —"

"You here for her?" BobbiAnne said with a flash of anger.

"No. I just looked in at her. She's the one who gave me your name."

"That bitch," BobbiAnne said.

"Why you say that?" I asked.

"Not a bitch but just sick," the Nordic girl amended. She moved into the room, put at ease, I guess, because I stayed stationary.

"Sick how?"

"She used Brawly."

"Yeah?"

"What are you going to do when you find Brawly?" she asked, changing the flow of the conversation.

I moved to a straight-backed wooden chair, indicating that I wanted to extend our conversation.

"The boy's in trouble," I said. "The police think he's going to go ballistic with politics, Isolda thinks he might have killed his father, and Alva just thinks that he's runnin' with the wrong crowd. For all I know, they might all be right."

Something I said got to the girl. A worried look invaded her optimistic features, and she took to the small sofa opposite me.

"Are you here to turn him over to the police?"

"I told you already that I'm here for his mother," I said. "Mothers don't turn their babies over to the cops."

"How did you find me?"

"That's the second time you changed the subject," I said. "Not polite, but I'll tell you that I wasn't looking for you. I asked around about Brawly and heard that he had a girlfriend lived in this building. Once I saw your name, I knew it had to be you because Isolda told me that you were Brawly's friend in high school. Now can you help me find the younger Mr. Brown?"

BobbiAnne had big, upstanding breasts and broad shoulders, crystal blue eyes and a stomach that protruded just slightly. All of this worked to make her more attractive as the moments went by. She was the kind of girl who would turn beautiful on you overnight.

Her face was worried, but still she didn't seem fragile or vulnerable. I liked that.

"I don't know where Brawly is," she said. "But he's not in any trouble that I know of. Nothing except that his mother doesn't understand him."

"Have you talked to him in the last day or so?"

"He called. He said that he was going to come by but first he had to see a . . . a friend."

"Anton Breland?" I said, remembering the alias Conrad sometimes used.

"How do you know him?" For the first time Miss Terrell's face showed real concern.

"Met him. He pulled out a pistol on me and left me stranded three miles away from my car."

"Oh. I didn't like him when I first met him," she said. "But him and Brawly have gotten pretty close. For the past six months he's really been getting into the black thing. He said that he realized that black people had to get the white man off their backs."

"Is that when he left you?" I asked.

"What do you mean?"

"Well," I said, "I didn't see his name downstairs."

"We never lived together."

"So Brawly isn't in any kind of trouble?" I asked.

"No," she said in an uncertain tone.

"I can't help him if you don't tell me."

"I don't even know you."

"The question is," I said, "do you know Brawly?"

"What's that supposed to mean?"

"It means that if the police come in here and find those guns up under your bed, they're gonna drag you off to jail. Especially when they find those army-issue M-ones."

"You searched my house?"

"Listen to me, girl," I said. "I don't care about you or those guns. I ain't a cop and I don't concern myself with politics. All I want is to figure out how Brawly is doing and get him outta trouble if I can. If you want to sleep with a thirty-year jail sentence up under your bed, it's okay with me. But if you know what's good for you, you'll tell me how I can get to Brawly and talk some sense to him."

"I don't know anything, Mr. Rawlins," she said.

"Are those his guns under your bed?"

She didn't answer that question.

"What are they for?" I tried again

"Just . . . just for self-defense, just in case."

"Have you touched them?" I asked.

"Touched what?"

"Those guns."

"No."

"Don't," I said, and then stood up.

BobbiAnne's whole body jerked at my sudden movement. It was the first real evidence I had that she was afraid of me.

"Brawly's in trouble," I said. "And if you aren't careful, he'll drag you down with him."

"I haven't done anything wrong," she said.

"If you can get a judge to believe that, you might only get fifteen years."

17 / *ANTON BRELAND* was in the directory. I looked him up in a phone booth at the back of a Thrifty's Drug Store. It was about two in the afternoon on a Monday. There could be no better evidence that I was losing my grip on the straight and narrow. As I sat there looking at the name in the white pages, I tried to convince myself that I had done my duty by John and it was time to go back to work. There was no reason for me to follow revolutionaries and murderers. Bonnie would be home in thirty-six hours. My life could be sweet once again.

But then I realized that in the past few days my waking hours had not been tinged with remorse about the death of my friend. Only my dreams revealed these feelings. As long as I moved forward trying to unravel the trail of Brawly Brown, I was in a kind of safety zone where guilt couldn't touch me.

I lit up a cigarette and tore out the page.

*A*NTON LIVED ON SHENANDOAH, a small tributary off of Slauson, in a house that looked like a brick bunker. The lawn was neat but dead. The four-inch-high grass was straw colored. I imagined that Anton first lost interest in the lawn about fourteen or fifteen months before, but it continued to grow because it was the middle of the rainy season. With the coming of summer, the lawn died, leaving what looked like a pygmy wheat field.

The driveway was empty and there was no green Caddy to be seen anywhere, so I decided to wait in my car awhile.

The house in that field of dead grass looked to me like many abandoned structures I had come across on the outskirts of Berlin at the end of the war. Not important enough to bomb or burn but too dangerous to live in.

I lit up another cigarette and waited.

It was winter in Los Angeles, the only time of year that the smog let up. Winds came in from the desert and cleared the skies. That same wind made the clouds a panorama of ever changing sculptures suspended in a brilliant blue background. One moment there'd be a one-eyed lion, prowling out toward the mountains, then it would transform into a multi-armed anteater rearing up on its hind legs to display clawed limbs.

Those drifting giants made me smile. I was too small for them to notice, just a black dot beneath their domain. It gave me the illusion of safety.

When I saw Anton/Conrad's green Cadillac drive up and him get out so nonchalantly, I realized that all safety is an illusion.

Conrad walked into the yard as if he were minor royalty living as well as could be expected among the poor. While he strolled toward his front door I considered my next move. Conrad had a gun and was reckless with it. He made decisions without regard for the security of his friends, bystanders, or even himself. I couldn't just ring the bell; he might shoot me through the door. On the other hand, walking up to him also caused problems. He was fool enough to pull out a gun in broad daylight. I might have been able to disarm him, but then his neighbors might see our struggle and intervene.

While I was wondering what my next move should be, a white man emerged from a brand-new Ford parked halfway up the block. I had noted the car but not the man in it. He was obviously waiting for Conrad, too. The man wore a comic-book green suit and moved stealthily at first and then very quickly.

Conrad had just opened his door when he sensed or maybe heard the white man moving behind him. Before he could turn around fully, the white man hit Conrad in the temple and the arrogant young man fell into his house. The door closed quickly behind them, and I was left to consider the new situation.

My first thought was to drive down to the corner, call the police from some phone booth, and drive away. Even in the days when I was a fixture of the shadier side of Watts, I knew better than to get involved with the business of the streets.

And this was definitely street business. The white man in the green suit wasn't a cop or a revolutionary, nor was he a member of the Klan or a jealous husband. He was there to perform a sort of criminal bookkeeping that used rope instead of ledger paper and brass knuckles instead of an adding machine.

I should have left but I had another kind of business at hand. There was my friend John and his need. There was the fever burning like a funeral pyre over Mouse's death in my mind.

I waited for fifteen seconds or so and then went to the house next door to Anton's. I pushed the buzzer but no one answered. I knocked loudly, just in case.

This house was a ranch-style wooden building. Freshly painted with a beautiful and delicate lawn surrounding it. The backyard had a large vegetable plot but most of the plants were dead. Only one hardy tomato bush still held about half of its green leaves — one medium-sized deep red fruit hanging heavily from an upper branch. There was a nervous hunger gnawing at my gut, so I plucked the tomato. California supermarkets never had tomatoes that tasted so sweet. They were all grown in hothouses without the benefit of nature.

While still swallowing the sweet flesh, I picked up a terra-cotta pot from the back porch of the ranch house and leapt over the waist-high wire fence that separated Conrad's lot. I went silently to his back door and pressed my ear against it.

"Please!" a man shouted. "I'ma have it by Sunday. By Sunday mornin', I swear."

There was a thud of a blow being delivered, then a groan, and then the heavier thud of a body falling to the floor.

"Mr. London don't wanna hear your nigger jive, Anton," another voice said.

Conrad groaned again, making me suspect that he'd received a kick in the ribs.

"Sunday, man. Sunday, I swear," Conrad whined. "It's all set up."

Another thud. Another groan.

"I know you gonna pay, nigger," the white man said. "I know because after I burn your ass, you won't ever forget to pay anybody ever again."

Maybe, if the thug stuck to his regular job, that is, a sound beating for a late payment, I might have stood by until he was through. My best bet was to wait for him to soften Anton up. And then, when he'd gone, I could come in and ask a few questions about Brawly. But anything having to do with ropes or fire when it comes to black-white relations was bound to set my teeth on edge.

Conrad's back porch was just a door and two concrete steps. I smashed the pot on the stairs and then plastered my back against the bricks. The first effect was complete silence, then fast steps coming toward the door. When he rushed out I caught him on the side of the jaw with a short right that had all of the evil intentions of Archie Moore. I followed with a left and then two more right hooks. The final punch missed because the white man in the ridiculous suit was already on the ground. His eyes were open but I doubt if they saw very much.

I lifted him by his garish lapels and let go long enough to connect with a powerful right hand. I kicked him twice when he was down and out. I didn't kick him out of revenge or rage, at least mostly those weren't the reasons. This was a dangerous man who knew how to inflict pain and, probably, death. The impact of those body blows would slow him up even if he regained consciousness.

I removed the pistol from his belt, dragged him inside the house, and closed the door.

Conrad had risen, propped up on his left hand. There was a pistol clutched precariously in the fingers of his right. I plucked it free and put it in my pocket to go along with the gangster's piece.

Feeling the weight of three pistols in my pocket made me smile. It reminded me of a well-spent and wasted youth in Houston. Many a night I carried my friend's weapons when they were likely to be arrested or searched.

Various odors wafted through the air. A garbage pail that should have been emptied three days before, a toilet that should have been flushed that morning.

Conrad writhed on the floor, wrestling with gravity and balance; it was a losing battle. The gangster was dead to the world, but breathing.

I knelt down and pinched Conrad very hard on the cheek. He came to full awareness with a painful start.

"What?"

"You might be dead now," I said. "If it wasn't for me."

"What?"

"Your boyfriend over there."

Conrad turned his head to catch a glimpse of his attacker on the floor next to him, then he toppled over.

"Shit," he said.

In the corner was a door that led to the fragrant toilet. I searched the unconscious gangster for any more weapons and then dragged him into the bathroom and closed the door after him. The window in the toilet was about the size of a cow's head, too small for a full-grown man to crawl out of, so I wedged a metal-framed chair against the doorknob, assuring myself that we wouldn't be interrupted.

Conrad had pulled himself up so that his back was against the wall. We were in a dark room that had once been a kitchen. *Dark* because there was only one small window and two forty-watt bulbs for light, and *once* because the stove was dismantled, the refrigerator was open and unplugged, and all the shelf space and the sink were piled with books and magazines, cans of paint, and various tools. The unfinished wooden table had one metal chair (which I'd used to imprison the thug), a typewriter, and various sheets of paper.

Conrad glared at me.

"I know you," he said.

"I guess that means he didn't knock the sense outta your head."

"What you doin' here?" he asked. "I mean, how'd you find me?"

"What's happening Saturday?" I asked him.

Conrad's attempt at looking innocent was enough to make me want to laugh.

"You know," I said. "You told that man beatin' on you that you could pay your debt on Sunday after you did something on Saturday."

"I . . . I . . . I was just talkin', brother. Tryin' to save my ass from gettin' kicked." Conrad looked away from me, trying to hide the lie in his eyes.

"Oh," I said. "I thought it had to do with those stolen guns you and Brawly took over to BobbiAnne's house."

Making no attempt to rise, Conrad looked up into my eyes. He did not blink.

"You and Xavier plannin' some kinda war?" I asked, just to keep up the pretense of a conversation.

"No. No. I'm gonna move them guns is all. Move 'em and then split the money with Bad Boy. On Saturday."

On a whim I asked, "What you got to tell me about Aldridge Brown?"

Again his eyes darted away.

"Did you kill him, or did Brawly?" I asked.

"I don't know what the fuck you talkin' about, man. I never heard'a no Alvin Brown."

"Where's Brawly?" I asked.

"I don't know."

"Does he have a room somewhere?"

"I only see him at the meetins," he said.

"You collect them guns at the meetins?" I asked.

"I don't have to talk to you," he said angrily. He was working himself up, getting ready to do something.

"The cops think that you're about to blow up City Hall, Anton."

"How you know?" he asked. "You a cop?"

I pulled out the gangster's gun. It was a long-nosed .22, a killer's caliber. I pulled back the hammer and Conrad's handsome Caucasian features blanched.

"Get up," I said, and he hopped to it.

"Take off your shoes and socks."

He obeyed that command, too.

"Turn out your pockets," I said. "And put everything on the table."

By this time there was the sound of movement coming from the toilet. Conrad glanced at the door fearfully.

"Okay, let's go," I said.

"Go where?"

"Out to my car."

We left the house and walked to my car. I stayed close to Conrad, with the gun always touching his side. I made him get in on the driver's side and scoot over to the passenger's seat.

"This gun don't make no more noise than a cap pistol," I told him, pressing the muzzle firmly into his side. "But it will tear your guts up."

As we drove I asked him the same questions. He told me again that he and Brawly were in the gun business, that they were going to unload the weapons on Saturday so that he could pay his gambling debt to Angel London, a bookmaker from Redondo Beach.

I HAD A KNOTTY PROBLEM. There was a semiconscious killer wedged into Conrad's bathroom. The killer now hated me more than he did Conrad. I couldn't let him see me or question Conrad about my identity. On the other hand, if I left Conrad in his house, he might have shot the gangster through the door or window. One way I'd be the target of a killer, and the other I'd be an accessory to murder.

So I decided to take Conrad on a drive up into Griffith Park. He was sweating and, I'm sure, expecting to be killed. So he breathed a sigh of relief when I kicked him out way up on a hillside. He didn't even complain about being let out with no wallet and no shoes.

"Next time maybe you'll give me a ride back to my car when I ask for it," I said before driving off.

I doubted that Conrad would go back home, and I was sure that the gangster was already on the street looking for my name.

18 / JESUS, FEATHER, AND I all got home at about the same time. I picked them up as they got off the blue bus at Pico and Genesee.

Feather had a homework assignment that she was so concentrated on, she didn't even take time for her snack before she was hard at work at the kitchen table.

"It's a book about a girl who fought in a war," she told me, "in Frenchland. I have to read it and write a book report."

"What girl?"

"Joan Arks," she said.

"Did she have a gun?" I asked.

"No, un-uh, a sword. A big sword."

"And did she cut off people's heads?"

"No. She just held it up over her head and ran after the enemy and they got scared and run."

It was a real book, about thirty pages, with large print and a black-and-white illustration every six pages or so. The cover showed Joan with the sword held high, men on their knees before her and men shouting her praises from behind. Feather studied each page with rapt attention.

"You want peanut butter an' jelly, sis?" Juice asked her.

"Um, uh-huh."

He made her the sandwich and poured some milk while I put rice on to boil and took frozen oxtails, which I'd cooked a week before, from the freezer. I also had a bowl of green beans and ham hocks on ice. When Feather had snacked and the food was all cooking, Jesus and I went into the backyard, where his long planks and sawhorses stood.

"So you still think you gonna build that boat, huh?"

"Uh-huh."

"And what about school?"

"I don't know," he said.

"If you wanna drop out, I got to sign a paper, right?"

"Yeah."

"Then you have to look me in the face and talk to me, 'cause I don't see any reason at all that you can't go to school when every other kid in Los Angeles seems to be able to."

"Not everybody," he said.

"No. Pregnant girls and juvenile delinquents don't go. Kids acting in the movies and little kids don't have no parents to show 'em the right way to go. But everybody else makes it."

Jesus turned away. He was probably going to leave, but I took his arm before he could make a move.

"Talk to me."

He sat on the grass and I did, too. When he started rocking back and forth, I put my hand on his knee.

"I love you, boy," I said. "You know when I was a kid I lost my parents, too. I know what it's like to be in the street. That's why I wanna see you get an education. What I never had."

He stopped fidgeting and looked into my eyes.

"I can't learn in class," he said.

"Of course you can," I said.

"No." His tone and demeanor could not be denied. "I don't want to listen to them anymore. They act like we should just listen and believe. They say things that are wrong. They lock the gates. I don't want to be there anymore."

"But you just have a little bit more than a year to go."

"I want to build my boat."

"Will you stay in school and try hard if I tell you to?" I asked him.

After a moment's hesitation he said, "I guess I will."

"Then let me think about it for a couple of days."

*W*E HAD A GREAT TIME at dinner. Feather regaled us with fragments of "Joan Arks" while we ate. After dinner she read to us from her paper. Jesus went to bed early, reading his book on how to build a single-masted sailboat. Feather and I watched *The Andy Griffith Show*. She loved little Opie.

"Because he's so nice," she said.

*D*ADDY? DADDY."

I had just walked into a graveyard's warehouse where dozens of occupied coffins had been stockpiled, waiting to be buried. It seemed that there was only one man, armed with just a shovel, whose responsibility it was to inter all those dead souls. I looked from one casket to another, but none had Raymond's name on the little bronze nameplate placed at the foot of each box.

Somebody called my name. Somebody held out a shovel. He wanted me to get back to digging.

"What?" I said. And then I remembered: I was the man in charge of burials, I was the gravedigger for all the dead black men and women.

"Daddy."

"What?" I said.

"You're asleep, Daddy."

I opened my eyes. There was a static buzz coming from the television. Feather was pressing against my chest with both hands.

"We fell asleep," she said.

I carried her to her room and put her under the covers fully dressed.

*T*HE PHONE RANG but at first I thought it was the alarm. Who set the alarm, anyway? I called out Bonnie's name. I knew that it must have been her, that she had some early flight and set the alarm and now was going to sleep through it.

"Bonnie, shut that thing off," I said.

And then I remembered that Bonnie was out of town. She was in an airplane somewhere. I imagined a plane high in the sky. I was sitting in the pilot's seat, looking out of the broad windows at the panorama of deep blue. There was no limit to the space overhead.

Then the phone rang again.

"Mr. Rawlins?" a deep voice asked when I answered.

"Who is this?"

"It's Henry Strong," he announced.

"Man, what time is it?"

"I must speak with you, Mr. Rawlins. It's urgent."

I looked at the night table. The clock's turquoise luminescent numerals read 3:15. I blinked and started to slide into that big sky again.

"Mr. Rawlins, are you awake?"

"There's a doughnut shop on Central at Florence," I said. "It's an all-night place that they use for the Goodyear tire plant down there."

"I know it."

"Be there in forty minutes," I said, and then I hung up.

I turned on my back and took a deep breath. *Graveyards and blue skies.* The phrase ran through my mind. It was a good title for a jet-age blues song.

19 / *I PUT ON WORK CLOTHES* so that I'd blend in with the crowd at Mariah's Doughnuts and Deli.

I made it in twenty-five minutes, my car rattling now and again along the way.

Strong wasn't there when I arrived. But the large room was half filled with workmen and -women smoking cigarettes and downing coffee.

It was way down in the black neighborhood, but the room was filled with all the races of L.A. Black and white, yellow and brown. All sitting together and talking. Norwegian, Nigerian, and Nipponese derivatives all speaking the same language and getting along just fine.

"Coffee," I said to Bingham, the nighttime counterman at Mariah's.

"How you want it, Easy?"

"Black as it gets."

He went to fill my order and I let my eyes roll over the three dozen or so late-night workers. The nearby Goodyear plant ran twenty-four hours a day, 365 days a year. The people who worked there had simple, straight-ahead lives. They got up an hour and a half before they were supposed to be at work, then they worked eight hours, and maybe a little overtime. They were citizens of a nation that had won the major wars of the century and now they were enjoying the fruits of the victors: mindless labor and enough of anything they wanted to buy.

Everyone in the room looked as though they belonged there. No one was looking at me, and no one was looking away.

I sat at a small table near the cash register and guzzled the strong coffee. Every word spoken or cup banged down exploded in my ears. My fingertips were numb, and if I moved my head too fast, my vision shook a bit.

After my third cup of coffee things began to settle down.

Strong came in the front door at 4:19 and strode up to my table. He had tried to dress for the occasion, wearing black slacks and a square-cut dark blue shirt with orange circles around the hem. But his head was too elegant for the clothes, and the clothes were too sporty for the twenty-four-hour diner.

Strong would have had a hard time fitting in anywhere he was not the center of attention.

"Coffee?" I asked him.

I gestured at Bingham, who called a waiter from the back to bring a plate of hot beignets and two fresh cups of coffee.

"You hung up on me," Strong said.

"You woke me out of a sound sleep."

The standoff lasted until after the young man had delivered our breakfast.

"I have to talk to you, Rawlins," he said.

"That's why I'm here."

"But not here. There's too many ears around here."

"Here is where they ain't gonna be listenin', man," I said, letting my country upbringing soak each word. "Here is where people mind their own business. They don't care about us."

Strong had a long face with deep, soulful eyes. He used those eyes on me.

"Are you a race man, Mr. Rawlins?"

"I can run if I have to," I said.

"That's not what I mean."

"I know what you mean. You one'a them better-than-thou kinda Negroes tryin' to explain everything by your own book. But I'm just a everyday black man, doin' the best I can in a world where the white man's de facto king. I got me a house with a tree growin' in the front yard. It's my tree; I could cut it down if I wanted to, but even still you cain't call it a black man's tree. It's just pine."

I had given him everything he needed to figure me out. If Strong was smart enough to read me, then I'd have to take him seriously; if not — well, I'd see.

His rubbed his fingers across his lips, digesting my words. He stared even more deeply into my eyes.

Then he smiled. Grinned.

"Okay," he said. "I'm not trying to convert you. I just wanted to know where you stand in relation to the First Men."

"Next question," I said.

"What do you have to do with Brawly Brown?"

"I'm looking for him. For his mother, like I said."

"Is that all?"

Strong was taller than I was and heavier by thirty pounds. His question had the hint of a threat in it. But I wasn't afraid.

"This is a waste of time," I said.

I sat back and bit into one of the best beignets I'd ever tasted.

"I'm worried about Brawly," Strong said.

"How's that?" I asked.

"I believe that he's part of a radical fringe in Xavier's group. Despite the name, the Urban Revolutionary Party is a cultural organization, Mr. Rawlins. They want to have better education for our children, to bring the proper nutrition and political clout to the neighborhood. But some of our youngsters aren't patient with the process. They're angry and want to lash out. I believe that Brawly is part of that element."

"How'd you get my number, Mr. Strong?"

"I got it from Tina," he said.

"I didn't give Tina my number."

"No, but you did give it to Clarissa. She went to Tina after you came to her house. She's worried about Brawly, too."

"She worried about his safety, and you worried 'bout what he might do to you."

"Not to me, but to the group. You saw what the police did the other night. You know what they're capable of. If we just get out in the street and urge people to vote, they break down our walls and put us in jail. What do you think they'd do if we formed into guerrilla squads armed to the teeth?"

"That's what Brawly's into?"

"I'm not sure," Strong said with all the honesty of a hungry crocodile. "I know that they're trying to raise money in order to buy weapons."

"Maybe they want the money for the school," I said.

"Don't talk shit, man."

"Okay. Okay," I said. "You the one should know."

"Why are you looking for Brawly Brown?" he asked.

"For his mother."

In years past when I did favors for people, I lied all the time. Gave the wrong name, never admitted to what my true purposes were. As a rule, people believed my lies. This was the first time that I told the truth consistently and the result was that no one believed what I said.

"If that's true," Strong said, "then you had better get to Brawly and take him back home. Because the only thing he's headed for is an early grave."

"At least we agree on somethin'," I said. "I would love nuthin' better than to get Brawly into a room with his mother. But, you know, I seen that boy once — he threw me across the room and I don't think he was even mad."

"Maybe if I came along with you," Strong said. "Maybe he'd listen to me."

"You think so?"

"It's worth a try. That Brawly's a hothead. With him out of the picture, I might be able to reason with the rest of them. And with you there representing his mother, he just might turn around."

From what I had seen, Brawly was more brute strength or blind hope — not so much a driving force. But what did I know? And even if my suspicions were right, that was no reason to disagree with Strong. If he was willing to help, then I was willing to let him.

"I know where he is," Strong said.

"Where?"

"I could take you to him."

*H*E PAID THE TAB and then walked me out to his car, which was parked across the street. It was an old Crown Victoria, as beautiful as the day it rolled off the production line. The radical leader was vain about his automobile. For some reason, that made me like him more.

But something was nagging at the back of my mind.

On the way I asked Strong, "Are Xavier and Brawly friendly?"

"I don't really know."

"No? I'd think the head of a group like the First Men would know all about what his people were doing and how they got along."

"I'm not the head of the organization. As a matter of fact, I am not, strictly speaking, a member."

"No? Then why they treat you like some kind of king?"

"I'm an activist from the Bay Area. I live in Oakland. I have a small following up there."

"But they said that you started the First Men."

"That was just an accolade of generosity," he said. "I was a good friend of a man named Harney, Phillip Harney. He was their spiritual model. His aura spilled over on me."

We drove down toward Compton. Down past Rosecrans Avenue and Alondra Boulevard not far from John's tract of homes.

The nagging doubt stayed with me.

When the road turned to gravel I looked up at the temporary street sign, which read A227-F. It made sense to me that Brawly would hide out in some empty house near the construction site where he was employed for so long. He knew the area, the security systems, and the schedules of the workers.

That's when it came to me. Strong didn't strike me as the kind of man to pick up the tab for some stranger. Maybe for a pretty girl or for some political big shot, but not for some man he didn't know and not for a fly in his soup like Brawly.

It wasn't yet five, so the skies were still dark. We pulled up in front of a house that was almost completed. When Strong turned off the engine my heart was already pumping. I was excited, at the end of my search, but I was also leery.

"Let's go," Strong said.

"Go where?"

"In the house."

"Excuse me for doubting you, Mr. Strong, but this isn't exactly what I had in mind. I mean, why is the house so dark?"

"It's dark because they're not expecting us," he said in a sensible, matter-of-fact tone.

"They who?" I asked just as reasonably, if a little more strained.

That's when Strong produced a pistol.

"We have just a couple of questions, Mr. Rawlins."

I held myself back from attacking the First Man. He was big, like I said. I didn't even know if I could have taken him if he was un-armed.

"Get out," he ordered.

I opened my door with him close behind, giving me no chance to slam the door on him or run.

We walked down what would one day be a concrete path to the house's front door.

"Don't get all worried, Mr. Rawlins," Strong said as we walked. "We just want to make sure that you are what you say you are."

I wanted to believe him, but the fact that there was no light on in the house made me doubt his intentions.

When we were halfway down that path the front door swung in-ward. I couldn't see into the house but I did hear a sound: a snick and crack. Then the self-professed race man yelled, "No!"

Six months of battle on the front lines under Omar Bradley and Patton are what saved my life. I hit the ground, rolled over twice, was up on my feet running a zigzag pattern down the length of the neigh-boring house-to-be. Strong was right behind me, wasting strength by yelling for his life. All this while shots were being fired. Bullets whizzed past my head. Strong's yell cut off on a sudden high note. I zigged to the right, heading for the cover of a house. I looked over where Strong had been. His body was on the ground and inert. A man was standing over him, shooting point-blank at his head. I took in that image in just a fraction of a second. Then I dove past the side of the house, jumped over a pile of rolled tar paper, and kept running hard. I heard at least two men yelling, and three shots were fired in my direction. But I kept running.

After two blocks I started wheezing. Maybe thirty feet after that I felt a terrible pain in my chest. I veered to the right and fell on the ground next to an unfinished porch. I laid flat in the shadows thrown by a security night-light, my ragged breath sounding like two vinyl records being rubbed together vigorously.

I almost lost consciousness.

After a few minutes a car drove by slowly. There was no flashing red, so I was pretty sure that it wasn't the cops. It took at least fifteen seconds for them to roll past.

After they were gone, and I had caught my breath, I walked six blocks to the main street. By then it was a little after five and the buses were beginning their routes. The bus I boarded hadn't gone more than four blocks when six county sheriff cars, sirens wailing and red lights flashing, sped in the opposite direction, toward the place where I'd almost died.

20 / *I GOT MY CAR* from Mariah's parking lot and drove down to Sojourner Truth. After parking in the lower lot, I held my hands in front of my eyes. They weren't shaking.

Then I made my way to the maintenance bungalow. We called it the main building as a kind of abbreviation and, maybe, as a comment on who really kept the school running. It wasn't even six o'clock. Nobody would bother me for over an hour and a half.

The custodians' bungalow was a storehouse of cleaning materials, locks and keys, paper items, and tools. Twelve day janitors and a night crew of five were needed to maintain the 132 classrooms, two locker rooms and showers, the gym, the garden, the auditorium, and seventeen office spaces that constituted the school. We had fourteen buildings, upper and lower asphalt recreation yards, and eighteen gates that had to be locked and unlocked every day to keep students in, and to keep them out, too.

My office nook was made up of a battered ash desk, a padded green swivel chair, two filing cabinets, and five key rings, with just under three hundred keys, hanging from a peg on the wall.

I brewed coffee in the twelve-cup percolator and set fire to a Chesterfield that I promptly snubbed out because when I was running from those gunmen I realized that smoking could kill me without the heart disease and cancer they were talking about in the papers. A man as short on breath as I was would surely die if he couldn't keep ahead in the rat race.

The coffee was great. Not too strong but full of the flavor of life. It contained the taste of my survival. There I was, alive and safely hidden in the bosom of Sojourner Truth.

I wondered who had killed Strong and why. Were they the confederates he had expected to question me? Did his friends lay a trap for him, too? Or were our attackers another group who were set against Strong and his First Men?

When I heard that bullet snap into the chamber, all my senses fled, bidding my body to follow. I didn't see the man who shot Strong long enough to have noted even the most general description. Height, weight, even his color were unknown to me. What I mostly saw was the flash of his pistol.

One thing I was sure of was that Strong was dead. I didn't feel bad about not going back. There was no saving him. And even if I could have helped, he had been holding me at gunpoint. My only worry was if someone had put me on their hit list, if I had somehow made someone scared enough to need me dead.

The men who fired at us had certainly meant to kill us both. It was also almost certain that they were the ones cruising around in their car looking for me. Maybe they thought Strong had told me something.

A normal working-class man would have been petrified in my position. But I had been through worse.

My childhood had been just as rough. Many a time I was sure that someone was going to kill me. But the threat of tomorrow was never as urgent as making it through today. So I was able to put the killers temporarily out of my mind while making the rounds of the school.

*E*VERY GATE that was meant to be locked was locked. Every can had been emptied of trash. No papers littered the yards, no lights were left on in the classrooms. My staff was a hardworking bunch of people. That was the early sixties, a time when men and women still knew that they had to work hard if they wanted to pay the rent and feed their hungering brood.

The only thing out of place was the metal shop in the shop building complex. All the chairs and even the large metal tables had been pulled out into the hall and stacked as if it were summer and we were preparing to strip and wax the floors.

I stood in the wide hallway wondering what flood or electrical failure might have caused my janitors to resort to this major job.

"Mr. Rawlins." The voice came from behind me.

I jumped a good yard, wrenching my shoulder as I turned to see my early-morning janitor, Archie "Ace" Muldoon. Short and balding, the little white man nearly glowed in the dark hallway. He had doffed his White Sox baseball cap in deference to his boss — me.

"Ace, you like to scare me to death."

"Sorry, Mr. Rawlins. I was just comin' down here to see if Terrance brought down the stripper."

"Stripper? Who told you to strip these floors?"

"Newgate." Ace said the name as if it was a whole sentence, a sentence used to explain 90 percent of the problems we had at Truth.

"What's wrong with him?"

"He came to me and asked where you were," Ace said. "When I told him that you were sick he nearly turned purple. I tell you, I've never seen a man get so apoplectic over the littlest thing."

"What does me being sick have to do with the metal-shop floor?"

"He told me to take him to all the rooms that were mine to clean. I walked him around the shops 'cause I figured he'd get tired'a lookin' behind all the heavy machines. I didn't mean to cause no problem."

Ace was from poor white farming stock in the Midwest. At one time I'd thought that he was after my job. It took me a while to understand that he respected me as his boss.

"I don't have a problem, Ace. But what bugged him?"

"He started looking behind the heavy machines and saw where there was a little wax buildup along the edges. I told him that it would take special equipment to move the heavy machinery, but he just kept shaking his head, saying that it wasn't my fault, that it was the supervisor who was responsible for this filth." Ace said the last word with real vituperation. I think that he disliked Newgate even more than I did. "Then he told us to prepare the classroom to be stripped and waxed."

"Don't worry about it, Ace. When Burns and Peña come in, tell them that I said to help you move this furniture back in the room before classes start."

"Okay, boss," Ace said. He went away happy that he was going to frustrate the arrogant principal.

---

*I*T WAS JUST after seven. I knew that Newgate would be stalking the office building, looking for kids smoking cigarettes or making out on some bench. Hiram Newgate loved to catch you doing something wrong. You could be a saint and he'd never notice it, but leave one spot on a leopard-skin coat and he'd be on you in a second.

*R*AWLINS, I WANT to talk to you," he called out three seconds after I'd sauntered into the eastern doorway.

He was half the length of the long hall away.

"What about, Hiram?" I called back.

Principal Hiram Newgate didn't like being addressed as *mister*. He certainly didn't like being called by his first name.

The tall and gaunt man strode the distance between us looking as if he were ready to throw down and fight. I smiled and let my eyebrows rise in innocent anticipation.

He wore a dark blue Brooks Brothers suit with a shirt that had the mildest blush of pink under mostly white. His dark tie had a white diamond off center, and his shoes were either new or the perfect example of a high shine.

Principal Newgate was a clotheshorse of the first order, but I can't fault him for that. I liked the tailor myself. Many a day I came in better dressed than he was. Those days he'd ask me about showing my custodians by example how to hose down the dusty yard or how to till the soil in the garden.

"I'll do that the day you take over an algebra class," I'd reply.

That man hated me more than Ace hated him.

"Where've you been?" the principal asked.

"Sick." I didn't cough but I brought my fingers to my lips as if I might.

"That's unacceptable."

"I'll send my intestines to you next time they feel like keepin' me in the toilet," I said.

"In management class," Principal Newgate said, "the first thing you learn is that an employee who takes his sick days at the beginning or the end of the week is abusing his privilege. That's what you call a malingerer."

"Oh?" I said. "And how many Mondays and Fridays have I taken off in the past year?"

"I'm only concerned with yesterday."

"So is it going to be a rule that nobody can get sick on Mondays and Fridays?"

"Of course not."

"Well then, how about making it a rule that you can't take off any more Mondays and Fridays than you can the other days?"

"That's more what I meant," the principal said, at sea in my friendly banter.

"I'll make sure I tell my staff."

"No one likes a wiseass, Rawlins."

"Especially when the wiseass gets so mad at his supervisor cursing at him that he makes a formal complaint."

"I was looking around the shop building with Mr. Muldoon," Newgate said, changing the subject. "I had him prepare the metal shop for a thorough cleaning."

"I know," I said. "I told him to put the furniture back into the classroom so Mr. Sutton can teach his class."

"I ordered them to remove the furniture." Newgate reminded me of a Captain Dougherty, who had sent four squads of soldiers into a firefight outside of Anzio, one per hour. Every member of every squad was slaughtered while we made no progress against the enemy. We knew that the good captain had been part of a wager between English and American officers about who would enter the city first. He started sending them at eight A.M. By ten to twelve he was hit with shrapnel from a Yankee grenade that went off by mistake.

"Lucky for you that I'm the officer in charge," I said. "Because Sutton was in Korea and he wouldn't like to see his classroom turned all inside out like that."

"I'm in charge of the whole school," Newgate said.

"Look it up in your handbook, Hiram," I said. "Supervising custodian makes the final decisions about plant procedure. You can complain about it, but it will be at maintenance headquarters, not with the administration."

Newgate had big veins in his neck, thick and cordlike. They stood out when he got really angry. That morning they even hinted red.

Watching him get so irritated gave me a moment of peace. I forgot about Brawly and Conrad, about bushwhackers and the secret arm of the L.A.P.D. Black men in America have always worked for white taskmasters. It had only been in the past few years that I could talk back without fear of losing my job, or maybe even a tooth or two.

Some men I'd known had died challenging their superiors. So Newgate's aggravation was a kind of balm. It soothed my symptoms, but the disease was still there.

21 / *"HELLO, MRS. PLATES,"* I said later that morning. Jorge Peña, Garland Burns, Troy Sanders, and Willard Clark had already come in, had coffee, and gone out again. "You're a few minutes late, aren't you?" I chided her but I didn't really care.

Helen Plates was a natural blond Negro, also from the Midwest. She had a complaint for everything from politics to drinking water, from poor blacks to rich whites. She could never get in to work right on time but she was my hardest worker, next to Garland, and Helen never minded if I asked her to do a little overtime. I think she liked to stay late because her husband was an invalid and she worked harder for him than she ever did at Truth.

"I'm sorry, Mr. Rawlins," she said. "You know I had to make sure Edgar took his pills before I left. His cousin, Opal, is fine to sit around and feed him soup, but she don't know how to dole out them pills. You know, he has to take his blue pill every three hours, his pink pills two at a time every five, there's the square white ones that he takes every hour, and the round white ones that he takes three times a day. The first time I left Edgar with Opal she just gave him all of 'em at once at ten-thirty. I called Dr. Harrell and he made us pump out his stomach at the emergency ward in the hospital."

"But if you can't trust Opal, then what are you going to do for the rest of the day?" I asked her.

"I have to call every time he needs to take a pill."

My next question should have been, *Well, if all you have to do is call, then why did you have to stay late this morning?* But instead I asked, "Do you have Mercury's address?"

Mrs. Plates's friendly patter petered out then. She sat back in her chair and turned her face away from me, as if maybe I was naked and should be ashamed of myself.

"That's a personal thing, Mr. Rawlins. I don't know if Mercury wants me to be handin' out his numbers like that."

"He didn't seem to mind you tellin' me that he was in trouble over that burglary he committed when it helped him out," I said.

"Shhh, baby. Mercury ain't like that no more. He's workin' construction in Compton and you don't know who might be at the door listenin'."

"Write down his address, will you, Mrs. Plates?"

"Why?" I could see in her face that she didn't want me to tell her the truth.

"I'm doin' some work for John — you know, the man Mercury and Chapman work for. He needs me to locate one of his employees, and I was thinkin' that Merc might know a thing or two."

"Is John's employee in trouble?"

"You don't even know his name, Helen. Why worry about him? Mercury isn't in trouble, either — that's all you need to know."

I SPENT THE MORNING wandering around the grounds, checking out pink slips that various teachers and administrators had left reporting problems with the plant. There was paint peeling off the ceiling of the girls' shower room and a faulty light in the teachers' lounge. Nothing serious. Nothing I couldn't handle with my eyes closed. I was having a good time.

At noon I went to the main building and took out the dirty and creased white card that Detective Knorr had given me. All it had was a telephone number with an Axminister exchange.

I dialed the number.

"D Squad," a woman's voice said.

"Detective Knorr, please," I said in a stern, barely civil, white man's tone.

"He's not in right now," the woman said. "May I take a message?"

"This is Grimes," I said. "I have a special expenses check for the detective that's come back three times. Can you give me the right address?"

"What address are you using?"

I gave her the address of the Seventy-seventh Street Precinct.

"Your records are obviously out of order," she snapped. My tone had gotten under her skin. She gave me Vincent Knorr's office address with vindictive pleasure.

I LEFT WORK at one. That was seven hours and I'd worked hard. I wasn't worried about Newgate getting mad at me. None of my custodians — or his teachers, for that matter — would tell him where I was. If he asked for me, the standard reply was "I saw him a few minutes ago. He was headed for the other campus."

*T*HE ADDRESS the angry secretary gave brought me to a building on Hope, just down the block from City Hall. Made from stone, the entrance brought me into a building-sized room that had a domed ceiling with a tiny colored-glass opening at the very top. A woman sat at a desk blocking entrée to the large circular room. Her nameplate read MISS PFENNIG.

Pfennig's copper-colored hair came out of a wash basin and she had probably been ugly even when she was a child, which was more than forty years earlier. Her long nose had gone awry, like a sapling grown under heavy shade, wavering this way and that in search for the light. Her eyes were a translucent gray. Her skin was gray also, but lusterless and drab.

I came in from the bright sun, so it took a few moments for my vision to adjust to the tomblike interior. Even the skylight couldn't brighten that dark globular room. With no windows and the roof at least thirty feet away, there was little possibility that it would ever muster any more than a dusklike gloom.

"What do you want?" Pfennig asked.

I ignored her rudeness, looking at the doorways along the edges of the perfectly circular room. The floor might have been fifty feet in diameter. I found myself amazed at the profound waste of space. I thought of Jackson Blue's lopsided room. At least he used the space he had for books and studying, for thinking, no matter how misguided. It struck me that Jackson might not have been so wrongheaded as I thought. After all, here I was in the medieval bastion of the special police squad assigned to hounding and destroying a black political group. How could someone justify being a law-abiding citizen after seeing something like that?

"I came to see Detective Knorr," I said.

"Who?"

"Detective Knorr."

"You must be mistaken," Miss Pfennig said. "There's no one here by that name."

"No," I said. "I'm not mistaken, you are. You're mistaking me for a black radical come here to blow up this building because of the conspiracy within these walls. You're mistaking me for an angry black militant tired of the lies and attempts to make your claims of our inferiority seem true."

I smiled, and fear blossomed in the ugly woman's face.

A man appeared from the shadows. He was tall and chiseled, blond on white wearing a tan suit and black shoes. An undercover cop if I had ever seen one.

"Is there a problem, Miss Pfennig?"

"This man was threatening to blow up the building," she said.

"No," I said again. "I said that you thought I was, when really I just wanted to speak to Detective Knorr."

"What do you want with Vincent?" The light-haired detective would never be a success in his job.

I handed over the card that Vincent Knorr had given me.

"He wanted me to drop by if I had any information."

The chiseled cop studied the card, turning it over two or three times. He was looking for a trick.

"There's no name on this card," he said at last.

"No. I guess you guys got some kinda secret goin' on around here. Vincent thought that I was the right kind of rat for your purposes."

"Come with me," the Aryan dream ordered.

"Hal," Miss Pfennig said. It was just one word but there was a lot behind it.

Hal ignored her and repeated, "This way."

We walked in a straight line to a door about sixty-two degrees up the circle from Pfennig's desk. Hal knocked and then opened the door without waiting for a reply. The room we entered had normal lighting. It also had a mahogany desk and a thickset secretary. She had long hair that would have looked better short and wore a pink dress that should have been battleship gray. Her eyes were round but still uninviting.

"Yes, Sergeant Gellman?" If I were a young man and had heard that deep and sensual voice on the phone, I would call back a few times, hoping for a way in.

"This man has a card he said he got from Detective Knorr. He's here looking for him," Hal said.

"And you brought him here?"

Hal's mouth opened as if he intended to speak, but there were no words in the pipe.

"You couldn't even leave him at the front desk?"

"He was being belligerent with Doris."

"Did you frisk him?"

Again Hal Gellman searched for words that did not exist.

Looking back and forth between those two, I began to have heart that change was possible in my lifetime. My enemies were both blind and small-minded, vain and unable to imagine me even though I was standing right there in front of them.

The nameless secretary pressed a button on a walnut box that sat on her desk.

A man's voice said, "Yes, Mona?"

"Ezekiel Porterhouse Rawlins came to the front door, and Sergeant Gellman brought him here. What should I do?"

Small-minded, maybe, but they did their homework.

A silence followed Mona's question. Hal stared at the wall above her head.

His glare and his situation reminded me of my father.

My father disappeared forty-two days after my eighth birthday. He went out to work at a lumberjack camp and never returned. I have very few memories of him, but what I do remember is cast in bronze.

He once told me that anything that happened to a man before he was sixty was a good thing.

"Not everything," I said, testing my own childish knowledge against his.

"Yes," he said, "everything."

"Uh-uh, not if you get your arm cut off."

"Even if you're right-handed and you get your right arm cut off," he said. "Even that will turn out to be a good thing if you're a real man."

"But how?"

"Because a real man will know that he has to overcome anything that gets in the way of him caring for his family. A real man will study the arm he has left. He will build its strength, learn how to use tools with it. He will make sure that he's a better man with one arm than other men are with two. And he'll make it so, no matter how hard he has to try. A real man can be beat only if you kill him. And with his dyin' breath he will try to overcome Death itself."

Standing there between those bickering police, I thought of my father and of Raymond Alexander, who never feared Death or her emissaries. Hal Gellman was being given a chance, though he probably didn't realize it. The deep-voiced Mona was helping him to see something. His boss's silence was telling him something.

I saw no awareness in his angry glare, though. That was my lesson.

The beech door behind Mona opened and a tall man, about my age, walked into the room. He wore a cheap dark suit with a white shirt and no tie. His shoulders were narrow and his gaze, behind the round wire-rimmed glasses, was intense.

"Rawlins?" he said.

I nodded.

He looked me up and down, decided by some unknown calculations that I wasn't a threat, and said, "Colonel Lakeland. Come with me."

He turned and walked back through the buff doorway.

As I followed I experienced a familiar feeling of elation. It's a reaction that black people often have when going into the slave master's quarters. In there, we imagine, is the place where freedom resides. And if we get the chance, maybe we could pick up a little of that most precious commodity when the man is otherwise occupied.

I smiled at my silly delight.

Mona mistook my smile as being for her. She sneered at me and I was jarred back to reality.

22 / *LAKELAND'S OFFICE CONSISTED* of a large space with a broad desk dead center. There were a dozen chairs or so at various attitudes around the room. A powerful lamp hung maybe five feet above the desktop, illuminating the counter-sized work area and leaving the rest of the office in a kind of twilight. The room smelled heavily of cigarette smoke. That was when I felt my first real twinge of withdrawal.

I noticed that there were half a dozen or so diplomas in frames hanging on the wall near the door. A bachelor of arts from UCLA, a master's degree from Caltech. I didn't have time to make out the other degrees but I was sure that Colonel Lakeland was the recipient of each parchment.

"Sit," Lakeland said as he made his way to a plush swivel chair.

I took a seat off to the left, not wanting to make it seem that I was the subject of our discussion. I was just another one of the guys, sitting on the edge of the project.

The nameplate before me read LT. L. LAKELAND. I just glanced at it and he said, "I'm a colonel in the army. I was tapped by city hall and Sacramento to run this operation."

"Intelligence?" I asked.

I guess he heard the sarcasm in my question, and that's why he passed it over.

"What are you doing here, Rawlins?"

"I could ask you that same question, Colonel."

Lakeland's face was also narrow. His lips seemed to belong on a corpse, they were so leathery and thin. His grin was a disgusting show.

"The Seventy-seventh Precinct captain thinks that you might be our man," he said.

"Your man for what?"

"Didn't Knorr tell you?"

"He said something about an insurrection. Sounded pretty crazy to me."

"It's not," Lakeland assured me. "They're stockpiling guns, shadowing the police."

"With the police following them," I added.

"It's our job to ensure the safety of the people, Rawlins. That's what they pay us for."

"What's that got to do with me?"

"Knorr offered you a job, did he not?"

"I'm no rat, Lieutenant," I said.

"Colonel."

"I'm speaking to the cop wants me to be a stool for him."

Lakeland considered me. I presented a problem. I knew what he was doing and where he was doing it from. But then again, I had come into his lair, unafraid.

"What do you want, Rawlins?"

"Brawly Brown."

"Again?"

"I got a friend named John. He's got a close friend named Alva. Brawly is Alva's son. He's a bullheaded young man but not bad as far as I've been told and as far as I could see. What I want is to pull him out of any trouble he's in with you and try to get him back home."

"What do I get in return?"

"I don't know."

Those dead lips grinned again.

"Not a very good trade, now, is it?" he said.

"As far as I'm concerned, Brawly and me are innocent bystanders," I said. "Just two black men in the wrong place at the wrong time. If I see something I think you need to know, I'll tell you about it. I won't be a rat for you but if we have some interest in common, I might let something drop in your lap."

"I need more convincing than that," Lakeland said.

"You won't be gettin' it from me, man. Listen, if I heard that there's going to be some ambush or bombin', I'd tell you in a minute, especially if innocent black people are about to get killed. All I'm askin' you for is Brawly."

Lakeland let his head loll to the side, to take me in from another angle.

"We could pay you. . . ."

"You could . . . ," I said, and then I experienced a moment of dizziness. I was just then realizing how far I'd climbed into that lion's den. I had taken steps, one after the other, without any real regard to my destination. I was speaking to a man who could have me killed, a man who was my enemy and my people's enemy. But there was no turning away. "But I'm here for only one reason, to get Brawly home."

"And what do I have to do with that?"

"I need some information."

"What kind of information?"

"Addresses for Christina Montes and Jasper Bodan, president and secretary of the Urban Revolutionary Party." I waited for a reply but none came. So I continued. "And some idea of what you have on Brawly."

"I ask you again, Mr. Rawlins. What will you do for me?"

"You've read my files, man. And you know how deep I can get into a situation just seein' me sit in front'a you. It wouldn't hurt you to have me worried about some conflagration. I mean, if the man you got in there now isn't doin' the job so you need another source."

"What do you know about our informants?" He tried to sound threatening but I could see the worry in those wormy lips.

"Just a guess, man. Only way you could keep tabs on one black man is through another one. That shit goes all the way back to the plantation."

"All you want is Brawly Brown?" There was humor in Lakeland's question. "And you don't want to be paid?"

"That's right."

"How can I be sure that you won't use what I give you against us?"

"You mean if I tell Tina where Xavier lives at?"

"Have you ever heard of Vietnam, Mr. Rawlins?"

"Yeah. That's over in Asia, right? Where the French got their butts kicked."

"There's red-blooded American men over there right now fighting for your right to vote and pray and walk down the street without being molested. Those men are black as well as white. I was with them only six months ago. I don't hate your people. I only hate the enemies of democracy. These radicals, these black revolutionaries are undermining the foundation of our democracy. I don't care that they have a valid complaint. We all have problems. But regardless of those problems, we cannot threaten the land that our children and their children will inherit.

"Brown is just a misguided pawn. He doesn't know anything. He follows whatever fool yells the loudest. People like this Xavier Bodan and his girlfriend Tina Montes, they have a whole army of young fools like him. If you can help us, we'll help him."

I was thinking that white America also had an army of young fools like Brawly, that all the young men in all the history of the world were like him. Young men fighting and dying for ideas they barely understood, for rights they never possessed, for beliefs based on lies.

"I was in the army," I said. "I know what it's like to fight a war. So believe me when I tell you that I know what you're talking about."

A buzzer went off and Lakeland picked up his phone. It flashed through my mind that the colonel was just talking to fill up the time, that he was having his people do some kind of check on me and now I was about to be arrested. I resisted the sudden urge to jump across the table and strangle the patriot.

"Yes? What?" he said. "No." Then he looked up at me and asked, "What do you know about Henry Strong?"

The room turned cold, which meant that I had begun to sweat.

"Only what I heard that night at the meeting," I answered honestly. "Never even heard of him before that night."

"Did you know him?"

I thought of the pictures that Knorr had of me at the First Men's storefront. Were there pictures of Strong and me at the late-night diner?

"Not really."

"What does that mean?"

"It means that I don't know anything about Strong."

Lakeland was suspicious of me. But he was suspicious of everybody right then.

"I have an emergency meeting to attend, Rawlins. Mona will give you the addresses you need."

I stood up, a little surprised that I had managed to maintain my freedom.

"But don't fuck with me," Lakeland said.

That was a long time ago, 1964, when most white men in suits didn't use the ghetto's slang.

"Don't fuck with me," he repeated. "Or I will burn your ass down."

23 / MERCURY HALL LIVED on Caliburn Drive. It was an ideal street for L.A. living, a road that went nowhere — a short street that ran in a kind of zigzag semicircle that both entered and exited on Eighty-eighth Place. All you ever saw were your neighbors and the occasional motorist who'd lost his way. Any suspicious character caused a flurry of phone calls because everyone was on their guard for trouble.

Blesta Ridgeway-Hall and Mercury had made a beautiful home. Lemon trees on either side of the front door and rosebushes at the curb. The grass was shaggy and just watered. It was a small house with a green roof and white walls. The front door was oak with a double wall. The outer surface had a tree and a crescent moon cut out of it.

A curtain on a window to my left fluttered.

"Mommy, it's a man," a child yelled from somewhere behind the closed door.

I had knocked on the door, just above the moon. The sound was a resonant tenor drumbeat.

I waited, counting the seconds of hesitation until the door opened.

Blesta was about five-five with light brown curly hair, light brown skin, and dark brown eyes. She was the beauty and the brains of the sisters that Mercury and Chapman married.

"Mr. Rawlins," she said. "Mercury ain't here."

"No? When's he comin' home?"

"Um, I don't know."

"Listen, B, I got to talk to him. But I understand if you don't want a man waitin' in the house alone with you. I could sit out in the car, no problem."

"I really don't know when he gonna be home, Mr. Rawlins. You know, two or three times a week him and Kenny go out for a drink and a game'a snooker after work." Blesta was almost pleading with me.

"I'll wait out in the car," I said.

"No. No, come on in. If you sit out there, all the neighbors gonna be yackin' back an' forth till one of 'em call the police and then Mercury get mad at me for gettin' you arrested." Blesta backed away from the door and I entered the small and perfectly ordered home.

The Halls' front door led right into the living room. Blesta had two yellow chairs with a matching sofa. The plush chairs had turquoise hassocks with walnut legs. The carpet was formed out of concentric ovals of dark blue and light green. A six-foot avocado sapling filled one corner and a big console TV sat in front of the couch.

The picture window beside the door looked out upon my green Pontiac. The room managed to be both peaceful and festive.

"Boo!" little Artemus Hall shouted at me.

The four-year-old jumped out from a doorway, yelled his scary word, and then fell down laughing.

I laughed, too. It was the funniest thing I'd seen in the past few days, days that seemed like months. I caught myself before the laughter turned hysterical.

"Go get your coloring book, Arty," Blesta said.

"No," he told her. And then to me, "Will you gimme a piggyback ride?"

"My back is a little sore today, partner," I said. "But why don't you come over here and make a picture for me?"

"Okay," Arty chirped, and then he ran full speed out of the room. I sat on the couch.

"Can I get you something, Mr. Rawlins?"

"Could you see your way to callin' me Easy?"

"Yeah, I guess."

"You guess what?"

"Easy." Blesta's smile was the axe that brought Mercury low. Her whole face seemed to ignite behind that grin.

Artemus came thundering back from his trove of toys with at least six coloring books under his arm. There was one of circus performers and animals and one filled with cowboys and Indians. He even had a coloring book of different kinds of houses throughout history.

I asked for a sad clown and he looked until he found one.

Blesta had to do work elsewhere in the house, so I sat with Arty while he carefully rubbed the Crayolas onto the newsprint outlines.

"Look at this, Mr. Raw-wins," he'd say, showing me the tangle of yellow lines he'd used to fill in the clown's upturned hands.

And . . . "Look at this" for the red eyes or the green mouth.

I sat there as peacefully as I had been at work earlier that morning.

I needed peace. There were two dead men on my mind: Aldridge Brown and Henry Strong.

I tried to think of what the two men might have in common other than Brawly — but nothing came to mind. Then I tried to figure why the boy would want to kill either man. Again I came up blank.

"Mr. Raw-wins, you like blue?"

"Yes, sirree," I said. "Blue is the color of music."

"Music don't hab no color," Arty said.

"Not when you're a boy," I replied. "But when you grow up it will be blue that you see when the music makes you cry."

Artemus gazed up at me with wondering, amazed eyes. Somehow my words made him think something that stopped everything else.

A car door slammed outside and Arty screamed, "Daddy!"

He jumped up and ran for the door. Blesta came in from the kitchen. I stood up. A few moments later the front door opened.

"Blesta, baby, somebody's car parked out f —" he said before catching sight of me.

Artemus grabbed onto his leg chanting, "Daddy, Daddy, Daddy . . ."

Blesta turned on that smile.

"Hey, Merc," I hailed, stretching out my hand.

He shook with me but there was suspicion in his eye.

Mercury was a shade darker and six inches shorter than I. He was truly big-boned, not fat or even chubby. He had the kind of build that professional boxers are trained to stay away from — powerful and low to the ground.

"Mr. Rawlins," he said.

"I just finished gettin' your wife to call me Easy, Merc. Don't mess it up now."

"He said he had to talk with you, honey," Blesta said, kissing him on the cheek. "I told him to wait in here 'cause old Mrs. Horner would sure call the cops if he stayed out in his car."

"Sit in the car?" Mercury said. "Easy Rawlins don't have to sit in no car in front'a my house. You want somethin' to drink?"

"No thanks, Merc."

"What you come by for?" he asked, all smiles and openness.

"I need to ask you a few questions," I said.

"Come on, Arty," Blesta said. "Come help Mama make dinner."

"I wanna stay wit' Daddy."

"I'm makin' frostin'."

Without another word Arty picked up his coloring book and ran from the room, his mother right behind him.

I returned to the yellow sofa while Mercury perched on a turquoise hassock.

"What you need, Easy?" he asked. "More about Brawly?"

"In a roundabout way," I said. "What you know about the houses they buildin' down a couple of blocks from where John's lots are?"

"Down where they got the pink flags hangin' from the eaves?"

"Yeah," I said. "How'd you know?"

"A man got shot down there last night."

"Who?" I asked.

Mercury shook his head. "All I know is that the cops come down and closed up any construction on that block. They didn't say who it was."

"Who's buildin' those houses?"

"I don't know exactly. It's another black investment group, though. I'm pretty sure it's one'a Jewelle's."

"She got them, too, huh?"

"Yes, sir. But I don't know their names. We all keep pretty separate out around there."

"So you never been over to that site?" I asked.

"No."

"How about Brawly?"

"Maybe, yeah. If John wasn't around, Brawly'd take him some long walks, if you know what I mean. He'd ramble around lookin' for someone to talk to. You know I don't have much patience for talkin' on the job. Brawly got along better with Chapman than he did with me."

"Chapman ever tell you what Brawly was talkin' 'bout?"

"Just shit, man. Brawly got an opinion on everything under the sun. Boy'd talk a blue streak and not say one goddamned thing."

"So you didn't like workin' with 'im too much then?"

"Man, I don't like workin' construction — period," Mercury said. "Matter of fact, I'm thinkin' that I'm gonna leave this whole thing."

"You quittin'?"

"Quittin', pullin' up stakes, an' headin' back down to where people talk like I talk."

"Back to Arkansas?"

"Maybe Texas," Mercury said. "There's gettin' to be some jobs down there. They havin' what you call a oil boom."

"Chapman leavin', too?"

"What am I?" he asked. "Chapman's keeper? Niggah can take care of his own business."

"You ever hear about a man named Henry Strong?" I asked in ambush.

"Yeah," he admitted, unperturbed.

"Where from?"

"A couple'a months ago. Brawly came by with him. They took me an' Chapman to Blackbird's for a shot or two."

"What he have to say?"

"Just all that black shit. You know, how we all should have what the white man have. He wanted us to come down to his meetin'-house. I told him no."

"What did Chapman say?"

"Why don't you ask Chapman?"

"I'm askin' you, Mercury. I figure you owe me one thing, at least."

"You have my gratitude, Mr. Rawlins. But I ain't tellin' you nuthin' 'bout my friends. No, sir."

Of course he'd told me volumes by refusing to talk.

"Why you askin' 'bout Strong and them places down the way?" Mercury asked.

"No reason really," I said. "I saw him down at the place where Brawly's been hangin' out. I tell ya, tryin' to get a handle on Brawly is givin' me more trouble than I figured."

"Yeah," Mercury said. "That Brawly's a mess."

"Well," I said. "I better be goin'."

I stood up.

"Okay," Mercury replied. "Honey, Mr. Rawlins's leavin'."

Blesta came out wearing a white apron over her housedress. There was a chocolate smudge under her left breast.

"Cain't you stay for dinner . . . Easy?"

"Got to go." I shook hands with her.

"This is for you," little Artemus Hall said, holding up the clown torn from his coloring book.

I took the leaf and stared at it. The clown's head was tilted slightly to the side. Artemus had made the face white and brown with big red tears coming out of the sad eyes.

"Thank you very much, Arty. I'm gonna put this one up in my kitchen. I gotta corkboard in there and I'm gonna put this one up on a tack."

I could see Mercury in the boy's smile.

24 / *THE NEXT PERSON* on my list was Tina Montes. She'd been kind to me the night the police broke in on the First Men and I pulled her out of there before they could crack her skull.

She lived in a rooming house on Thirty-first Street. The woman who owned it, Liselle Latour, was a pal of mine from the old days in Houston, Texas. Liselle had been born Thaddie Brown but changed her name when she ran away from home at thirteen. She'd turned to prostitution and had become a madam by the time she was twenty-five. She left Houston in '44 with her partner/bodyguard/boyfriend Franklin Nettars. Frank had been pestering Liselle to leave Houston for years. He told her that the black folks up in L.A. made real money and that a small whorehouse around there would make them rich.

Liselle would have never left but for a fight that had come to pass in her house of ill repute. A white man — I never got his name — had a disagreement with one of the whores and wound up with a knife in his throat. The woman was arrested. Liselle managed to stay out of jail but she knew her name had been placed on the police list. And once you went on the police list in Houston, you either died, went to jail, or left town.

They took a sleeper cabin in a special colored car on the *Sunset Express* from Houston to L.A. The whole way Franklin was telling Liselle how great it would be when they got to California.

"He'd be sayin'," Liselle told me, "that you could live pickin' fruit off'a the trees while you was walkin' down the street." She always smiled when she mentioned his name.

The porter dropped by their cabin to tell them that they were just about to cross the California line.

"Ten seconds after that," Liselle said, "he got a heart attack. Hit him so hard that he only felt it a few seconds before he was dead."

I never thought about Liselle loving Franklin. I mean, they seemed more like business partners than soul mates. But when Franklin died, Liselle was a changed woman. She took her life savings and bought the place on Thirty-first. She made it a rooming house for single women and didn't even let a male visitor past the ground floor. She never even dated another man and became very involved with the dealings of the church.

Liselle became virtuous and solitary but she didn't forget her old friends. Neither did she pretend that she'd come from some upstanding moral background. Liselle told everyone what she had been because, as she'd say, "I don't want you findin' out someday and then gettin' mad that I lied to ya."

She was happy to see her old friends and even share a drop of spirits with them.

That's why I felt no trepidations approaching her home.

There were two doors to the three-story wooden building, one up front and the other on the side. The front door was for the women and girls; the side was Liselle's private entrance.

When I knocked, Liselle opened up almost immediately. Her front door was across the way from the inside door to the entrance hall of the rooming house. Liselle spent most of her day sitting in between the doors, sewing or reading her Bible. From there she'd greet her boarders and make sure that no man snuck upstairs.

"Easy Rawlins," she cried. "Baby, how are you?"

"Just fine, Miss Latour. And you?"

"Workin' off my sins one ounce at a time," she said gladly.

The years had not been kind to Liselle. Her face had crossed over into middle age, and for every ounce of sin she'd lost she put on an ounce of fat. I hardly recognized the beautiful young woman that the men in the Fifth Ward used to throw their money at.

"What you doin' here?" she asked. Her eyes narrowed.

"Why? Cain't I come by and shout at an old friend some evenin'?"

"I don't think so."

"Why not?"

"What you want, Easy?"

"I want to sit down."

Reminded of her manners, Liselle gestured toward the chair across from hers. She closed the hall door and slapped her hands down on her knees.

"Well?" she asked.

"I don't get it," I said. "Why you think I'm'a be here for some kinda business?"

"Because trouble follows you, Easy Rawlins. It always has, and it always will."

"You talkin' like I'm some kinda gangster," I said. "But you know

I'm not like that. I got a job at Sojourner Truth Junior High School and I've raised two kids on my own. What kinda gangster does that?"

"You the one said 'gangster,' not me. I just said that trouble follows you. Whenever I hear about you, I hear about somebody outta jail or back in, somebody gettin' killed or robbed or beat up by the cops. Even them kids you got come outta worlds where adults would be hard-pressed to survive — that's what I heard.

"But most of all, I know you married to trouble because of Raymond Alexander. Everybody who ever been anywhere around Mouse know that there's some kinda mess on to brew. Young women cain't help it. They see a man like Raymond an' their tongues start to waggin' an' their panties get wet. But men who ran with Mouse are either fools or magnets for trouble their own selfs."

"Mouse is dead," I said.

"And if the stories I hear is right, you the one dropped the body off on EttaMae's front grass."

I had forgotten how thorough the grapevine was.

"Many a day," Liselle continued, "I had to shoo Mr. Alexander away from my girls' door. He come up at me all blustery, but I shook my broom at him. An' you know evil as he was, he always backed down.

"But you know," she added, "I don't think that he really is dead."

"You don't? Why not?"

"Just how Etta left. I believe that if he had died, she would'a made a funeral, invited everyone who ever loved him and everyone who wanted to make sure that he was gone. 'Cause you know Mouse had many enemies. Like you have, Easy."

"Now I got to look over my shoulder?" I said, trying to sound amused.

"Man who travel in bad company got to expect grief and misery at the do'."

"I can see that I knocked on the wrong door today."

"I'll tell you what, Easy," Liselle said. "I will prove to you that you come here because'a trouble."

"All right, prove it."

"Christina Montes," she said.

That brought the curtain down on my repartee. I think I managed to keep my mouth closed, but still Liselle smiled.

"Am I right?"

"Yes, ma'am," I said with a sigh that I felt down in what the doctors called my bronchioles.

Liselle grinned and sat back in her wooden chair. She stretched her hand behind her and plucked a pint bottle from the edge of a bookcase. There was a small juice glass on the floor next to the chair. This she filled halfway with the amber fluid. She knew that I had given up drinking and so didn't offer me a drink.

"What's wrong with Tina?" I asked.

"Same thing that's wrong with all women."

I raised my eyebrows to ask for the other shoe.

"Men," Liselle said. Her tone was more lascivious than it was angry. "Men mornin', noon, and night are the bane of women and the joy of their lives."

"She see a lotta men?"

"You just need one bad apple, Easy. You know that."

"Does this bad apple have a name?"

"I call him the X-man," Liselle said. "But she call him Xavier."

"And how is this Xavier trouble?"

"Oh, don't get me wrong, Easy. He's a good boy. If I was his mama, I'd swell with pride every time he walked into a room or opened his mouth. He's skinny as a rail but brave and proud as a lion. That's the kinda man a good woman want to have around."

"So Tina's a good woman?"

25 / *FEATHER RAN AT ME* the second I came in the door.

"Daddy, I got a B-plus on my Joan Arks book report," she shouted. She ran up and tackled me around the waist.

"Do you have to jump all over me?" I complained.

"I got a B-plus, Daddy," she said again, ignoring my objections.

"Let me go," I said.

Feather backed away from me with pain in her eyes.

The little yellow dog came up behind her, baring his teeth.

"I got a B-plus," she said, and the first tear appeared.

"I'm sorry, baby, but I had a hard day. That's good about your B. It's good."

"It's a B-plus."

"Hi, honey," Bonnie said from the kitchen.

It struck me then that there was the smell of cooking in the a

"Good as they come. Manners and charm. She got it all. Know how to fold a napkin on her lap and cleans up after herself without bein' asked."

"Don't sound like trouble to me," I said innocently.

"Yeah. You talk that sweet talk, baby. But you know the cops been to me askin' about her, throwin' dirt on her name" — I didn't know but I had suspected as much — "an' you know that the First Men been comin' by with com'unist leaflets and rough talk about killin' and burnin' down the street. I asked 'em was they gonna burn down my house and they said no, but how you gonna start a fire an' ask it to skip the houses you want to save? Once the flames get goin', they burn down everything."

"What did the police say?"

"That she was a revolutionary and could they search her room for arms."

"Did you let them in?"

"Hell no. Shit. I got two guns under my own bed and another one in the hall closet. What the hell do it mean to have a gun?"

"How about a man named Henry Strong?" I asked.

"Yeah. Yeah. He was here. She introduced me to him as if he was a bowl of ice cream in the middle of the Sahara Desert. It wouldn't have surprised me if she would tell the X-man that she was goin' to the beauty parlor and spend the afternoon studyin' revolution at Henry Strong's feet — on her knees."

"That's all?" I asked.

"Yeah . . . sometimes that Conrad come by, but usually he was with his uncle."

"Uncle? What uncle?"

"I don't think that they were really related. He come to the door one day and I asked him who was that with him and he said his uncle, but then he smirked like it was some kind of joke."

"What he look like?" I asked.

"Husky man. Thirty-five, maybe even forty. He looked all right but never spoke a word in my presence, never talked to anyone at all."

"He have a name?"

Liselle twisted her face, trying to remember. All she came up with was the memory of the whiskey in her hand. She took a sip and said, "No. I don't remember a name. A heavyset man. Big, you know, and dark."

"Could the name have been Aldridge?" I asked.

Liselle shook her head. "I don't remember," she said.

I sat back then. The yen for a lungful of smoke hit me hard, but I refrained from asking Liselle for a cigarette.

"Do you know Tina very well?" I asked.

"Uh-huh."

"Do you trust me?"

Liselle stalled and then said, "I know that you aren't a bad man, Easy. But like I said, you hang around some real hard times."

"There's been two murders already," I said. "Those cops came here are more like vigilantes than they are law."

"What you want with her?"

"You know John the bartender, right?"

"Yeah?"

"His girlfriend, Alva, got a boy named Brawly. He's all messed up in the First Men. I'm tryin' to get him outta trouble. But if I can help Tina, I'll do that, too."

"And how is Christina messed up in all'a this?"

"She knows Conrad, who's a dirty piece'a work. . . ."

Liselle hummed her agreement.

"Brawly's father was killed and the other man, Henry Strong, was murdered just this morning —"

"What?" Liselle said.

"So I think anybody on Tina's side would be welcome."

"What you want me to do, Easy?"

"I want you to talk to her, tell her who I am and what you think about me. If she hears that and wants some outside help, have her call me at home."

"She ain't been here in a couple'a days," Liselle said. "But she bound to show up. All her clothes still up in her room."

I wrote down my number on an egg carton that Liselle had thrown out.

When I opened the door to leave, Liselle put a hand on my arm and said in a conspiratorial tone, "I told you 'bout you an' trouble now, didn't I, Easy?"

"Yes, ma'am."

She was wearing a yellow wraparound dress with a red and blue silk cloth coiled in her hair. Her feet were bare.

"I forgot you were coming home today," I said.

"You say that as if you want me to leave."

"No. No, baby."

Feather moved over to Bonnie and leaned against her side, frowning and staring at my shoes.

"Did you hear about Feather's B-plus?" Bonnie asked.

"Yeah," I said. "That's really great. I mean, I think we should have some special ice cream for dessert after a grade like that."

Feather's frown softened and she looked up as far as my shoulder.

I heard the faint sound of sawing coming from the backyard.

"What's that?"

"Jesus working on his boat." It was Bonnie's turn to frown.

"We're talking about it," I said.

"A child does not have the right to make up his mind whether or not he's going to school," she said.

"Jesus been a man as long as I can remember," I told her. "If I died tomorrow and you disappeared, he would raise Feather all by himself. You could bet the farm on that."

"Are you sick, Daddy?" Feather asked.

"No, honey. I'm fine."

"All I'm saying," Bonnie continued, "is that he needs to finish his education. He needs to understand how important it is."

"How the hell you gonna tell me what that boy needs an' you didn't even know he was alive six months ago?" I said. "You don't know. You don't know what he's thinkin' or where he's goin'. There's all kindsa people up and down this block got education way over me. But we still livin' on the same street, goin' off to work every day. How am I gonna tell Juice that he got to do somethin' I ain't never done? How am I even gonna believe that shit?"

"Easy," Bonnie said.

She glanced down at Feather, who was transfixed by my anger. "I just mean let me work this out on my own, okay?"

"I'll get dinner," Bonnie said.

She headed for the kitchen. Feather followed in her shadow.

I reached for my shirt pocket but it was empty. I'd discarded the pack of Chesterfields earlier that day. There was half a carton on the top shelf of the hall closet, I knew. But I clenched my teeth and sat in my recliner. Nothing was going to beat me. Not Jesus's demands or Lakeland's designs, certainly not a flimsy little cigarette.

The fabric of the chair smelled of tobacco smoke. So did my fingertips. For five minutes all I could think about was smoking, or not smoking.

When I finally calmed down, Brawly Brown was waiting there in my mind. Big and clumsy, strong and easily influenced. Or was he smarter than he seemed? Was he the First Men's fool, or was it John and Alva who were fooled by him? I couldn't trust Alva's opinion. John only cared about his woman.

If the heavyset man who'd come to Tina's with Conrad was Aldridge, then I had at least one other person who was connected to both men.

I took a deep breath.

Something was missing.

What was I missing?

A cigarette.

"Dinner," Bonnie called out the back door.

Brawly had to be involved in something serious. That's the only way I could see the ambush set up outside of the housing tract near John's places. There was no other way. Anyway, Strong told me that he was bringing me to Brawly, but that could have been a lie.

But if Brawly tried to kill me, if he murdered Henry Strong, then there was nothing I could do to help him. At least there was nothing I should do.

"Sure I killed him," Mouse once said to me about a man who had been his friend. "Motherfucker turned on me. An' you know once a dog taste your blood, he always got a hunger for more."

How could I put a murderer back in the house with John? Back on the street with the rest of us?

"Easy." Bonnie was standing there over me.

"Yeah?"

"Didn't you hear me? Dinner's ready."

*B*ONNIE'S LASAGNA WAS always a treat. The tomato sauce was dark red and spicy. She used four kinds of cheese and shredded veal rather than ground round. The salad had lots of Parmesan cheese and garlic in the dressing. The food tasted wonderful but it was somehow weaker than usual. I craved a cigarette. I kept taking deep breaths through my nose, but still I had the feeling of slow suffocation.

"Is something wrong, Easy?"

"No," I said sharply. "Why you keep askin' me that?"

"Because you keep sighing," she said.

"Listen, if a man can't sit down to a meal and take a deep breath, then maybe he shouldn't even come home. You been pesterin' me since I come in the door. What do you want?"

That silenced the table for more than a minute. It would have been even longer but I spoke again.

"I'm goin' out for a while," I said, standing up from the table.

"Don't go, Daddy," Feather pleaded.

"Where are you going, Easy?" Bonnie asked in a maddeningly reasonable tone.

I took another deep breath that came out in a sigh.

"To the market," I said. "For our B-plus special ice cream. You want pistachio or chocolate chip, Feather?"

"Both," she said.

*T*HE LITTLE MARKET down the street was always open until ten. Mr. Tai was a night owl and everyone around the neighborhood knew that his was the only place, besides the overpriced liquor stores, where you could get prepared and packaged foods after eight.

"Sweet tooth tonight, Mr. Rawlins?" Tai asked when I brought the two half-gallon containers up to the register. I also had a pint of vanilla, which was for me.

"Good grade," I said. "Feather got a B-plus."

"That's good. I got one girl get really good grades. She likes the books and the homework."

"What about your other kids?" I asked.

I liked Tai. He had a slight build and a gentle disposition but he also had a vicious scar down the left side of his face. I'd once seen him throw a six-foot drunk on his ass out in front of his store.

"Two more girls. They will get married and make my grandchildren. One boy who fail everything," Tai snickered. "Everything. If they gave him a test on what he ate for breakfast, he would fail that, too."

"Doesn't that bother you?"

"No."

"What are you going to do?"

"I wait till he's sixteen and then he come here and work with me. Eight o'clock we open up and ten we go home. If that don't make him go back to school, then I have a partner. Tai and Son."

The grocer gave me a wide grin.

26 / *I MANAGED NOT TO BITE* anybody's head off over ice cream. Feather spent most of her time eating from her bowl on Bonnie's lap. Jesus, who probably knew me better than any other living being ever had, stayed away from me. He didn't talk about his boat or dropping out. As a matter of fact, I don't think he said a single word. All those early years as a mute had given him a close kinship with silence. Silence and patience at being understood.

After the children were in bed Bonnie made me a drink, a concoction made from a scoop of ice cream, vanilla flavoring, milk, eggs, nutmeg, and honey. In the old days I would have added a shot of bourbon to top it off.

We sat in the living room listening to the late news. There was a story about a Negro named Henry Strong who died instantaneously from a gunshot wound to the head in the early-morning hours. He lived at the Colorado Hotel on Cherry and was a native of Oakland, California.

"Do you want me to leave, Easy?"

"What?"

"Do you want me to move out of your house?" Bonnie asked.

"What are you talkin' about, Shay?"

"You haven't even touched me since you came in." She was close to tears.

I moved over to the couch and put my arm around her.

"I was just . . . just . . . I was just preoccupied," I said.

She shook off my arm and shifted away from me.

"We haven't known each other very long, Easy. I know that when you helped me that your friend got killed. . . ."

"No one's even sure that he's dead," I said. "And even if he is, that was between me and Raymond. We been livin' up near the front lines ever since we were children. It ain't nobody's fault the way we lived. You didn't ask him for nuthin' and you weren't there when the shit went down. You were there for me, though. You been there for the kids."

"You needed somebody to love you, Easy. You were hurting and you were kind, too. But just because you're grateful doesn't mean you want me. I will leave if that's what's best. I will."

"That's not what I want. No."

Bonnie's face was like the drawing of a black goddess from some Polynesian myth. The eyes slanted upward, her full lips perfectly shaped. Those lips parted and for a moment I forgot the hunger in my lungs and the pain of Raymond's death. Even the trouble I'd burrowed down into didn't seem like much.

"I been doin' somethin'," I said.

"What?"

I told her about John and Alva, about Brawly and the First Men.

I told her about Aldridge and Henry Strong but refrained from letting on that I was at both murder scenes.

"It sounds too dangerous, Easy," she said after I was done.

"Like when you were in trouble," I said.

She kissed me and I kissed her, and then she kissed me again. I'd had an erection ever since her lips parted.

*L*ATER THAT NIGHT we were in the bed, still kissing. Cigarettes must have something to do with sex somehow, because my desire for tobacco was completely gone for an hour and a half. All I needed was my baby. I could have taken that on the radio.

"So you're upset because of the police and the political group?" Bonnie asked me between smooches.

I think she was looking for a way to talk me out of helping John.

"No," I said. "I'm upset because I haven't had a cigarette since early this morning."

"Why don't you have one then?"

"Because this is some serious business. I might have to move fast and I know from the stairs at Sojourner Truth that I don't have much of a wind. I couldn't trot around this block if I wanted to."

"You're a full-grown man, Easy," she whispered into my armpit. "A man shouldn't have to run."

"Maybe there's some white man somewhere think he don't have to skip out now and then, but a black man anywhere in this United States better be able to run a mile and then another one."

"I don't want you out there running after trouble," Bonnie complained.

"Then you don't have to worry about me. I'm the runnin'-away kind."

"That's not true," she said. "I wish it was, but it's not."

"You really wish that I was a coward?"

"I love the man," she said. "Not the man who saved me, but the one who cared that I was okay."

I looked into her eyes but her heart was too vast for me to comprehend.

*W*HEN THE PHONE RANG I was deep in a dreamless sleep. I heard it jangling but there didn't seem to be any reason to answer. My left foot was hanging out of the bed, feeling a slight chill, and my right thigh was pressed against Bonnie's butt, warm as toast. Everything was right with the world.

"Easy. Easy."

"Hm."

"Easy."

"Yeah, babe?"

"It's the phone. A woman named Tina."

I remembered the ringing. It seemed like many years ago. The only thing that mattered was my cold foot and warm thigh.

"Easy."

And then I was awake, craving cigarettes and aware of the danger I'd crossed over into.

"Hello," I said.

"Mr. Rawlins?"

"Uh-huh."

"This is Tina Montes. We met the other night at the First Men."

"I remember. Your people pulled a gun on me and threw me out of the car."

I could feel Bonnie stiffen against my leg.

"I didn't want that. Conrad and Mr. Strong get kinda rough sometimes."

"What can I do for you, Miss Montes?"

"Miss Latour said that I could trust you."

"You sure can do that," I said. "On one condition, that is."

"What's that?"

"You can trust me if you don't lie to me."

"Okay."

"What time is it?"

"One," she said.

"In the morning?" I said with a sigh. "Tell Liselle to get the parlor ready. I'll be over in less than an hour."

I put down the phone and sat up in one motion.

Bonnie didn't say anything until I was dressed and ready to leave.

"Easy?"

"Yeah, babe?"

She stood up all naked and womanly. From her purse she took a Camel cigarette. She always carried a pack because she sometimes smoked with her girlfriends. She lit the cigarette, took a drag, and then put it between my lips.

She kissed my cheek and said, "You need to be calm out there, Mr. Rawlins. Give up smoking some other time."

"Aren't you upset about some woman calling me in the middle of the night?"

"No," she said. "You wouldn't give our number to some bird you took a fancy to. You wouldn't hurt me like that. I am worried about someone pulling a gun on you, though."

"He wasn't serious," I said. "Just tryin' to show me who was boss."

27 / *LISELLE MET ME* at the front door. She looked even older late at night. The flesh under her eyes hung down and her shoulders did, too.

But, weak and tired as she was, she grilled me before allowing me to set foot past the threshold.

"I don't want you worrying her now, Easy," Liselle said. "You know that girl has enough problems. And I don't want you bringing her down just because you wanna help that broodin' Brawly boy."

"You know Brawly?" I asked.

"He been here. Yes, he has."

"What do you know about him?"

"Just that he's sullen and childish. Start talkin' to anybody like they supposed to care how he feels. Told me that he liked me 'cause I wasn't cold like his mother. I told him that it's much easier for a stranger to be nice than a mother who got to listen to a boy's boasting he's a man while she washin' the shit stains outta his drawers."

I laughed. "What he say to that?"

"Just frowned an' never even said hello to me again."

"I won't hurt Tina," I said. "I promise you that."

Liselle held my gaze with her drooping, watery eyes for a good five seconds before leading me into the old-fashioned parlor, where Tina was seated on a straight-backed walnut chair.

The young radical was wearing baggy blue slacks and a coral-colored top that was also loose-fitting. Tina had a small nose and medium brown skin. She was pretty because she was twenty, more or less. By thirty she'd be no more than handsome, and by forty she'd be considered plain.

But right then she held the strong attraction of vulnerability. She looked up at Liselle and me like some condemned prisoner hoping for a reprieve but expecting the worst.

"Here he is, baby," Liselle said. "But if you don't want to talk no more, just stand up and come in to me. Just come in to me."

"Thank you, Miss Latour," Tina said.

Liselle walked into her small apartment, leaving her door slightly ajar. I waited a moment before walking over and pushing the door closed. Then I came back to the chair across from Christina Montes.

"How are you doing?" I asked.

"Okay. But you know three of our brothers are still in jail. One's in the hospital."

"Why'd the cops break in on you like that?"

"I don't know," she said. "Thanks for helping me get away."

"No problem."

"Conrad shouldn't have put that gun in your face. Xavier says it's because people think he looks white that he always feels he has to prove himself."

"I'm not worried about him," I said. "Liselle told you that I'm tryin' t'help Brawly, right?"

"You told us that you were lookin' for him in the car the other night."

"Yeah, I forgot. Well, she told you that I'm all right, I guess."

"She said that you could help people out if they're in trouble but that I should be careful because you move with dangerous people."

"I can't argue about that," I said. "But you put me to shame."

"What do you mean by that?"

"You got Conrad and Brawly stackin' up guns with Brawly's girlfriend —"

"Clarissa?" Tina was really surprised.

"No, the white one, BobbiAnne."

"You got that wrong, Mr. Rawlins. Clarissa is Brawly's girl," Tina said. "He loves her."

"I don't know what the word is that he does to BobbiAnne, but she's his girl, too," I said with a great deal of authority in my voice.

"I don't know anything about that or any guns, either. All I know is that Henry Strong is dead and I'm scared, scared for Xavier and the others."

"What about Aldridge Brown?" I asked.

"What about him?"

"Did you know him?"

"Sure I know him. He's Brawly's father. A couple of times he bought us dinner at Egbert's Coffee Shop."

"So Aldridge was in the Party, too?" I asked.

"No. Really I don't think he cared about politics. But he had a lot of trouble with Brawly when Brawly was a boy, and they were tryin' to make up for it."

"Do you think whoever killed Strong killed Brawly's father?"

"The police killed Henry, but what do you mean about Mr. Brown?" If she was lying, she was a master at it.

"He was killed two days ago at a house owned by a woman named Isolda Moore."

Tina shook her head slowly.

"Don't you read the newspaper?" I asked.

"Why would I? It's all lies anyway," she said. "Why be blinded by white men's lies?"

"Because you might read something that has something to do with you," I said. "That's why."

"I don't know what to tell you, Mr. Rawlins. I've been staying at different friends' houses since the night the cops busted up our meeting. Mr. Strong said that we should keep moving because the police had us all on a list and the leaders might be killed. I only came here tonight to get my stuff and move away. Miss Latour has always been kind and friendly. She told me I should talk with you, but really I don't know anything about guns and murderers."

"Why do you think the cops killed Strong?" I asked her.

"Because he's so important to the movement. He told us that the police would try to eliminate our elite either by framing them or by assassination."

Before I visited with Colonel Lakeland I would have sneered at the possibility of such a conspiracy; now, I didn't know.

"What about Aldridge?" I asked. "Why would the cops kill him?"

"I don't know. He never went to our meetings or anything. He just picked up Brawly sometimes and took us out for coffee."

"But him and Brawly got along okay?"

"Yeah," she said. "I mean, they had a bad history, like I said. But that was all worked out. You could tell that Brawly was still a little distant, though."

I tucked her words away. It was a puzzle with too many pieces. Even if one thing seemed to fit, something else was left to the side.

"What about you and Strong?" I asked.

"What do you mean?"

"You know what I mean. Did he ever come by here without Xavier knowin' it?"

"A few times. But there's nothing wrong with that. Men and women are free to know each other and see each other and —"

"How much did you show to Mr. Strong?" I asked.

"What business is that of yours?"

"Because after this talk here I'm gonna ask you to go with me to see Xavier. I don't wanna say anything that will make him so mad that he loses reason."

"Why would I take you to Xavier, anyway?"

"I didn't say I wanted you to take me to him. I know where he lives. On Hoover." I told her the address. "What I need is for you to pave the way for a calm conversation. Now how are we going to be calm if in the middle of it, it turns out that you've been beddin' the master?"

The intensity of Tina's eyes told me that Liselle's suspicions were right.

"It wasn't nuthin'," Tina said. "He was lonely down here and we liked to talk. One day he put his hand on the back of my neck. . . ."

I didn't care about the details. I didn't care that they had been together at all.

"Where?" I asked.

"My neck."

"No. Where were you when you first . . . um . . . kissed him?"

"At his place."

"The Colorado Hotel?"

"No." She gave me a Watts address, not far from Central Avenue.

"Okay," I said. "We don't have to talk about that with Xavier. But did Henry say anything other than he thought he was gonna be assassinated? Killed?"

"No."

"He was shot over by some tract houses goin' up over in Compton," I said. "You ever go there with him, or he ever talk about it?"

"Brawly was out there," she said, hesitating over the memory. "I think Henry went out there with him once, maybe more times."

"Why?"

"Henry liked Brawly. He said that he was a revolutionary in the rough. He told me that he was cultivating him for the movement."

Like he was doing with you, I thought.

"You wanna go see Xavier?" I asked.

"Why?"

"Because I know things that he should know. Because somebody's killin' people close to you and it would be good to find out who."

"I know who it is," she said.

"You think you know," I said. "But you can't put a face on 'em. You think you know, but why would the cops kill Aldridge Brown? Why kill Strong? He's from Oakland. Xavier's the head man. Why not him or you — or Anton Breland?"

"How can I trust you?" Her question cut all the way down to my core. I thought of Mouse and how he went out with me and never came back. And he was my friend.

"You can't," I said. "How could you? You don't know me. You don't know who I know. All you know is that I knew where to look for you and that I know where to find Xavier. Come with me, watch me, and maybe you'll find out if you can trust me or not."

28 / JASPER XAVIER BODAN lived on the third floor of a rooming house on Hoover. He was at the end of a long hall lit by a single bulb.

There was a strip of light showing at the foot of his door.

"Who is it?" he asked after Tina knocked.

"Tina," she said. "And the man who pulled me out of the storefront the other night. Easy Rawlins."

The door opened inward. The room beyond seemed to be empty. I followed Tina with my hands visible at waist level. Xavier was standing behind the door with an extremely small pistol in his hand.

He pushed the door shut and glowered at us.

"Why you bring him here?" he asked Tina.

"He already knew your address," she said. "He invited me to come with him."

"Why you talk to him in the first place?"

"He found my address, and Miss Latour said that he was good at helpin' black folks out when they're in trouble," Tina said. She was another young woman pleading for her black man to listen to reason. "I brought him because he says that he wants to help."

"I don't need your help," he said to me. "I should have let Conrad shoot you the other night."

When he held the pistol up in my face, it didn't seem so small anymore. The proximity of the muzzle affected my lungs. I could breathe in just fine, but my exhaling ability seemed to be paralyzed.

"Put that gun down, Xavier," Tina said. "He came here to talk to you."

"I don't need to talk."

"Yes, you do," I said. Forcing the air out of my lungs was one of the most difficult physical tasks I'd ever performed. I was dying for a cigarette. "There's things you don't know. Things that will put all of this in a different light."

"Listen to him, baby," Tina said. She moved next to the skinny kid. When she put her hand on his gun arm, I flinched, afraid that he might clench up and shoot me by mistake.

When Xavier let his pistol down to his side, my whole body relaxed. I realized that I had to use the bathroom but decided that it wasn't a good time to ask where the facilities were.

"Can I sit?" I asked.

"Over there." He pointed to a solitary wooden chair.

I sat down and reached for my pocket, remembering again that I'd thrown my cigarettes away.

"You got a cigarette?"

Tina reached into her purse and came out with a filter-tipped smoke.

"What you got to tell me?" Xavier said as Tina lit a match for me.

I inhaled deeply and my throat and lungs felt a strange cold burning all the way down. For a second I was afraid that I'd been poisoned but then I realized that it was a mentholated cigarette.

"The cops," I said, choking on the strange smoke.

"What about 'em?"

"They came to me and asked me to spy on you," I said.

"Why they want to put a spy on me?" Xavier asked.

I shrugged.

"Then why come tell me about it?" Xavier asked.

"You the one thinks the cops killed Strong," I said.

"He says that Brawly's father is dead, too," Tina added.

"Aldridge? Why'd anybody wanna kill Aldridge?"

"That's a good question," I said. "But I got even a better one for you."

"What's that?"

"I went down to the cops and told them that I was willing to help them, to share information —"

"You what?" When Xavier's gun came up again I was less afraid, but not foolish.

"Hold on, man," I said. "I already told you that I'm tryin' to help Brawly. When the cops came to me and started talkin' 'bout the Urban Party, I wanted to find out what they had on him."

"That's what you say." Xavier kept the gun leveled at my chest. "But I don't know you. You might be planning to turn me over."

"He already knew your address, baby," Tina said. "I told you that. He didn't need to come here to get you arrested."

"Then maybe it's something else."

There was sweat on Xavier's upper lip. He was no more than twenty-two years old but he was standing up pretty well under the pressure of the situation. I glanced around the place while he considered my possible duplicities. You could have called it a compartment rather than an apartment. The most outstanding feature was a small window looking out on a club's red neon sign — MERRIAN'S. There was an aqua-colored vinyl couch that I'm sure he slept on and a table with stacks of books and papers on it.

"There is a special squad assigned to you," I said. "D Squad they call it. It's headed up by a man named Lakeland. He's from the army, but they tapped him to watch you."

It was too much for him to come back at me with doubts or challenges.

"Oh no," Tina said, looking at her man.

"We don't know if what he's sayin' is true," Xavier said.

I was proud of him for trying to stay on top of the growing problem.

"But Henry said that they were trying to kill us," Tina reasoned.

If I were planning to overpower them, that would have been the moment. Xavier turned his eyes on Tina. Maybe it was because she called Strong by his first name. Maybe it was his anger that she wanted to believe what I was saying.

"They didn't kill Henry," I said.

"Now how the hell you gonna know that?" he said.

"Because I was there, in their office, when they found out about it. They were surprised. For cops, they were even upset."

"Where's their office?" Xavier asked.

"I got to urinate," I replied.

Tina giggled. She was close to hysteria.

"What?" Xavier asked me.

"I got to go, man."

"No," Xavier said. There was power in his voice and even the trace of an evil smile on his sweaty lip. He moved closer to me and said, "You sit here till I get the answers I want."

That was too much.

I slapped his gun hand with my left and socked him at half strength with my right. I grabbed his wrist, twisted, and pulled the gun away from his loosened fingers.

"Stop!" Tina shouted.

I turned toward her with my hands in the air.

"I'm just goin' to the toilet," I said. "Fuck a niggah keep me from my bodily functions. Where is it?"

Tina's eyes darted at a door that stood perpendicular to the window. I went into it and relieved myself without closing the door behind me.

When I came out Tina had propped Xavier up to a sitting position on the floor, but he was still too stunned to rise.

"I'm sorry I had to hit you, man," I said. "But you don't treat somebody like that. You don't push a gun in his face when he ain't done nuthin' to you."

Tina was too scared to talk and Xavier was still seeing double, wondering which image of me was the one talking to him.

"Can I take another cigarette?" I asked Tina.

She nodded and I picked up her purse from where she'd dropped it on the floor.

"Gimme one, too, will ya?" she asked.

I lit two at once and handed her one.

Xavier groaned and put his hand to his head.

"You didn't have to hit him," Tina said.

"No. Instead I could have peed in my pants. But let me tell you, it take a badder motherfuckah than your boy here to make me do that."

"What do you want?" Xavier managed to get out before he grimaced in pain.

"I been tellin' you the whole time, man," I said. "I been asked by

Brawly's mother to make sure he was okay. If he isn't in too deep, I'm gonna try and rectify the situation. The only thing I care about the First Men is that Brawly is a part member."

"I don't know where Brawly is," Xavier said.

He held out his arm and Tina helped him to his feet. I doubt if he weighed more than she did.

"I know that. I know that. But maybe you could help me anyway."

"What?" Xavier wasn't afraid even though I had his pistol and proved my superior strength.

I really liked the kid.

"First," I said. "What are you guys doin' with them guns?"

"What guns?"

"The guns at Brawly's girlfriend's place. Guns like this one here." I took out the .45-caliber pistol I'd taken from underneath Bobbi-Anne's bed.

Both kids were impressed by the size and heft of the gun.

"You got that from Clarissa's place?" Xavier asked me.

"No, from BobbiAnne's."

"Who's BobbiAnne?"

I went through the same talk with Xavier that I'd had with Tina. Both of them claimed that they didn't know of any white girl that Brawly ran with.

"We don't make people do anything, but it's frowned upon when one of the Party takes a white woman over one of our black sisters," Xavier said. "We wouldn't say he couldn't be with her but we would damn sure know if he was."

"And what about Henry Strong?" I asked.

Tina stiffened and Xavier asked, "What about him?"

"How long has he been down here?" I asked. "The other night it sounded like he was just down from Oakland to give a talk to your organization. But from what I've heard since then, it seems like he's been here for a few weeks at least."

"Why?"

"Because somebody murdered him," I said. "They murdered him not five blocks away from where Brawly worked up until a few weeks ago. That ties in Brawly, so I'd like to know how."

"Mr. Strong is connected with various political organizations in the Bay Area," Xavier said. "He'd been watchin' us for a while and wanted to bring some money down our way. You see, they had some supporters in Berkeley that liked what we were doing. The special thing we wanted to do was to start a school for kids from the first grade to the eighth. We were going to buy the old Kleggman Bakery on Alameda but we needed more money."

"And Henry was going to get you that?"

"He's been coming down for the past few months, havin' meetings with some of the officers of the First Men," Xavier said.

"Then why would he ever know Brawly?" I asked.

"Brawly said that he knew builders and contractors that were black," Tina offered. "When he first came to us and he heard that we wanted to make the bakery into a school, he started talking to us about his mother's boyfriend and the project he had down Compton."

"He said that John could help with your school?"

"At first he was just bragging," Tina said. "You know, how he was a contractor and he could get together a good black crew. We didn't listen until he said that there was a woman, a black woman who helped finance his mother's friend's project. When Henry heard about that, he began talking to Brawly."

"You don't say," I mused.

"How did you find out where we lived?" Xavier asked.

"Lakeland," I said. "He got your picture, your history, your numbers, and all the gold fillin's in your teeth noted down on paper in a file cabinet."

The lovers clasped hands.

"Tell me about this school," I said. "From everything I've heard and read so far, I thought you guys were trying to bring down the system, not educate children."

"That's just your fear talking," Xavier, the flyweight, said. "If you really listened, if you really read our manifesto, you'd know that the school is our first priority. We want to start a school, a publishing house, a community center, and a lunch program for our children and our elderly."

Tina's eyes were fastened on her skinny boyfriend's profile. I wondered at her — in love with two powerful men. She was at the center of everything she loved and held dear.

After a while she got into the conversation. She said that black women had to learn to love their own beauty and their men.

"We can't let them dictate how we live and love and learn," she said. "That's our responsibility and if we don't take the reins, we'll never be truly free."

I wondered who she included with *them*. Was I one of the ones holding back the black race?

29 / WE TALKED FOR QUITE A WHILE. Xavier was a dreamer, that much was sure. He lived in the possibilities scrawled down by idealistic philosophers far from the front lines and battlefields. He wanted free hospitals and schools and no war whatsoever. The Urban Revolutionary Party was the first step in his broad global plan. People like Handsome Conrad and idealistic Brawly were a part of that plan, though they may not have completely understood the goals.

Xavier was the mouthpiece and the visionary, but Tina was definitely the smarter of the two.

"If we don't do anything," she said, "then the world will pass black people by. We'll still be takin' the bus while other people will be takin' rockets to the moon."

Her argument reminded me of Sam Houston telling me about my rattling automobile.

"This BobbiAnne told me that Conrad and Brawly had brought the guns to her place," I said. "You think that they would be so different from you that they'd plan to do it with guns rather than schools?"

"There you go with that BobbiAnne shit again," Xavier said. "Brawly don't know no girl but Clarissa."

"He wouldn't even let me kiss him good-bye," Tina added. "There's no girl on his mind but her."

"Big girl," I said. "Red-blond hair and freckles comin' down off her nose . . ."

Xavier shook his head but Tina said, "That could be the girl that's been hangin' around Conrad. What was her name?"

"Yeah. Conrad's friend," Xavier said. "She's been coming around for a couple'a months now. Mostly she'd just be sitting in the car, waiting for him. I don't know if he ever even said her name."

"I know where she lives," I said.

It was closing in on four in the morning.

*T*HE FRONT DOOR of the building was locked late at night. We rang the bell, figuring that Conrad or BobbiAnne would open up for the secretary of the Party. But there was no answer.

I did my card trick on the door and once again winded myself on the stairs. I tried to hide my weakness from Xavier, but I didn't need to worry about him. He was concentrating so much on the acrobatics of his mind that I doubt he would have noticed if I stopped and put my hands on my knees.

There was no answer to our knock on BobbiAnne's door.

*T*HE GUNS WERE GONE and the closets were empty, but she didn't take the photograph of her and Brawly when they were teenagers.

"Is this the girl?" I asked the revolutionaries.

"Yeah. Yeah, that's her," Xavier said. "But this is an old picture."

"You think it's a coincidence that this woman is Conrad's girl now and that I saw a box of weapons under her bed?"

"No guns there now," Tina said.

"So if you can't see 'em, then they don't matter?" I asked.

From the corner of my eye I thought I saw the doorknob jiggle. Then the door flew open.

When I saw the doorknob turn, a dozen thoughts went through my mind. The first was that it was Anton/Conrad with BobbiAnne and Brawly, all of them armed to the teeth and prepared to end our lives. That's when I thought of going for my pistol, but there wasn't enough time. By then the first uniformed cop was in the room and I was glad I hadn't tried to shoot him through the door. I was even glad that I wasn't with Mouse, who would certainly have killed the man and, probably, his partners. Then I remembered that Mouse was dead and that I was carrying a concealed weapon. These last thoughts drained all of my will to resist.

"Police!" the second cop shouted.

"Hands in the air," the fourth one said.

We were shoved against the wall, disarmed, handcuffed, and dragged down the stairs.

"What is the meaning of this?" Xavier asked, trying to stand still. "You have no right —" he commanded before he was struck in the head with a truncheon.

Christina Montes cursed those officers with language I couldn't imagine coming from her mouth. I was forced to my knees. I stayed there, knowing when to pick my battles.

After Xavier was propped up between two cops, we continued our downward journey.

Tina was dragged from the building and put in the back of a

cruiser. Xavier and I were also put in a backseat. He, knocked senseless for the second time in one evening, and I trying to understand
the forces at work.

The policemen didn't talk to us much. Xavier was completely
malleable, and I did as I was instructed.

We were separated at the downtown station. I was taken to an office and manacled to a heavy metal chair.

Through the slatted blinds I could see various uniformed policemen and plainclothes detectives sitting at desks, drinking coffee,
talking on the phone. No one looked at me. No one cared that I had
to go to the bathroom. I could see a clock through the slats — two
hours had gone by. Somewhere there must have been a window because I could tell that the sun was coming in.

I would have paid a five-hundred-dollar fine just for a cigarette.

A squat man came in at last. He wore a cranberry-colored suit
with a nametag that said LT. J. PITALE. I didn't know how to pronounce the name and I didn't try. I didn't ask for a toilet, a cigarette,
or a reason that I was chained without being charged.

"Rawlins," the squat man in the ugly suit said.

"Lieutenant," I replied.

"Possession of a concealed weapon," he said as if I had asked for
the charges. "Breaking and entering. Resisting arrest. Assault on an
officer . . ."

I must have frowned at the last charge because Pitale said, "Officer Janus sprained his thumb subduing your pal with his club."

I let out a chuckle.

"You think this is funny, Rawlins?"

"No, sir," I said simply.

"Then why do you laugh?"

"To charge a man for assault when you break your fist beatin'
him," I said. "I will use that story to teach my kids how to survive."

"You got kids?"

I didn't answer.

"Because I don't think your children will be seeing their father for a long time."

I sighed for a cigarette.

"Officer Janus can still swing that stick," Pitale warned.

"What do you want from me, Lieutenant?"

"Why'd you break into that apartment?"

"The door was left open," I said.

"What were you going to do with that gun?"

"I found the forty-five on the living-room table. It bothered me that it was right out in the open like that, so I picked it up. When I heard people outside the door I shoved it in my pants, not knowing what to expect. What we intended to do was call the cops and get them to come down and investigate where BobbiAnne was and why that gun was just out lyin' around." Two hours chained to a chair gives you lots of time to think.

It was Pitale's turn to smile. He was accustomed to the stories concocted by felons.

I saw a flames from the windah, Officer. And I was climbin' up on the fire escape to see if anyone needed savin'. And . . . and you know when I saw that fine new TV, I thought that the owner would have wanted me to save it. . . .

The story I gave was solid. I didn't think that a judge would ever have to hear it, but a little insurance is always good to have.

"What were you doing with members of a communist organization?" he asked.

"Communist?"

"You heard me."

"Yeah," I said. "You said communist. That's the first I heard of any communist. Xavier and Christina are friends of my friend's adopted son. I never knew that they were Russian."

"You could die in this room, Rawlins," he told me.

The threat didn't bother me so much, but when he took out a Pall Mall I almost came to tears.

"May I make my phone call, Lieutenant?"

Pitale agreed to dial any number I gave him and hold the phone to my ear.

I had two things going for me: one was that I have a good memory, and two is that I was pretty sure that D Squad was a twenty-four-hour operation. I called Vincent Knorr's number and when a man answered I said, "This is Easy Rawlins callin' for Knorr. Tell him that me, Xavier Bodan, and Christina Montes have all been arrested and are being held at the main downtown station. And tell him that Lakeland wouldn't want me languishing here. Languishing." I repeated the word because the early-morning cop seemed to have a problem with it.

"Knorr your lawyer?" Pitale asked me when he took the receiver from my ear.

"In a way," I said.

"Funny that such an innocent man would have a lawyer ready to jump to his defense any hour of the day or night."

"You been a white your whole life, Lieutenant?" I asked.

"What the hell do you mean by that?"

"I mean that *Father Knows Best* don't need no lawyer. But you know *Amos 'n' Andy* got to have one. You'd know what I was talkin' about if you were ever chained to this here chair."

I believe that I saw a glimmer of comprehension in Pitale's face. I think that he understood me, which wasn't necessarily a good thing. The one edge black people have always had over whites was that they never truly understood our motivations. And just because a man understands you, that doesn't make that man your friend.

"It doesn't matter how I feel or what I know," Pitale said. "What matters is what you were doing in that apartment and where that gun came from."

"I already answered that question," I said. "And I don't want to say any more until my lawyer comes."

"By that time you won't be able to talk . . . ," Pitale replied.

I didn't ask the question, but I believe that my eyes betrayed my fear.

". . . with your teeth being knocked out and all." Pitale finished his sentence with a smirk.

I was wondering when Officer Janus would be called in to increase the charge to double assault when the phone rang.

It was a big black phone with five or six lights along the bottom. Pitale turned his head, watching for the next ring. When it came, one of the center lights flickered. The lieutenant grunted and picked up the receiver.

"Yeah?" he said, and then went quiet. While listening his face became softer, almost submissive. "But, Captain, we got 'em redhanded on B and E. But . . . Yes, sir. Immediately, sir."

He hung up the phone and stared at me.

"Who'd you call just now?"

"My insurance agent," I said.

"What the hell is going on? What are you guys into?"

"Can I leave now, Officer?" I asked.

I couldn't help smirking.

30 / "OLYMPIC AND SOUTH FLOWER," I said into the pay phone. "Could you come and get me?"

"Sure, honey," Bonnie said. "I'll be there as soon as I can."

"And don't forget to bring me some cigarettes from the closet," I added.

I waited on a bus stop bench until Bonnie could get to me. Sitting there in the chilly morning dew, I thought about how alone I had been for most of my life. Mouse had been my closest friend, but he was crazy. The kids and I had a bond as deep as it gets, but they were still children with needs and desires that kept them from understanding the adult world.

But Bonnie was in every way my equal. She took life head-on, and though I had known her for only a few months, I felt that I could call on her no matter how bad it got.

She sidled up to the curb and I jumped into her small blue Rambler. My knees were up against the dashboard and there seemed to be space for only one of my arms, but I didn't care. Bonnie gave me a deep soulful kiss and then took off down the street with no idea or care for where we were going.

The first thing I did was open the pack of Chesterfields and light up. That was good. Six months later I would think back on that first drag with the memory of deep pleasure.

"I got arrested last night," I said after a few blocks.

"Do you have to come back for a trial?"

"No. They didn't have anything on me and just cut me loose."

"Where are we going?"

"My car's parked over on Grand," I said. "I'm sorry 'bout this."

"Is this boy worth the risk you're taking?" she asked me.

"I'm not sure," I said. "But I'm not doin' it for him."

"Then who?"

"Partly it's John. You know we been friends for over thirty years. There was times that I'd go to John and ask him to hide me. He never asked me why and he never said no."

"What's the other part?"

"You were right when you said I've been sad. I know I got to get out there and find out what happened after EttaMae took Raymond from that hospital. But it's been hard to push myself there. While I'm lookin' for Brawly I kinda like lose myself in his problem and maybe, when it's all over, I'll find the old Easy and he'll be able to go out there and find out the truth."

Bonnie didn't say anything. And after a while we came to Bobbi-Anne's apartment building.

I kissed her again.

"Call me in sick at work," I said, then opened my door.

"Easy?"

"Yeah?"

"You said that you lose yourself."

"Yeah?"

"That's not right," she said. "What you should be doing is finding yourself, not this boy."

I DROVE DIRECTLY over to John's place. I knew he'd be gone to work, but that was what I wanted.

Alva opened the door with hope in her eyes. But when she saw me, the hope turned to fear.

"What is it?" she asked.

"Can I come in?"

I took the hassock I'd sat in a few days before while Alva put on water for tea.

After composing herself over the stove, she came to sit across from me.

"What is it, Mr. Rawlins?"

"We need some straight talkin', Alva."

"Is Brawly hurt?"

"Not that I know of, but I'm pretty sure he's in trouble. He is in trouble," I repeated myself for effect, "and only you tellin' me the truth is gonna help me help him."

"What kind of trouble?"

"The kind of trouble that comes from hotheaded young men with wild women and guns everywhere."

"Oh."

It was the short syllable that preceded a big fall. I didn't want to hurt her. From the beginning, my job had been to keep her from unbearable pain. But sometimes you have to feel pain before you get better. I hoped that this was one of those times for Alva Torres.

"Why is Brawly mad at you?" I asked.

"He thinks I don't love him," she whispered. "He thinks that I abandoned him when he was a child."

"Why he think that?"

"Because I sent him to his father. He was so headstrong and physically he was strong, too. I'd tell him to go to bed or come back in the house and he'd just push me aside, just push me aside like I was one of the kids at the playground. And then . . ." She let her words trail off and stared at a point somewhere behind me.

"Yes? And then what?"

"His uncle died in a bank robbery attempt."

Alva caved in on herself in the chair. She wept. I wanted to touch her, to reassure her, but I didn't. The pain she felt was beyond my reach.

"When was this?"

"Nineteen fifty-four," she said. "It was a Bank of America down on Alvarado. He went in there with a stocking mask and they shot him in the street with forty-two hundred dollars in his pocket."

"Were him and Brawly close?"

"Yes, they were. Leonard would come over and Brawly would act right. Brawly and me both loved Leonard."

"So what happened after he died?" I asked.

"The police kept comin' ovah, askin' 'bout what I knew about Leonard and his partner."

"What happened to this partner?"

"He got away with most of the money. And the cops thought I knew about it. They kept comin' over until I just couldn't take it and they had to put me in the hospital." Alva clutched her hands together.

"You let yourself get that sick rather than turn in Aldridge?"

Alva looked up at me with both surprise and relief in her eyes.

"I didn't know until a long time later that it was Aldridge," she said. "I would have never sent Brawly to live with him if I knew."

"How did you find out?"

"Aldridge told Brawly and they fought."

"When Brawly was fourteen?"

Alva nodded. "He told me when he came down here to live."

"He didn't tell you when you were in the hospital?"

"I don't think so. But I don't remember everything," she said pitifully. "They give me drugs. Brawly said that he came and saw me and I told him that I wasn't his mother and he should go away. But I don't remember that. Then he went to stay with Isolda."

Hatred replaced sorrow in Alva's voice.

"And what happened then?"

"She twisted him," Alva said. "She did dirty things to him and turned him against me."

"Why she do that?"

"Because she's wicked, that's why."

There didn't seem to be much further I could get with that line of questions, so I switched gears.

"When did Brawly move away from Isolda?"

"When he was sixteen he got in trouble with the police. They said that he stole a radio out some store and put him on trial. If he was a white boy, they would have threatened him and let him go home. But bein' black up there, they put him on trial and convicted him. He had to live in a residence for delinquents and report to this juvenile detention center until he was nineteen. He was on probation until twenty-one. That's when I told him that he could come down here and I'd help him finish his high school degree and go to college. After he dropped out, John said that we could rent him a room in our building and he could work for us."

"Did he steal the radio?" I asked.

"Yeah. But it was just a boy's mistake. Brawly ain't no thief. He's just angry. And why shouldn't he be? He had his childhood taken away from him."

"Why'd you and Aldridge break up?" I asked.

"What's that got to do with anything?"

"Well," I said, "that's why Brawly lost his childhood, ain't it? Maybe that's the key to me talkin' to him when I finally pin him down."

Alva looked at me then. Before that day I had always thought that a man or woman who had a mental breakdown was weaker than other people. But I could see in her eyes the strength to handle more pain than I could imagine.

"It was the same old thing" — her voice wavered — "same old thing. He couldn't keep his hands off the girls. Finally he found someone he liked so much that he didn't even come home half the time. I put his things on the front yard one night, and in the morning they were gone."

Many thoughts went through my mind but I kept them to myself.

"Can you save my son, Mr. Rawlins?"

I reached out and took both of her hands in mine.

"If it's at all possible, I will bring him back here to you, Alva," I said. "Even if I have to hog-tie him to the roof of my car."

She giggled, and then she grinned.

"Thank you," she said. "I'm sorry I misjudged you, Mr. Rawlins."

I smiled and patted her hands. I nodded, accepting her apology, but I knew she had not misjudged me. She had seen me for what I really was. The only mistake she'd made was believing that she'd never need my kind of help.

31 / I DROPPED BY Colonel Lakeland's office at about ten that morning.

Miss Pfennig wasn't happy about it, but she sent me on through to Mona, who was, if anything, even less enthusiastic about my presence. But Mona called her boss, and he had her send me right in.

Detective Knorr was seated at the table, in the same chair that I had chosen to keep from being the center of attention.

"Yes, sir," I said without being asked anything.

I took a seat, also uninvited.

Knorr gave me his assassin's smile. Lakeland was more honest and simply frowned.

"What do you have for us?" Lakeland asked me.

"Not too much," I said. "Nothing solid."

"How'd you get arrested?" Knorr asked.

"Just like I told them," I said. "Me and Jasper and Christina had gone to see BobbiAnne, but she was out and the door was open. I've been havin' a weak bladder lately and —"

"Cut the shit, Rawlins," Lakeland said. He took a familiar-looking .45-caliber pistol from somewhere behind his desk. "What in the hell is this?"

"I found it on the table in that woman BobbiAnne's living room," I said.

"That the story you told Petal?" he said.

I knew he was talking about Pitale. Maybe that was the way he pronounced his name.

"No story," I said. "It was sitting right there in plain sight."

"How'd you like to spend thirty-five years in a federal prison, Mr. Rawlins?" Lakeland asked.

"No thanks."

"Because this, this gun, was stolen from a federal facility in Memphis, Tennessee, and that's the sentence for the theft."

"I think my paternal grandfather was from Tennessee," I said. "The story goes that he killed a white man and had to relocate to Louisiana for his health."

Knorr's light eyes regarded me as a child might stare at the wing he was about to pluck off a fly.

"It was on her coffee table," I said. "I picked it up, put it in my pocket, and then the cops busted in. Why were they there, anyway?"

"Petal works for Captain Lorne. They're also keeping watch on the First Men's members," Lakeland said.

"They were camped outside of BobbiAnne's apartment?" I asked.

"Apparently," Lakeland said. "When they saw Bodan and Montes go in, they hoped they could get them on something and break up their organization. But the real question is, what were you doing there?"

"I found out that BobbiAnne was Brawly's friend from back in high school in Riverside, so I went there with Xavier and Tina to talk to her."

"About what?" Lakeland asked. Both he and Knorr leaned forward, almost imperceptibly, to hear clearly how I lied.

"They were scared," I said.

"Scared of what?" Knorr asked.

"Whoever killed Strong. Tina had been moving from place to place, and Xavier was sitting behind his door with a pistol in his hand."

"So what's that got to do with BobbiAnne?" Knorr asked.

"I told them that Brawly's father, Aldridge Brown, had also been murdered and that I thought that his death had something to do with Strong's and that BobbiAnne knew something about it because of her connection to Brawly."

"What's she got to do with Strong's death?" Lakeland asked.

"Hell if I know," I said. "Like I told you half a dozen times already, the only thing I'm interested in is Brawly. Tina and Xavier knew BobbiAnne, so I thought they could get her to get me with Brawly."

"But what's that got to do with the shootings?" Knorr asked.

"Ain't that the question I just answered?"

"So you know nothing about Strong's death?" Lakeland said. "You just lied to them so that they would take you to Brawly."

"I lied to 'em," I said. "But that don't mean I don't know nuthin'."

I waited, wanting them to feel that they were mining information and not being spoon-fed.

"What?" Lakeland asked.

"The same thing you should know if you were listenin'," I said.

"Tina's scared to death and so is Jasper. They both loved Strong and believe that he was murdered by the government, the police, or by both. They sure didn't have anything to do with it. All they want is to build schools for black children."

"Schools where they'd teach children hate," Knorr said.

Lakeland turned his head to Knorr as if his words were the clarion call. Then he turned back to me.

"That's all you know?"

"So far."

"So you walk in here and tell us that you don't think these people are involved with murder," Lakeland announced. "Who did kill him?"

"Somebody scared, somebody stupid," I said. "Somebody that he knew and that he could harm. That's always the way, now, isn't it, Colonel?"

The officers of the law were stumped by me speaking their language.

"Are you gonna keep on this?" Lakeland asked me.

"If you mean, am I gonna keep on looking for Brawly and trying to get him back home with his mother — the answer is yes."

"We got you out of jail," the colonel said.

"And I told you everything I learned from Xavier and Tina."

Lakeland lifted up the pistol and bounced his hand. "Was this the only weapon you found in the apartment?"

"Yes, sir."

"Do you need to know anything from us?"

"I'd like one more address," I said.

"What?"

"Where did Strong live while he was down here?" I had heard the address they'd given on the news. It wasn't the same one I'd gotten from Tina.

"The Colorado Hotel," Knorr said. "On Cherry. But you don't have to worry about going over it. We already searched."

"Does where he live mean something to you?" Lakeland asked.

"No. I mean, I thought I might go by there and ask if Brawly been around. You know that's my prime target."

"I thought you were a janitor," Lakeland said. "But you sound like some kind of detective."

"Do you know how to sew, Officer?" I asked in response.

"What?"

"I don't mean darn," I said. "I mean could you piece together a pattern and stitch the seams of a shirt or a pair of pants?"

"No."

"Can you bake a cake from scratch or lay a floor in an unfinished room?" I continued. "Or lay bricks or tan leather from a dead animal?"

"What are you getting at?" the colonel commanded.

"I can do all those things," I said. "I can tell you when a man's about to go crazy or when a thug's really a coward or blowhard. I can glance around a room and tell you if you have to worry about gettin' robbed. All that I get from bein' poor and black in this country you so proud'a savin' from the Koreans and Vietnamese. Where I come from they don't have dark-skinned private detectives. If a man needs a helpin' hand, he goes to someone who does it on the side. I'm that man, Colonel. That's why you sent Detective Knorr to my house. That's why you talk to me when I come by. What I do I do because it's a part of me. I studied in the streets and back alleys. What I know most cops would give their eyeteeth to understand. So don't worry about how I got here or how to explain what I do. Just listen to me and you might learn somethin'." I closed my mouth then, before I said even more about what I'd learned in a world that had already passed those cops by.

They were both staring at me. I realized that any chance I had of them underestimating me had passed by also.

"So who do you think killed Strong?" Lakeland asked.

"I don't know anything about it, Officer," I said. "It could have been somebody in the First Men, but not those two kids."

32 / "BACK THEN OUR CUSTOMERS were Jewish gangsters and white girls who wanted to be starlets," Melvin Royale told me. "Now we got a mixed clientele of a lower pedigree."

Melvin was a Negro, large and verbose, just the way I liked it. He had worked as a bellman at the Colorado Hotel and Residences for twenty-seven years. Twelve of those years he was the head bellman.

I met Melvin after asking at the front desk if there were any jobs open for nighttime porters or bellhops. All hotels need people for the graveyard shift, so the carrottop clerk sent me down into the basement office of Mr. Royale.

The reception area of the hotel was small but elegant in a worn-down-but-comfortable sort of way. There were two potted ferns on either side of the carpeted stairway leading to the rooms. The banister of the staircase was mahogany, with a shiny brass cap at the first step.

But the stairs going down to the basement were moldy and damp. Melvin's office was barely large enough to hold him and the end table that he proudly called his desk. The chair he had me sit in had its two back legs sticking out of the door.

"You ever work as a bellman before?" Melvin asked me.

"Yes, sir," I said. "At the DuMont in St. Louis and at the Mark Hopkins in San Francisco."

"You move around a lot, huh?"

"I come outta Mississippi," I said. "At first I went up to Chi, but you know that wind was colder than a mothahfuckah up there. St. Louis was better, but they still had snowflakes for three months and I spent half my salary on coal. Now, it never snowed in San Francisco but I was still wearin' a heavy sweater half the time in August. L.A. got warm weather and you see colored people almost everywhere you go."

"They might not got a sign keepin' us out, but you better believe that there's places you better not be."

"Oh yeah," I said. "I know. I ain't no fool."

Melvin laughed. We were getting along just fine. Old friends.

"You kinda tall for a bellhop, ain't you, Leonard?" he asked, using the name I'd given.

"I've done my share of hard labor, Mr. Royale," I replied. "Heavy stones and eighty-pound sacks of cotton. A suitcase or two is more than enough for me."

Again Melvin laughed.

"You got the right attitude," he said. "Ain't no reason to bust your hump for these white peoples. Shit. You strain your back or break your leg and they'll drop you just like that." He snapped his fingers, causing a loud report. "They don't care. I had a boy workin' with me in here twenty-some years, Gerald Hardy was his name. Gerry would do anything these people asked. One time I remember he worked thirty-two days straight. Thirty-two days! And half'a that was double shift. He worked like that for years. Always happy and willin' to do some things that weren't quite legal and willin' to overlook other things that was downright wrong.

"One day Gerry gets the flu. He calls in sick, sayin' that he cain't pull himself out the bed. The boss man, Q. Lawson, says okay, take it easy. But the next day he's on the horn wonderin' why Gerry ain't here. They had a function that night and were relyin' on Gerry's overtime. Well, to make a long story short, four days went by and Gerry was fired. I lent him money for two months' rent, but you know I couldn't go no further than that.

"Gerry was dead in five months' time. Kicked outta his house and sick inside somehow. Every maid, porter, bellhop, and waiter in this buildin' was at his funeral, but do you think Q. Lawson sent even a lily to the grave? No, sir. You better believe I ain't gonna strain my back or damage my health for him or any other white man."

"But you got colored tenants in here now, right?" I asked.

"Couple of 'em," Melvin said. "But they all special cases. If they got some tap dancer in a Hollywood movie or some delegate from a foreign nation. Sometimes when a rich white person is stayin' at some hotel in Beverly Hills, they send what they call their *nonessential staff* to be down here. I mean things is changin', ain't no doubt to that. Marion Anderson or James Brown could stay just about anywhere they please. But your everyday Negro still have the door shut in his face."

"But didn't that man get killed down Compton live in here?" I asked. "That's what made me wanna come ask for this job. When I read that a nice hotel had colored residents, I thought to myself — Leonard, that would be a good place to work for."

"No, brother," Melvin said in a friendly but condescending tone. When he leaned back in his chair his oily face glinted in the electric light. His skin had the color and radiance of wood resin. "No, brother. Only special Negroes stay here. An' they less likely to spare a kind word or an extra coin than the white residents."

"So that man . . . that . . . that . . ."

"Henry Strong."

"That's it, that's the name. Henry Strong. He was a movie actor or somethin'?"

Melvin pursed his big brown lips and frowned, ever so slightly. I was a hair over the line, but just that. Not enough to be out of order. Not enough for him to think that I was anything other than Leonard Lee, hopeful to be a bellhop at a hotel where famous Negroes sometimes stayed.

"Naw," Melvin Royale said. "He was some kinda gangster turned rat. I mean, they said in the papers that he was a political communist or somethin', that he worked with a group of black protesters. But you know the only peoples that came up here to see him were white men in cheap suits and white prostitutes."

"Really?" I said, widening my eyes as if the idea were too strange to comprehend.

"Uh-huh. On'y white people. The men paid his rent — in cash."

"Why you say 'rat'?" I asked.

"Because them men brought him here had badges, they said that they wanted to keep Strong on the quiet."

I whistled and Melvin smiled at my country naïveté.

"Damn," I said. "A month's rent in a nice place like this must be a whole lotta money."

"Month?" Melvin said. "Hank Strong been here over a year — on and off."

"Oh," I said, thinking of Alva and how much information could be held in just a word.

I FILLED OUT the application form that Melvin gave me. I put down a Social Security number, an address, a phone number, three references, and a job history going back seven years. It was all lies. I told him that I'd come in at eleven that evening, ready for work. I said that all I needed from him was a red cap size seven and three-quarters. I said all that and walked out the door.

*T*HE APARTMENT BUILDING where Strong seduced Christina was on 112th Street, four blocks down from Central. It was a wood-frame building covered with plaster and painted to look like stone brick. Henry's apartment was toward the back, its door facing a small concrete path half obscured by untamed bushes. There was nowhere to hide around his door. I was sure he took the place for just that reason.

The lock was too sophisticated for my card trick, but the door was so cheap that my forty-four-year-old shoulder was good enough to break it in.

The room seemed to be oval shaped. I think that was due to a failure of architectural design. There was a bed and a coffee table, a rocking chair and sink. None of the furniture matched, and there was a thin layer of dust over everything. He had three good suits in his closet and six pairs of shoes. There was a brown and black Stetson hat hung on a nail in the wall and a box of Havana cigars on the floor next to a glass that once held bourbon whiskey. There was a small metal box with a red cross on it under his bed. In there was the half-drunk pint of whiskey, a pack of three condoms (with one gone), and a straight razor.

There was nothing in any pocket, nor was there anything under the mattress. There were no books or newspapers or even a drawer where he could have hidden some kind of note. I had searched the whole place in less than ten minutes. And then for some reason I went back to the bed. It was neatly made, like a soldier's bunk. The fitted sheet over the mattress, another sheet and blanket folded back under the pillow so that you could see all the layers of bedclothes.

I patted the tight fitted blanket from top to bottom.

Something was there between the sheets and mattress.

I pulled off the blanket, finding nothing but the covering sheet. I pulled off the second sheet, revealing nothing but the pristine whiteness of the fitted slip. But under that I found something that might have been the best sleeping aid a poor man could have: rows of twenty-dollar bills fanned out under the sheet. Under the twenties was a layer of fifties and hundreds. When I'd finished counting, it came to just under six thousand dollars.

Under the money I found an envelope and a slender notepad. The envelope contained two tickets for the Royal Northern cruise liner headed for Jamaica.

The tickets were issued to a Mr. and Mrs. J. Tourbut, the date of departure was Friday afternoon. The names meant nothing to me. The notepad was empty except for a memo scrawled on one of the center pages.

Saturday A.M. 6:15, 6:45.

The time meant nothing, but the day reminded me of something Conrad had said while he was being beaten. The money looked nice. It had its own special mathematics. It might have been money that Strong was holding for the Urban Revolutionary Party and other revolutionary organizations. But it might also have been a nest egg for Mr. and Mrs. Tourbut — provided by the man who had been paying his rent.

I wondered if Tina knew that the money was under her bottom when Henry was touching her neck.

I rolled the cash into two big wads and shoved them into my windbreaker pockets. I took the tickets and the note, too. Then I got into my emerald-colored car and headed for a place that most black people weren't aware of in 1964.

33 / ON MY WAY to Laurel Canyon I considered the money that was now under the carpet in my trunk. It was probably from the white men who also paid Strong's rent in cash. It smelled like a police payoff to me. I mean, it might have been money that Strong intended to give Xavier to fund his brave new world — but I doubted it.

I had already refused money from the police, but this was different. They hadn't given me this money. They'd lost it betting on a rat. I decided that I'd wait and see if any of Stone's heirs could be found. If they couldn't, then I'd have Feather's college tuition in a foil-lined paint can at the back of my garage.

*M*OFASS AND JEWELLE lived on an unpaved path that cut away from a tributary off the main canyon road. The little artery probably had a name, but I never knew it. Jewelle liked to keep a low profile because even though she was hardly out of childhood, she had made dangerous enemies. There were members of her own family who hated her for freeing her elder boyfriend, Mofass, from their control.

Jewelle had taken Mofass's fairly meager real estate investments and turned them into something resembling an empire. Through Mofass's real estate company she controlled and managed property all over Watts, including two small six-family dwellings that I owned. There was a group of white businessmen, the Fairlane Syndicate, who worked with Jewelle because she had a knack for finding just the right deal and knew how to exert leverage to make that deal come through.

She was no more than twenty but she had proved to me that the color line was a minor impediment in America if you knew how to deal with the credit line. I had played with the idea of trying to become a real estate mogul. But once I saw Jewelle in action, I knew that I was not equipped to compete.

*M*OFASS ANSWERED the door.

"Mr. Rawlins," he said in that deep gravelly voice. Then he coughed for half a minute, bent over almost in half with his perpetual housecoat hanging open, revealing a big brown belly and faded blue boxer shorts. When he regained his composure he ushered me into the living room, across the vast tiled floor to a small table they had against a window that ran the full length of the wall. Seated at that table, we had a bird's-eye view of the Los Angeles basin.

"How's it goin', William?" I asked my onetime apartment manager.

"Every twelve weeks the doctor tell me that the emphysema's gonna get me in three months," Mofass replied. His voice sounded like the old baritone, only with a towel shoved down his throat. "Then, when the time's up JJ brang me back down to him and he looks at me and says, 'You got twelve weeks.' JJ say, do I wanna go to a different doctor but I tell her, hell no. I could live another thirty years with a doctor like this one here."

I laughed and Mofass choked. I hadn't seen him outside of that house or in real clothes in over a year. He was like one of those tough old alligators that could dive to the bottom of a river and not surface for weeks. You think, *He must have gone by now*, but still you take the long way down to the bridge rather than set foot in the water.

"Mr. Rawlins," a girl's voice called.

Jewelle still dressed in one-piece, square-cut dresses. This one was light brown, about her color, and loose. She had pigtails with red ribbons at the end. But I also noticed that she had been wearing lipstick within the last few hours. Her lips seemed fuller and there was something in her eyes that denied her childlike appearance.

"Jewelle," I said. I stood up and kissed her cheek.

"Watch it now," Mofass growled. "That's my baby there."

"It was just on the cheek, Uncle Willy," she said with a giggle. "Can I get you somethin' to drink?"

I didn't need anything. Neither did Mofass.

We all sat down around the small table and looked out over the smog-choked city.

"So what you need, Mr. Rawlins?" Mofass asked.

Jewelle did everything. She cooked and cleaned, made sure that the maintenance was kept up on the house and car. She ran the business and kept the bank accounts. All Mofass did was sleep and eat and bask in the warmth of that young girl's blind love.

That was the way things really were with them. But in Mofass's mind things were different. In his mind he was the chief of the tepee,

Jewelle did his bidding, and without him she'd have been lost. She never contradicted his account. Jewelle fell in love with Mofass when she was fifteen and he would be her god for the rest of her life.

"I needed to know some things about those tract homes you're building down with John," I said.

"What for?" he asked with all the solemnity of a judge.

"Well." I hesitated for effect. "You see John's girlfriend, Alva, has got a son, Brawly Brown, who's in trouble. He was workin' for John down there but stormed off in a huff — some kinda tiff with his mother, you know."

"Kids today don't have no kinda idea how hard life is," Mofass said. "I see 'em on the TV shimmyin' and shakin' and losin' they minds. They need to get a job and stay on it."

"We had some trouble at one of the sites, Mr. Rawlins," Jewelle said. "But it was a couple'a blocks over from John's lots."

"Are you interruptin' me, JJ?" Mofass scolded.

"Sorry," she said.

"That's what I'm here for," I said to Mofass. "I was wondering if the trouble down the street could have had anything to do with Brawly."

"I see," Mofass, the king of the blind, said. "That's something to think about. You know, um, I oversee the whole operations, not every little detail. I'm tryin' to train JJ here so that one day she can run the whole kabob. But she still just in trainin'."

"Do you think she would know anything?" I asked the paper lion.

"Can you help Mr. Rawlins, JJ?" he asked.

"I think I can," she said with real deference in her voice. And then to me, "Robert Condan and his cousin Renee the ones buildin' over where the trouble was. They got a record store down on Adams.

They had a shootin' two days ago at about four or five in the morning. The police came over and shut us down for the day. But it wasn't nuthin'. You know, just some thieves or drug addicts usin' the place as a hideout for the night."

"But the man killed wasn't a thief," I said. "He was a political organizer."

"I know that's what they say in the paper, but the captain I talked to told me different."

"What captain was that?" I asked.

"How many police captains you know, Mr. Rawlins?" Jewelle said with a challenging grin.

"More than I would like to admit," I said. "For instance, I'd bet that the cop you talked to was Captain Lorne."

"Wow," she said. "Yeah. It was him. Tall with silver hair?"

"I've never seen him," I said. "But his name came up on the sunny side of the storm."

"Uh-huh," she said, not really understanding. "That's all I know."

There was a loud snort right then. We both turned to see that Mofass had fallen asleep. His head had slumped down to his chest and he was drooling slightly. JJ jumped up and ran from the room. Mofass snored three more times and she was back with a blanket and a towel to wipe his face. Touching him lightly on the sides of his head, she got him to lie back in the chair. She covered him up to his chin, smiled, and kissed his forehead.

I knew many people who thought that a love affair between a child like her and a man almost sixty was a disgrace. I would have agreed if I hadn't known them. But as gruff and overbearing as Mofass was, I knew that he loved that girl with all his heart. And JJ needed a man to go through the motions of being the one in charge.

"What about the police that patrol the area?" I asked when she was through with her ministrations.

"You mean the cruiser cops?"

"Uh-huh."

"They're there mainly for the Manelli family."

"Who's that?"

"It's the big contractor. They got seventeen different building sites around Compton. They buildin' sixty-two blocks over the next three years, over six hundred employees."

"And they got the police workin' for them?"

"Yeah," JJ said. "The Manellis think that people been stealin' from 'em. So they got the police questioning everybody not on their payroll."

"I know that," I said. "They braced me a few days ago."

"I'm sorry to hear that. You know, they usually leave us alone."

"Why's that?"

"A couple'a times when Manelli had to push some overtime to finish their model homes, John and his team lent a hand. John did it 'cause his own budget was tight and he might'a had to lay off Mercury and Chapman. So instead, he let Manelli pay their salary for a couple'a weeks."

"John always knew how to make ends meet," I said. And then, "Well, I better be goin'."

When I stood up, Mofass opened his eyes. I got the feeling that he'd been pretending to be asleep.

"You got what you need, Mr. Rawlins?" he asked.

"You better believe it, William. That JJ's gonna be a terror one day."

"One day," he said. "You can let yourself out. You know I get tired in the afternoons."

JJ walked me to the door.

"Is there gonna be any problem out at the sites, Mr. Rawlins?" she asked when I reached out to shake her hand.

"I don't think so, honey. But if there is, I will call you, okay?"

"JJ!" Mofass called from across the big room.

"Comin', Uncle Willy," the woman pretending to be a child said.

34 / *THE NEXT STOP* I made was Clarissa's apartment. There was at least two days of mail in her box and no answer to my knock.

*P**ROBLEM WITH THE COLD WAR* is not when it's cold but when it gets hot. . . ." Sam Houston was regaling some poor soul who just wanted his lunch in a brown paper bag to go. The man wore blue jeans and a red checkered long-sleeved shirt. His sparse hair was curly gray, and his skin was black under a layer of fine white dust.

The googly-eyed restaurateur was about to make some other global pronouncement when he caught sight of me.

"Excuse me," he said to the silent workman.

Sam took off his apron and lifted the door-board to the kitchen. Then he strode out to meet me in the middle of the room.

I had never seen Sam come out from behind his board, so I girded myself for war.

He had two inches on me in height and reach, and his thin body might have carried more punch than it appeared. I had learned, when I met a man named Fearless Jones years before, that some thin men could be stronger than bodybuilders.

"You know it ain't right to come in someplace and sneak around a man's back," Sam said, touching my chest with a long, accusing finger.

The men sitting to my right discontinued their conversation to behold the encounter.

I didn't want any eavesdroppers, so I said, "Why don't we step outside, Sam?"

That took him off guard. He was angry at me but had no reason to think that I'd come back hard. For my part, I didn't know how to shut his big mouth without taking it outside. And I didn't know how to take it outside without saying so.

Sam stalked off toward the door while the patrons began gabbing. I stayed two full steps behind him, taking a glance back at the kitchen as I went. Clarissa was nowhere in sight.

Once outside, Sam turned around quickly and I took one step to my right. He took a little hop and fired off a right hook that missed my head by less than an inch. I let the fist go by, then shoved his shoulder lightly. The force of the push, added to the momentum of his swing, picked Sam up off the ground and dropped him on the pavement.

When he thrust his right hand up under his apron, I put my hands in the air and said, "I'm not here to fight with you, man."

He was breathing hard.

"Then why we out here in the street then?" He stopped fumbling. I offered my hand and he took it.

"I didn't want nobody to listen to what we had to say," I said while helping him to his feet.

"Why not?"

"Do you like Clarissa?"

"Hell yeah," he said. He was slapping imaginary dust from his arms and chest. "That's why I'm mad at you sneakin' around, talkin' 'bout one thing but then stalkin' my girl."

"Your girlfriend?" I asked.

"No. Clarissa's my cousin. Everybody work for me is family, you know that."

"Listen, Sam," I said. "I don't know what you been told, but I didn't lie to you. I was lookin' for Brawly and I found him — with her."

"What you mean, 'with her'?"

"He's her boyfriend. Didn't you know that?"

That shut Sam's mouth for a good five seconds. It might have been the best comeback I'd ever had with him. Even though I was involved in a life-and-death situation, I took a moment to savor his confusion.

"That ain't right," he said at last. "She said that you followed her and tried to get over on her at her apartment. She said that she cain't be comin' in to work 'cause she scared you gonna be on her here."

"I did go to her place but I was followin' Brawly, not her." The lie was not really so bad. I *had* seen her with Brawly at the Urban Party's gathering. When I followed her, it was only to get to him.

"You lyin' to me, Easy Rawlins?"

"Come on, Sam, you know better'n that."

"Not when it come to pussy I don't," he said. "Niggah work a eight-hour day six days a week and pray to God on Sunday, but when pussy walk by he might just lose his mind."

As I said, the maddening thing about Sam Houston was that he was almost always on target. He had a good mind, just no real direction to point it in.

"I am not after Clarissa," I said. "Least not the way you say. I got me a woman and I don't need to go skulkin' around after some girl-child."

There was the ring of truth in my words. Sam squinted so that his eyes were hardly larger than a horse's orb.

"Then why she wanna lie?" he asked.

"You tell me, Sam. Would you have been upset to see her with Brawly? Would you have done something about that?"

"No. I mean, I might'a given her grief. I might'a said a thing or two."

"But," I said, "if you knew she was with him and I came to you and said that the boy was trouble, you might have been willin' to help me get a line on her."

"What you sayin', Easy?"

"I'm sayin' that since I last talked to you, two men have been murdered and Brawly's in it somewhere. I don't know where exactly, but I do know that it's bad."

"Murder?"

"Murder. Two men. Dead as doornails."

"Who?"

"Henry Strong, the mentor of the First Men" — Sam spit at the mention of the radical organization — "and Aldridge Brown." I continued: "Brawly's father."

"Who killed 'em?" Sam asked.

"Hard to say. The cops think it was the First Men. The First Men think it was the cops. Brawly's cousin has nominated him for at least one of the killings. It's all up in the air. I'm just lookin' for some shelter before it come back down to earth."

Sam pulled at the collar of his gray T-shirt and moved his chin around as if he couldn't get enough air. He wasn't used to being on the short end of the conversation.

"So what you want?" he asked.

"Brawly Brown," I said for the hundredth time, it seemed.

Sam put his left hand on top of his head and his right hand on his chin.

"She's just a child," he said. "Him, too."

"They're all children, Sam. All of 'em. But you know in the Stone Age most'a your people only lived long enough to see twenty. They were old men and women by twenty-five."

I knew the scientific explanation for the problem facing us would hearten Sam.

He smiled and said, "Yeah, Easy. You right about that. You sure are."

They were words I never expected to hear come out of Sam's mouth.

"So what you doin' here?" he asked me.

"I got to find Brawly again. Clarissa's my best bet," I said. "I went to her house, but she was gone. Do you know where she is?"

"She told me that she was scared'a you, Easy. She went into hiding."

"I told you why I'm lookin' for her."

Sam's face contorted so that it looked like a wizened brown fruit ready to drop from the tree. At first I thought he was having a heart attack but then I realized that that was the way he must have looked when he was thinking. His mouth twisted with distaste and his shoulders rose, making him look like a comical scavenger bird. Finally he shuddered like the great vulture he resembled, shaking dust from its feathery frame.

"Yeah," he said. "Yeah. I can see it in my mind. Brawly comin' in, sittin' near the kitchen, comin' on through to go to the bathroom out back. And Clarissa always hoverin' somewhere nearby. Uh-huh. Uh-huh. She used to stay late every night, talkin' to her first cousin Doris, helpin' out with the cleanup even though she didn't have to. But after Brawly started comin' around, she always left right on time. Yeah. You right, Easy. Clarissa been seein' that sour boy for three months at least."

"You know where she is?" I asked.

"No. No, I don't but I know who does. Doris. She's been Clarissa's partner in hidin' this from me the whole time."

I realized that Sam was angry because he had been fooled by his employee, that the whole time he was being superior with his knowledge, reading, and reasoning ability, they had a secret right out in plain sight.

"You wait here, Easy," he said, and then he strode back into the restaurant.

I lit up a cigarette and remembered again how good a smoke could feel when you had been denied. Then I remembered running with my lungs aching and then Henry Strong getting a bullet in the head. The silhouette of the assassin had some heft to it. It could have been Brawly, but I wasn't sure.

I thought about Mouse. He would have tagged along with me on this adventure, laughing the whole time.

"What you doin' messin' with this boy, Easy? He just sowin' his wild oats."

"But he's in trouble, Raymond," I'd say.

"We all in trouble, Ease" would have been his reply. "Shit. If it wasn't for trouble, life wouldn't be no fun at all."

I stubbed out the ember of my cigarette and returned it to the pack. A few minutes later Sam came out.

"I know where she is," he told me.

"Where?"

"Hold on now, Easy. I believe you and everything, but you cain't go see Clarissa without me comin' with you."

"This ain't restaurant work, Sam," I said. "People gettin' killed out here."

"Clarissa's my family," Sam said. "Doris is, too. When I asked Doris how I could get to Clarissa, I told her not to worry, because it was me goin' to her."

"Okay," I said. "It's your funeral."

35 / "*YOU KNOW, EASY,*" Sam Houston said. "I was surprised to see you when you walked in the other day."

"Yeah?" I asked. "How come?"

We were on Highway 101, on our way to Riverside, already outside of L.A., traveling through the rolling green hills of the southern California countryside. Oak trees appeared here and there on the landscape. I like the oak because it's a brooding, solitary tree. It grows within sight of its brethren, but rarely do you see one sidled up to a mate.

"'Cause I thought you'd be dead by now," Sam said.

"Dead? Why dead?"

"Because the only reason a lotta mothahfuckahs out there didn't come after you was because'a Raymond," Sam said. "They hated you but they were more scared of Mouse. Some'a the peoples come in my place called you all kindsa dog, but they knew better than to even say sumpin' to you. Shit. Easy Rawlins got a guardian angel from hell, that's what they said."

Part of the reason Sam was riding me was that he was jealous of my friendship with Mouse — everybody was. Raymond Alexander was the most perfect human being a black man could imagine. He was a lover and a killer and one of the best storytellers you ever heard. He wasn't afraid of white people in general or the police in particular. Women who went to church every week would skip out on Sunday school to take off their clean white panties for him.

And I was his only friend. I was the one he called first. I was the only one who could tell him no. If Mouse was going to kill a man, I was that poor soul's last court of appeal.

But that wasn't all that was eating Sam. He was a talker, a thinker, a man who read the newspaper every day — but Sam was not a man of action. He stayed behind his door-board and stared down the bad men who came into his place. In his restaurant he was the king. But on the street he was just another guy, a frightened black man in a world where being black put you below the lowest rung of white society.

There were no black men in tuxedos playing the violin at the symphony or elected to the Senate or at the heads of corporations. There were no black men on the board of directors or representing our interests in Africa, and very few cruising up and down Central Avenue in police cars. Black men, as a rule, were not scientists or doctors or professors in college. There was not even one black philosopher in all the history of the world, as reported by our universities, libraries, and newspapers.

If you wanted to be an important black man, you had to take a risk and go your own way. You had to challenge a man who outnumbered you ten to one. And every one of that ten was armed with the latest weapons while all you had was a slingshot. That's why David was such a famous biblical character in the black community, because, against all odds, he brought down the giant.

That's what Sam Houston dreamt of doing, standing tall and making a difference. He saw himself as an important, intelligent man but he was afraid, with good reason, to stand out from the herd and be heard.

"Well, you know, Sam," I said, "I been through some pretty hard times without Raymond at my side. I mean, I made it through a whole world war and five years in L.A. when he was still down in Texas. And then there was that five years he did for manslaughter. Naw, man. Those people talkin' to you have had their chance before now."

It wasn't the words but the tone in my voice that kept Sam from one of his snappy replies.

"What you want from Clarissa?" he asked.

"Whatever it is she knows and I don't."

That wrinkled look took over Sam's face, and I knew that he was thinking again.

"What?" I asked him.

"This is what you used to do? Run around sniffin' after what somebody might know? Drivin' all over hell?"

"Before I settled down to a job," I said. "Yeah."

"But somebody like John cain't pay you. I mean, John cain't hardly cover the price for the materials he usin' to build them houses."

"That's true," I said. "Sometimes I'd be out there findin' some-body's missin' wife when all I was gettin' out of it was a free tune-up for my car. But every now and then I'd open some door and some-body'd be on the other side offerin' a thousand dollars just to close it again."

"That's crazy," Sam decreed.

"Yeah, you better believe it. More than that," I said. "*Crazy* ain't even the word."

Sam brought me to a small house in Riverside, on a street called Del Sol. The lawn was unruly and the bushes that grew around the walls had become ragged. From the design of the house, I was sure that it was built by the people who had first lived in it. Arc-shaped and multileveled, it was two stories to the right of the entrance and only one to the left. When Clarissa opened the front door she fell back and I could see that there was another door behind her. The glass in that door revealed a green backyard. It was a home with its own personality. I broke out a cigarette to accent my pleasure at the unique design.

"What are you doing here?" she asked. "Doris called but she just said that you were comin', Sam."

"It's okay," Sam said. "I know you been lyin' to me, but Easy here done broke it down. I brought him to find out about Brawly, but he ain't gonna do nuthin' to hurt either one'a you."

Clarissa's shoulders slumped and she led us into the living room, which was in the two-story part of the house. The room had been straightened up recently. I could tell that the once pristine white carpet had seen a spate of stains and cigarette holes, but all of that had been vacuumed and cleaned to show its best face. The rosewood furniture was old and well cared for, except at one time the spilled glasses had been set upon the surfaces with no coasters and the cigarettes that fell to the floor first were set on the corners, where they left bullet-shaped black smudges along the edge.

Everything that could be reached was dusted, but there were cobwebs along the ceiling and thick dust at the top of the drapes.

Clarissa was wearing blue jeans and a white T-shirt with no bra underneath. She was a good-looking girl. Her skin was dark and her light eyes large and translucent. If I had to guess her thoughts, I would have said that she was hoping that she could close her eyes and when she opened them we would be gone.

"Sit down, Clare," Sam said.

She did as she was told.

The fluffy tan sofa and chairs had been vacuumed also. The suction hole had left neat lines across each fabric surface. I took to a chair while Sam sat down next to his cousin on the couch.

"Mr. Rawlins has some questions to ask you," Sam said.

"I ain't talkin' to him," she said.

"Why not?" A sharp tone came into Sam's voice.

"'Cause I ain't," she declared, and I was reminded of Juice.

"They killed Henry Strong," I said. "You know that, right?"

Clarissa looked up at me with hatred in her eyes.

"I didn't do it, sugar," I told her. "But whoever did is still out there."

"What's that got to do with me an' Brawly?"

"The first one killed was his father," I said. "Somebody beat him to death at Isolda Moore's house."

For an instant the bright-eyed girl froze.

"Isolda Moore," I repeated. "She's Brawly's cousin, used to live up here. You know her, don't you, Clarissa?"

"Bitch," she uttered.

"What kinda language is that?" Sam said.

"Let her use any language she need to, Sam," I said. "Is this her house?" I then asked Clarissa.

"No."

"Then it must be BobbiAnne's," I said. "BobbiAnne Terrell's house. What is it, the parents dead? Moved away for good? They can't just be on vacation, not with the mess this place was in before you cleaned it up."

Clarissa was stunned by my simple deductions. Sam was, too.

"How you know all that?" he said.

"Did they bring the guns out here?" I asked Clarissa.

She shook her head.

"What guns?" Sam wanted to know.

"How long was Conrad livin' out here?" I asked.

Clarissa started to cry.

"I didn't tell you," she sobbed. "I wouldn't."

"Of course you wouldn't," I said in a soothing tone. "You'd never betray your man. But you kids are in it deep. It doesn't matter that he thinks he's invisible, that he believe the cops and the government don't know what he's doin'. He thinks they don't even know he's out there, but he's in plain sight, like a sittin' duck, like a fish in a barrel, like —"

"Stop it," Clarissa cried. "What do you want from me?"

"It's like I told you from the start," I said. "I'm workin' for Brawly's mother. She thinks he's in trouble, and I think she's right. What I need from you is to help me help him outta the mess he don't even know he in."

"He told me not to talk to you."

Sam reared up and opened his mouth, but I put up a hand before he could holler.

"I know," I said. "I know. You love him and you think he loves you. And if you go behind his back, he might get so mad that he'll just walk away — you might not never see him again. But that ain't nuthin'. You're a pretty girl and good in your heart. You'll find another boyfriend and Brawly will still be breathin'."

"He said that you were the police" was her reply.

"Honey," Sam said. "You know that man I always talked about — Raymond Alexander?"

"The one they called Mouse?"

"Yeah, that's the one. You know all them stories I said about him. About when he faced down and killed three armed men in the Fifth Ward and all he had was a stick. About when the police heard that he was holed up in a house outside'a L.A. and said that they couldn't go because it was across the county line."

"And when three of his girlfriends," Clarissa added with a grin, "made his birthday party with bows in their hair."

"That's him."

Clarissa smiled and said, "So?"

"This here Easy Rawlins was Mouse's best friend. They ran together for almost thirty years, since they were kids. If there's anything I'm sure of, it's that Mouse would never have run with a man that could turn another black man over to the cops."

"I thought you said that Mouse was dead," Clarissa said.

"Nobody ever saw a body or went to a funeral," Sam replied. "And even if they did, that wouldn't turn Easy here into no rat."

Clarissa considered for a moment and so did I. I wondered at the strength of character and will of a man like Raymond who could reach out beyond the grave to help me in that Riverside hideout.

36 / "NO," CLARISSA WAS SAYING, "he didn't ever tell me what he was doin'. All I know is that they started to work with Mr. Strong on somethin'. They were like a special group inside the Party, and only a few of them knew what was goin' on."

"What were they doing?" I asked again.

"I don't know. Conrad would come over and pick Brawly up at all hours. They'd go off and meet with Mr. Strong —"

"Did he meet with anybody else?" I asked.

"I think so," she said. "But I never knew who. I mean, I figured that they were in the group but it was all secret."

"Now why they wanna keep somethin' like that a secret?" Sam asked his cousin.

"Sam," I said, "I let you come along but this is my party."

He didn't like to hear it, but he sat back on the couch.

"But you did know about the guns," I said.

She looked down at her knotted hands and nodded.

"How'd you know?"

"One day Brawly had Conrad's Cadillac," she whispered. "He had let Conrad off at somebody's place and they didn't want his car to be around there, so Brawly took it. He brought me out there and showed me in the trunk. It was six or seven rifles wrapped in army blankets."

"What he say they planned to do with them?"

"He said that those rifles would take the first shots in the revolution." She began to weep.

I believe that as she spoke to me, the full meaning of Brawly's words hit home. Sometimes you have to hear yourself saying something out loud before you understand it.

"Did he say what they planned to do?"

She shook her head.

"Did he tell you what he did with those guns after they took them out from BobbiAnne's place?"

Again, no.

"How did BobbiAnne and Conrad get together?" I asked, thinking that a change of tempo might get me closer to what I didn't know.

"Conrad got in trouble with some men who he had been gambling with," Clarissa said. "They was gonna bust him up and so Brawly called his high school girlfriend and asked her to put him up. You were right; her parents both died last year. Him of a heart attack and then she just faded away."

"And after that is when BobbiAnne moved down to L.A.?"

"Yeah," Clarissa said. "She moved down to be near Conrad."

"And do you think that she was a part of this special group that Strong started?"

"No," Clarissa said. "They didn't have no white people in the First Men. White people couldn't come in the door, that was the rule."

The image of those policemen breaking through the windows went through my mind.

"Where's Brawly?" I asked.

"I don't know."

"You got any idea? Any at all?"

"No, sir."

"What about Isolda?" I asked.

"Who?" Sam chirped.

I ignored him, staring at Clarissa's downcast face.

"What about her?" she asked.

"Why do you hate her?"

"Because'a what she did to Brawly."

"What's that?"

"It's not for me to say."

"If you want me to try and help him, you better believe you better tell me somethin'."

Clarissa looked at me with real spite in her eyes. I could see that she was going to tell me something, and somehow she believed that I would be hurt by it.

"She took him in when him and his father fought, and then she tried to make him into her husband," she said.

"Who?" I asked.

"Brawly," she said, sneering. "She'd walk around the house with no clothes on and come into his bed with him at night. She'd get him all hot and make him love her."

I sat back in my chair.

"What you say?" Sam asked.

"She had sex with him until finally he stole a radio out of a store so that the county would take him away," Clarissa said.

"She had sex with him." Sam repeated the words as if they were some intricate puzzle.

"Do you know where Brawly is now?" I asked again.

And again Clarissa shook her head.

"Is he going to call?"

"Not until Sunday," she said.

"That'll be too late," I muttered.

"What you say, Easy?" Sam asked.

I took a deep breath and stood up. "You gonna stay up here?" I asked Clarissa.

It was the first time she thought that she might leave the house where Brawly had hidden her.

"Yeah," she said, darting a glance at Sam.

"Come on back down with us, baby," Sam said. "You can stay with me and Margaret. You be safe there."

"Two people dead already," I reminded her. "And none of us know who's doin' it."

*T*HE RIDE BACK to L.A. was almost completely silent. Clarissa sat in the back.

When we got in range of L.A.'s radio waves we listened to KGFJ, the soul station. James Brown and Otis Redding serenaded our bruised minds. Once Sam asked me if I ever heard from EttaMae — Mouse's wife, the mother of his son, LaMarque, and one of my best friends.

"No," I said. "She's gone."

He didn't follow up the question and I didn't offer any explanations of my guilt.

"WAIT UP A MINUTE, Easy," Sam said to me.

I was parked in front of his house off of Denker at about eight. He walked Clarissa into the house and I laid back and shut my eyes. A pattern was beginning to appear in my mind. It wasn't a pretty picture, nor was it very clear. I still didn't know where Brawly fit, or if I could save him.

I had a clear path of investigation, though. I knew what I was after and I knew who and what might be after me.

Sam came out and climbed into the passenger's seat.

"You think you could drop me off back at the restaurant?" he asked.

"Sure."

I didn't do anything, though. I didn't start the car or move very much at all.

"So we gonna go?" Sam asked.

I lit a Chesterfield.

"This ain't bar talk, Sam."

"What ain't?"

"Not one thing you heard today," I said. "Not that Riverside house or Brawly Brown or the mention of army rifles. Loose lips 'bout any'a that shit get the man who said it dead."

Sam brought his hand to his long throat, trying to hide his fear with a contemplative pose.

"Get his cousin killed," I continued, "and be a threat to my own peace'a mind."

I turned to him with whatever it was my face looked like when I was deadly serious. "This shit can get you killed."

"I ain't sayin' a word, man," Sam said.

I stared at him until he looked away.

Sam never tried to get under my skin again after that day. When I'd come into Hambones he'd be friendly, but there was no more sharp-edged banter or superiority on his part. I missed our old arguments but, on the other hand, I appreciated his fear.

37 / *BY THE TIME* I got home the children had eaten and gone to bed. Bonnie was curled up on the sofa, reading a French novel in tight pants and a blue velvet shirt that was buttoned only halfway up the front.

When I walked in she came to me and kissed me. She didn't ask why I was late or where I had been. She knew. She didn't need me to apologize for being me. I felt, at that moment, that Bonnie had known me for my whole life.

Dinner was waiting on the stove. Baked chicken and rice under a peach gravy with brussels sprouts on the side. We ate and talked about her travels in Africa and Europe with Air France. She was a black stewardess working in three languages in a country I once considered living in because it seemed so much better than America.

"It's better in some ways," Bonnie once said when I suggested that we live together in Paris. "But it's not without prejudice."

"Do they hang colored people in the countryside?" I asked.

"No," she said. "But that's because in France they aren't afraid of blacks, just certain that we are from a lesser culture. We are interesting, but in the end just primitives. At least here in America the white people I've met are afraid of Negroes."

"And that's better?" I asked.

"I believe so," she said. It was a turn of a phrase that she'd learned along the way. Bonnie picked up things from the way people spoke and then used them in her own manner. "If you're afraid of someone, then in some way you are forced to think of them as equals. It is not a child but a man you face."

She was a deep soul and I was lucky for the time I had to spend with her.

That night we didn't make love but just held each other. I listened to her breathing until it turned deep and I knew she was asleep. I drifted on behind her, murder just a distant thunder in my mind.

I HAD TWENTY-SEVEN sick days accrued at that time and a pretty good union, so I called in sick the next morning and drove off to see John at his construction site.

He had on white overalls and old alligator shoes, one of which had worn through over the little toe. He wore a tool belt and a wristwatch with a thick gold band, and he was hammering away at a nail in an awkward, one-handed fashion.

"Hey, John," I said.

"Easy."

"I hope you using enough nails on that sucker," I said.

"I done had to buy so many nails that I do believe these here houses could be called armored homes."

We both laughed and clasped hands.

I suppose I was sensitive around that time. John and I rarely shook hands. We were real friends with no need to express our peaceful intentions. But that day there was an obstacle, maybe more than one, between us. We held on to each other to make sure that we didn't get separated.

"I heard that you were out by my house yesterday," he said.

"I needed to get the truth from her, John. You know I couldn't do that with you in the room."

"That truth gonna help you find Brawly?" There was an angry edge in his tone.

"Findin' him ain't gonna be nearly as hard as savin' him."

"What's that supposed to mean?"

"Alva was right," I said. "Brawly's in sumpin' bad."

"It's them First Men," John said.

"Some of 'em," I agreed. "But it's more than that, too."

"What more?"

"I'm not sure yet," I said. "But did you know that Henry Strong, one of the mentors to the First Men, used to come around here and see Brawly?"

"No."

"Did you know that Aldridge Brown used to come around to see his son, too? They had lunch together more than once."

"I don't believe it. Brawly hated Aldridge."

"Did he tell you that?"

"Alva did," John said. "He's her son. She should know."

"Your mother's still alive, ain't she?" I asked.

"You know she is."

"You tell her everything you feel? You always tell her the truth? I mean, Brawly knows how his mother feels about Aldridge. Why would he tell her if they squared up and started talkin' again?"

"Maybe that's true," he said. "But even if it is, how'd you find out?"

"I came out here one day when you were gone and talked to Chapman and Mercury. They told me because I asked."

"And here they supposed to be my men."

"They wouldn'ta said anything if I didn't ask, John. And you know we go back. Me an' Mouse pulled their fat outta the fire when they robbed those dockworkers."

"Okay," John said. "So Strong and Brawly's father came out here. So what?"

"So what if Brawly killed Aldridge? Strong, too? I caught a glimpse of the man who shot him. It could'a been Brawly, I don't know."

"So? What you sayin'?"

"If Brawly killed them people, he's way past a good talkin'-to and sowin' his wild oats. What you want me to do if he's a double murderer?"

John looked at me, taking long, slow breaths. I had counted six exhalations when he asked, "How was Strong killed?"

"Ambushed, chased down like a dog, and then shot in the back of his head."

John did not like that.

"Could you just walk away?" he asked.

"I'm in it already, John. The police know I'm in it. They are, too."

"I knew I shouldn'ta called you, Easy. I didn't want to, but Alva needed to feel like she was doin' somethin'. She had lost him for so many years and there she was, losin' him again." John bit his lip and shook his head slowly. "She asked me to bring you in, so what could I say?"

"I don't know."

"Find out, Easy. Find out what happened."

"And if she lose the boy?"

"She still got me," he said.

Mouse had been my closest friend since I was a child, but I never respected any man as much as I did John. He was taciturn with a mean temper, but in the end you could always count on him to do what was right.

"Mercury and Chapman out around here someplace?" I asked.

"Chapman is," John said. "Mercury quit."

The fever I'd been feeling for days broke at that moment. Half the puzzle fell into place and I wondered, as one always does in hindsight, why hadn't I seen it before.

*C*HAPMAN WAS APPLYING A ROUGH COAT of plaster to a three-beamed wall when John and I walked in.

"John," Chapman said. "Mr. Rawlins."

He had a splotch of plaster on the side of his broad nose and plaster in his hair. Chapman had straightened hair that he combed down the back of his neck. With his light skin, heavy features, and straight hair, strangers often had trouble guessing his racial background.

John moved to stand against the wall on the other side of Chapman. He noticed that we had cut off his avenue of escape.

"I hear that Mercury quit," I said.

"Yeah," Chapman said. "Yeah, he sure did. Been threatenin' to move down to Texas for so long that I guess he felt he had to do sumpin' about it."

"He left town?"

"That's what he told me he was doin'."

"But you his best friend," John said. "Best friend should know for sure about his partner."

"Have you called his house?" I added.

"He said he was goin' to Texas, to look for work. Bought me a drink to say he was leavin' the next day. Why I'ma call him if he supposed to be gone?"

"Supposed to be," I said. "That mean you don't believe him?"

"What is this? Some kinda police interrogation?"

"I was out at Mercury's house the other day," I said.

"So?"

"You know, that's a nice house he got."

"So?"

"Where do you live, Kenneth?" I asked the ex-burglar.

"Over on One-sixteen. The LaMarr Towers."

"That's projects," I said in mock surprise.

"So what?"

"So how come you in the projects and Mercury got a house over in the nice part'a the slum?"

"He got some money from an uncle that died back in Arkansas."

"Did you know his uncle?" John asked.

"Yeah. I went with him to the funeral."

"Was he rich?" I asked.

"Rich enough to leave Mercury ten thousand dollars, I guess."

"He bought the house for cash?" I asked.

"That's what he said," Chapman answered. I could see that an old suspicion was rekindled in his mind.

"I hear that they got extra police patrols because of thefts out around the sites," I said.

"So what?"

"So maybe you two didn't go as straight as you said you did."

"You listen to me, Easy Rawlins," Chapman lectured. "I put up my burglary tools right after you and Mr. Alexander got them men off'a us. I even took the five hundred you gave me and donated to my mother's church. I already told you where Mercury said he got his money. That's all I know."

"When I was out to his place I asked him about you and Henry Strong and Aldridge Brown," I said.

"Asked what?"

"Didn't you use to hang out with Brawly and them?"

"We had drinks once or twice, but it was Mercury hung out with them. Why? What'd he say?"

"That you were thick as thieves with all three," I said. "That they'd come and pick you up after work and you'd go off together."

"That was him. Not me. No. I don't like Aldridge, 'cause he's a braggart. And Strong made you feel like he was keepin' secrets. I don't like a man like that. That's why I never hung out with you, Easy."

"How's that?"

"Nobody ever know what you thinkin'," Chapman said. "That day we went out to see them union men, we didn't know that you was gonna bring Mouse along. And then when you made them pay us . . . I ain't complainin' about the help, but I knew right then you was too deep for me."

"And you felt the same about Strong?" I asked.

"That's right."

"Why?"

"He had a way of gettin' you to talk about stuff. Merc and me don't like to brag that much about the old days, but the first night we saw Strong, Mercury started in on how when we were teenagers we'd break into candy stores. Strong wheedled it outta him. I was always too busy for drinks after I seen that."

I glanced at Chapman's plastering job. It was excellent. He used a circular motion of his knife to make every application neat and perfect. The swirls were all of equal size and depth. When he came back to level the wall, it would be just right.

"Blesta told me that you and Merc would go off and play snooker after work a few times a week," I said.

"Used to," Chapman said. "Used to, but we ain't played in months."

"Where you think he been goin' lately?" I asked.

"Gettin' his hambone greased," Chapman said. He looked me in the face.

"Who wit'?"

"He never said a word about it," Chapman replied. "I just knew by the way he was actin' that he was gettin' it on with some girl."

Chapman looked me in the eye for a second and then he looked down.

"That all you got, Easy?" John asked me.

"Yeah."

"Then I got a question," the bartender said to Kenneth Chapman. "Why didn't you tell me when Brawly's father come around here?"

"Brawly's a man, John," Chapman replied. "I cain't be workin' with him and treatin' him like a child, too."

"Do you think Merc left town?" I asked Chapman.

"I don't know."

"You still don't wanna help me after what I told you?"

"What you said is just talk, Easy. And talk is cheap."

J OHN WALKED ME down to my car after our chat with Chapman. "What you think about Mercury?" he asked me.

"Once a thief . . . ," I said.

"What's that got to do with that group Brawly's messed up with?"

"I don't know," I said. "Maybe nothing."

"What's that supposed to mean?"

"Maybe I been lookin' at this whole thing wrong. Maybe you were right from the beginning. Maybe Brawly's tied up with a bunch'a thugs and thieves."

"What are they gonna steal?"

"If Mercury's in it, it's likely to be a payroll. There any big ones out around here?"

"Manelli," John said. "They're big and they pay once a month — in cash."

"Oh yeah," I said. "That's the top of the list. You know when the next payday is?"

John just shook his head and scowled.

38 / WHEN I KNOCKED on Mercury Hall's door later that morning, I had my hand on the .38-caliber pistol in my pocket. Blesta opened the door as far as the guard chain would allow. She stuck her face into the crack and so did little Artemus two feet below.

"Boo!" the child said.

"He's gone," Blesta said.

"Say what?" I asked her.

"Down to Texas to get a job," she said.

There were bags under her eyes and a strained quality to her voice.

"He said he's gonna send for us," she added.

"Can I come in?"

"I'm sorry, but no, Mr. Rawlins," she said. "You know with Merc gone, I got to be careful."

"Careful of me?"

Her stare was all the answer she offered.

"What's wrong, Blesta?" I asked.

"Mercury told me not to talk to you," she said. She was an honest young woman. The truth was a balm to her.

"Lotta men been sayin' that about me lately. You think I might hurt your man?"

"Where's Daddy?" Artemus asked. Maybe it was the first time he realized his father was gone.

"Not now, Arty," Blesta said.

"You tell Mercury, when he calls you from the road, that I'm out here lookin' for him. Okay?"

"I don't think he's gonna call for a few days," Blesta said.

"Not till Sunday?" I asked.

Blesta nodded, though I believe it was against her will.

"Where's Daddy?" Artemus asked in an anxious tone.

"If he calls you before then, you tell him what I said."

Blesta looked down to avoid my gaze. She closed the door.

"Where's my daddy?" Artemus shouted from behind the door.

I walked down to my car, hoping that Mercury really was on the road down South.

*I*SOLDA ANSWERED her shanty apartment door in nothing but a bathrobe. That was at eleven o'clock in the morning. I wondered how she managed to pay her nickel rent — or her dollar mortgage, for that matter.

When she smiled at me the questions in my mind dimmed somewhat. Sexual charm will do that to a man.

"Mr. Rawlins."

"Miss Moore."

Her kissing lips turned into an inviting smile and I found myself in a chair on her little island of luxury amid the shambles of the room. The smell of lilac was in the air, and a frosty glass of iced tea was soon to find its way into my hand.

"Have you found Brawly?" she asked.

"I just don't understand it," I said.

"What?"

"Why a woman like you — so beautiful and able to create beauty even in a hole like this — why would you need to seduce a fourteen-year-old boy?"

Isolda Moore was no pushover. Her smile diminished slightly. Her head tilted a bit to the side.

"You're right," she said. "You don't understand." Five words that she meant to be a confession, an explanation, and absolution.

But I wasn't having it her way.

"No, I don't," I said. "I don't get that at all. I got me a teenager up in the house right now and I could tell you this — I wouldn't stand for no woman north of thirty with her hands in his underpants."

"It wasn't like that," Isolda said. "It wasn't like you said."

"How else could it be?" I asked angrily. I wasn't really mad, at least not at what had happened to Brawly all those years before.

"He called me from a phone booth on Slauson. Called me collect. I was all the way up in Riverside and he was cryin' his eyes out and mumbling because of his swollen mouth. I broke every speed limit comin' down to get him. I found him sittin' on a park bench with the tears still in his eyes. The first night up at my house he didn't even want to sleep alone in his own bed. He begged me to sleep with him and when I said no he crawled in next to me when he thought I was asleep."

"Why didn't you send him away?" I asked.

"Send him where? His mother was in the madhouse and his father nearly broke his jaw. If it wasn't for me, they would'a put him out as a foster child or in the orphanage." Isolda's voice was full of passion that she had not shown before. "And after a couple of nights in the bed together I felt his want. I knew it was wrong, but he needed me."

"His girlfriend said that you walked around naked, that you seduced him into your bed."

"That's the way he has to remember it," Isolda said with a nod. "Because after it went on for a while I told him that it had to end. I told him that he needed to have a girl his own age. That's when he took up with BobbiAnne. But, you know, even when he had been with her he'd come back home and wanna climb in the bed with me." There was pride in her voice. "And when I refused him he got mad and blamed me for the way he felt."

It was a solid argument, good enough to have been in a play. Sometimes you did things bad because of love and hurt the people you cared for most. Maybe if Isolda was some bucktoothed third-grade teacher, I might have believed her. But every part of her life was so perfectly arranged, I couldn't see her giving in to the whirlpool of someone else's passion.

"Is Alva mad at you for sleeping with her husband or her son?" I asked then.

"Why don't you ask her?"

"I'm askin' you."

"I ain't told her about either one," Isolda said.

"Did you know Henry Strong?" I asked.

"Never heard of him."

"Hm."

"What?"

"Nuthin'," I said. "It's just that somebody's been lyin' to me."

"Who?"

"Maybe Kenneth Chapman."

For the first time she stumbled. It was no more than turning her head away from me, looking off for something easy to fall from her tongue. She turned back, but still she wavered.

"What'd he say?" she asked at last.

"That you and him and a man named Anton Breland had drinks with Strong and Aldridge." I was lying to force her to admit some kind of connection between the murdered men. ·

"I don't know what he's talkin' about."

"But you know Chapman?"

"Once when I went to pick up Brawly for lunch, he introduced me to him and a stocky man named Mercury. They worked with Brawly. But I ain't never been out with them. And I don't know no Henry Strong."

"I see. Yeah. Uh-huh." I was just making noise while Isolda floundered in my suspicions. She was telling me the truth about not going out with Chapman while lying about Strong, I was sure of that. But I needed more.

"What did this Chapman say?" she asked.

"Just that you had been with them. And when I asked him about Aldridge he told me that Brawly and Aldridge got along just fine, even after that fight you said they had."

"They did have that fight," Isolda protested. "I ain't lyin'."

"Yeah," I said. "Yeah. I'm sure that it's Chapman lied to me. Sure of it. You know him and Mercury was burglars a long time ago. I thought they give it up, but you never know with crooks."

Isolda let her bathrobe fall open so that I could see her left breast. She was thirty-five if she was a day, but gravity hadn't touched her yet. It was the breast of a twenty-year-old. Any male from six weeks to ninety years old would have had trouble resisting. If I hadn't had Bonnie in my life, I might have crossed the line — for just a kiss. But instead I took out a Chesterfield and sat back, out of range of her charm.

She acted as if the robe had fallen open by mistake and covered up.

I inhaled deeply, feeling of two minds about the benefits and detriments of smoking. On one hand, tobacco robbed me of my wind, but on the other, it gave me something to do while the devil was tempting me.

I stood up.

"Time to go," I said lamely.

"Where?" she asked, rising and coming toward me.

"To talk to Chapman again, I guess."

"What about his partner?" Isolda asked. "Mercury."

"He left town," I said. "Probably the smartest one of the bunch."

39 / *JACKSON BLUE* was in his bathrobe, too.

I shook my head when he came to the door. "What's wrong with you, Easy?" he asked.

"Don't nobody work?" I said. "I mean, am I the only one who thinks he got to get up in the morning and at least put on a pair of pants?"

Jackson grinned. White teeth against black skin has always had a soothing effect on me. It made me happy.

Jackson led me down the stairs into his house.

"I'm workin'," he said as he went. "Been readin' about a guy named Isaac Newton. You ever hear about him?"

"Of course I have," I said. "Every schoolkid knows about Newton's apple."

"Did you know that he invented calculus?"

"No," I said, not particularly interested.

I took my seat at his table and he took to the one-piece school desk. He stretched out in the chair like a cat or an arrogant adolescent.

"Yeah," he said. "I mean, at the same time this dude name'a Leibniz came up with the same calculations, but Newton invented it, too. Newton was a mothahfuckah."

"How long ago did he live?" I asked.

"Died in 1727," Jackson said. "A rich man, too."

"So he did his work," I said. "You just sittin' 'round here in your drawers."

"But, Easy," Jackson said with that grin. "I'm learnin'. I know things. I know things ninety-nine percent'a your white people don't know."

"I know about gravity, Jackson. Maybe I didn't know about calculus, but what good is it knowin' that, anyway?"

"It's not just that, Easy. It's not knowin' one thing. It's understandin' the man. If you understand him, then you got somethin' to think about in your own world."

He had me then. Just like Sam Houston talking about newspaper articles, Jackson made claims that made me want to stop and understand.

"Okay, man," I said, looking at my wristwatch. "Two minutes to hear what you mean."

I expected Jackson to smile again, but instead he put on his serious face.

"It's like this," he said. "Newton was a religious man, what they called a Arianist. . . ."

"A what?"

"It don't matter, except that it meant that he was a heretic in England, but he didn't let nobody know. He was a alchemist, too. Tryin' to turn lead to gold and like that. He lived through the plague years.

And at the end of his life he was the president of the science club and the head of the national mint."

"All that?"

Jackson nodded almost solemnly. "As the head of the mint he was in charge of executions. And all them things he discovered — he kept 'em to himself for years before he let the world know."

"So what, Jackson?"

"So what? This is black history we talkin' here, Easy."

"So now you sayin' Newton was a black man?"

"No, brother. I'm sayin' that all they teach in schools is how a apple done falled on Isaac's head and that's it. They don't teach you about how he believed in magic or how he was in his heart against the Church of England. They don't want you to know that you can sit in your room and discover things all by yourself that nobody else knows. I'm down here collectin' knowledge while some other Negro is outside someplace swingin' a hammer. That's what I'm sayin'."

"Swingin' a hammer is more than you do," I said out of reflex. I didn't really believe it. Jackson Blue's rendition of Isaac Newton reminded me of me, a man living in shadows in almost every part of his life. A man who keeps secrets and harbors passions that could get him killed if he let them out into the world.

"You a fool if you believe that, Easy."

"And you just a fool, Jackson," I said.

"How you see that?"

"This man you talkin' about kept his secrets — for a while. But then he let the world know — that's the only reason you know it today. When are you gonna let the world know?"

"One day I might surprise ya, Easy. Uh-huh."

"Well," I said, "until that day comes, I need you to do somethin' for me."

"What's that?"

"Before I get into that, why don't you answer my question?"

"What question?"

"How come you in your house in your underwear in the afternoon? I mean, who pays the rent?"

"Somebody who thinks that my studies are something important, that's who."

I could tell that he wasn't going to reveal his golden goose. And it really wasn't any of my business, so I went back to the reason I had come.

"I need you to apply for a job, Jackson," I said.

"A job? I don't know what the fuck's got into you, brother. But I done worked more in my forty-two years than most white men twice my age. An' I'm a lazy mothahfuckah."

I had to laugh. It was funny and it was true. I celebrated the moment of joy by lighting up a cigarette.

"I ain't askin' you to work. I mean, maybe one day, tops. I just want you to apply for the job and then take it. But you don't have to build up no real sweat or nuthin'."

"What kinda job?"

"Construction."

"Construction? Damn, Easy, that's the hardest work out there. Just spendin' the day out under that sun like to give me heat stroke."

"Two hundred fifty dollars for one day," I said.

"Where do I sign up?"

"Manelli Construction Company down in Compton. You can use John for a reference."

"What you wanna know from them?"

"Everything you can find out. Who's in charge. Who's workin' there. I wanna know about payroll and catering trucks and who's on duty what hours. I wanna know about security and what anybody knows about Henry Strong's murder three nights ago."

Jackson digested the order, nodded.

"This about Brawly and the First Men?"

"Strong got killed out to there. John's crew worked for Manelli when John couldn't make the paychecks and they needed help. Somehow Mercury and Chapman got sumpin' to do with what's happenin' with Brawly. I just need to know."

Jackson nodded again and then extended his palm. I laid one of Mr. Strong's hundred-dollar bills across it. That made Jackson smile.

We settled up quickly after that. He'd go down to Manelli's that afternoon and show up for work the next day. Because the amount of time crossed over two days, I promised to pay for his expenses, as long as they didn't get out of hand.

After that we talked about Newton some more. Jackson told me that the kind of calculus Newton created was called *differential calculus*. He tried to explain that mathematics was the language of the way things worked, that that was the real secret men were always going for — to speak in the language of things. I barely understood him, even on an everyday level, but I knew that he was saying something that was important to my life.

40 / *I CAME HOME* to find Jesus and Feather in the front yard with Bonnie. They were trimming rose-bushes that I'd cultivated on either side of the front door. Bonnie loved the apple-sized, mottled red and yellow roses. When she agreed to come live with me, she'd said, "Only if you promise to keep those roses by the door. That way I'll think that they're flowers you give me every day."

Feather was collecting the roses in a tin pail that looked too big for her to carry. She was laughing while Jesus used his shears on one of the bushes. It was getting close to sunset and the sky was full of clouds that were a brilliant orange and black with the light at their back.

"Daddy!" Feather cried. She ran at me and tackled my legs. "I got another B-plus."

"That's great, baby." I lifted her over my head and then brought her down for a kiss on the cheek.

Bonnie was taking off her thick gardening gloves, but Jesus kept hacking at the bush. He was doing a good job of it, too. I had taught him when he was Feather's age. I didn't need him to work, but he wanted to. He wanted to work with me, eat with me, walk with me down the street. If he was out in the world in trouble, I'd do anything to save him.

By then Bonnie was kissing me.

"Are you okay?" she asked, looking deep into my eyes.

"Okay," I said, turning away as I spoke.

I went in the house, followed by Feather. Her B-plus paper was about "Betsy Washington" and the flag.

While I made us grilled-cheese sandwiches, Bonnie and Jesus joined us in the kitchen. I offered them sandwiches, but Jesus never had much of an appetite and Bonnie didn't eat between meals.

"I know," Feather said when we were all together. "I could read you my paper out loud."

"Not right now, baby," I said. "First I got somethin' to say."

Feather flashed an angry glance at me. The woman she was to become flickered a moment upon her face. She pouted and looked down. Then she took Jesus's hand and leaned against his side.

"I wanted to talk to the family," I said. "I want to say something to the kids."

They were all looking at me. I took a bite out of my sandwich. I felt a little dizzy.

"School is the most important thing in the world," I said. "Without an education, you can't do anything. Without an education, they will treat you like a dog." I glanced at the cabinet and saw the little yellow dog's snout sniffing out my scent. "I expect you to go to college, Feather. Either you'll become a teacher or a writer, or something even better than that. Do you hear me?"

"Yes, Daddy," she said.

We were staring at each other.

Jesus was staring at the floor, clenching his fists.

"All right," I said. "That's important because Juice is going to learn in a different way. From now on he's going to study being a boatbuilder. He's found his calling in that, and I won't stand in his way. But if he's going to do that, he has to study even harder than if he was in school. I know all of the curriculum for school and I'm going to make you read out loud to me for forty-five minutes every night. And after you read, then we're gonna spend another forty-five minutes talking about what you read. You hear me? And if you ever stop working on that boat, you have to get right back in school. I don't care if you just turned eighteen, you still have to go back. You hear?"

Jesus looked up then and nodded with the kind of conviction that only young men can have. If he was any other child, I would have dismissed the hard look in his eye. But I knew my boy. Not only would he finish the boat but it would be seaworthy and so would he. And he would read to me every night. And he would love it. I realized that he wasn't the type of child who could learn from white strangers who couldn't hide their natural contempt for Mexicans. I had seen it at Sojourner Truth. Most children ignored the signs or connected with the two or three teachers who really did care about them. But Jesus wasn't like that. He was connected to me, and it was my job to make sure that he learned what he needed to make it through life.

"I'd rather you stay in school," I said. "'Cause you know it ain't gonna be easy goin' through your lessons every day. Some days I might be late. Some days I might miss, and then you'll have to do double duty the next night."

Jesus grinned and I realized that this was what he had always wanted.

"I'll help on nights that you can't be home," Bonnie said.

"You got them papers up in your room?" I asked Juice.

He nodded.

"Leave 'em on the table for me. I'll read 'em after you go to bed."

*A*RE YOU REALLY going to do all that, Easy?" Bonnie asked me after I'd signed the papers and we were both in bed.

"What?"

"Read with Jesus every night."

"Oh yeah. Now that I made the promise, I got to do it. That's our deal."

"What do you mean? What deal?"

"When he came to live with me. He couldn't even talk, because he'd been through so much. But he'd sit by my side and listen to every word I said. And if I said somethin', then he took it for truth. If I said to jump off a building 'cause he wouldn't break his leg, then he would jump. And if he hurt himself, he would know that I had tried to tell him what was right but somehow had made a mistake. And if I told him to jump again — he would. That kinda faith makes a truthful man outta you."

"But suppose you can't do it?" Bonnie asked.

"Can't do what?"

"Can't keep your word."

"But I will keep my word," I said. "That's what you don't understand. I have to keep my word to that boy."

"But what will you teach him?"

"The *Iliad* and the *Odyssey, Twenty Thousand Leagues Under the Sea, Treasure Island.* Anything with a boat and a man in it. That's what I'll teach him first. And then I'll take whatever math he's got to know to make the boat and try and make sure he understands it. Work with what you have, that's what I always did."

"But wouldn't it be easier if he just stayed in school?"

"No, baby. I mean, I understand what you sayin', but what me and the boy got between us is hardscrabble road as far back as we can remember and as far up as we ever gonna go. If Jesus don't trust you or like you, he won't let you in. He sure as hell ain't gonna learn from teachers he doesn't respect. And anyway, while I been lookin' around for Alva's son I found out a couple'a things that helped me come to this decision."

Bonnie was already convinced. I knew by the way she put her head on my shoulder. But she asked, "What's that?"

"First it's just Brawly himself. I haven't seen the boy more than five minutes but I know from lookin' that he's a mess 'cause he didn't have a mother or a father the way a boy needs to have parents. He was abandoned and then, when he was found, he was abused. He could have the best education in the world, but it wouldn't help him. I knew that when I saw the diplomas on a killer cop's wall. He got the education but he ain't learned a goddamned thing."

*A*FTER BONNIE WAS ASLEEP I got up and called Liselle Latour.

"Yeah?" she said in a sleepy voice.

"Hey, Liselle. It's Easy."

"What time is it?"

"'Bout ten-thirty," I said. It was really ten to eleven. "I'm sorry to bother you, honey, but did Tina come back in?"

"They had her in jail."

"Tell her that I'ma come by tomorrow morning, about eight-thirty. If she doesn't wanna talk to me, maybe she should already be gone."

"Okay," Liselle said.

Her breath sounded as if she might have had a question, but I cut her off with thank-you and hung up the phone.

41 / *TINA WAS WAITING* for me at the door. I liked that. I've always been a punctual man. It was my army training. If a man said 7:59, you got there on time because by eight you might be dead.

When she opened the door I saw that she had a raised bruise on her right temple. There was a small scab at the center of the bump, surrounded by yellowish skin.

"Let's get away from here," she said to me at the doorstep.

"Where to?" I asked.

"I don't know," she said carelessly. "Down Central."

We went to the car and drove off.

"How long have you been out?" she asked me.

"They let me go a few hours after they caught us," I said. "How about you?"

"Just over a day. They had me in a cell with drunks and women livin' on the street."

"That's where you got the knot on your head?"

Instinctively, Tina brought up her hand to cover the injury.

"Yeah," she said. "Yeah. I got in a fight with a woman who got mad at me for not having a cigarette."

"I'm sorry," I said. "They shouldn'ta done that to you."

"How did you get out so fast?" Tina asked.

"I called the man city hall's got on you. He sent word upstairs and they kicked me aloose."

"So you were working with the men who arrested us?" she said, not so much accusing me as verifying what she'd already believed.

"No," I replied. "The men who arrested you think that they're the ones on you, but really it's a secret squad, the one I told you about. They got a soldier been to Vietnam runnin' it. They're the ones you got to worry about. They tapped me because they think I'll turn you over."

"If that's true, then why would you tell me?"

"Same reason I called Liselle last night," I said. "Because I don't wanna push you or trick you. You got enough people on your ass."

"Who else?"

"Even though he's dead, there's Henry Strong. Whatever he was doin', it might'a looked like it was for you but really it would'a led to your downfall. I'm ninety-nine percent sure that he was a stool for the cops. And then there's the secret group he was workin' with inside the First Men —"

"What secret group?" Tina asked. There was a deadness to the question, almost as if she didn't care if I answered.

"Conrad, Brawly, and Strong are the only ones I'm sure were in it. And whatever they were planning to do, it has to do with them guns Brawly and Conrad were hiding at BobbiAnne's."

Christina Montes was quiet for a moment then. She gazed out of the passenger's window at the stores on Central.

"They had me rent them a house," Tina said.

"What?"

"Brawly and Conrad. They had me rent them a house on One thirty-six."

"When?"

"Yesterday. Conrad gave me two hundred and fifty-five dollars."

"That almost proves it," I said.

"But you said that Henry was workin' for the cops," she said.

"Yeah," I said. "Whatever they plannin', I'm sure the police know their every move and that they plan to discredit your group."

"I don't believe it," Tina said.

"You should. I'm the only man tellin' you the truth."

"It's too crazy. Why would they go to all that trouble?"

"To make it look like you're crazy killer criminals. To have people, both black and white, happy when you get run down like dogs and thrown into prison for the rest of your lives."

There I was, the conservative veteran explaining a campaign of subterfuge to a revolutionary.

"Where's the house you rented at?" I asked.

"I . . . I don't know if I should say."

"What you should do," I said, "is give me the address, pack up your boy Xavier, and haul outta town. Go to San Diego or 'Frisco. Anywhere but here."

"You're just trying to scare me."

"Why'd you wait for me to come this morning, Tina?"

"Because . . . because you asked me to."

"That means in some way you trust me, right? I mean, you trusted me to come. You trusted me not to bring the cops."

"No," she said, in a rather peculiar tone. I turned my head and saw that she had a small pistol pointed at the side of my chest.

"You plan to shoot me?" I asked her.

"You're the one who's been against us the whole time," she said. "You killed Henry and probably Brawly's father, too. Henry called me to ask me what you had said at the meeting, before the cops came. I told him that you'd talked to Clarissa and she gave me your number. When I was in jail I started thinkin' about it. Henry was going to see you the night he was killed. That's why I agreed to meet you."

"To kill me?"

The fact that she didn't answer caused sweat to sprout on my brow.

"What do you plan to do?" I asked her.

"Just drive."

We were still headed south on Central, in the Sixties. I took a deep breath through my nose and gritted my teeth.

I had been in some tough situations in my life, with and without Mouse. And I knew that it wasn't in the hardest moment that you were likely to lose your life. A small girl with a baby gun might not have frightened most men. But I realized that she could kill me or bring me to my death just as easily as the recently deposed champion, Sonny Liston, could knock my head off.

"So, you been a part of the secret group the whole time?" I asked.

"No, Conrad and them just told me when we got outta jail," she said. "They told me about you. Conrad told me how you brought Henry out to Compton and shot him in the back of the head."

"Yeah?" I said. "And how would Conrad know that?"

"He saw you. He was hiding in the house. He said that you

must'a fooled him to get him to bring you to where they were meeting, just like you fooled me an' Xavier into gettin' arrested."

"So then they told you to kidnap me?"

"No," Tina said with a sneer. "You called on me. I would have stayed away from you, but you stuck your nose out once too often."

"So now you're in with the gang," I said. "Now you plan to use those guns Brawly and Conrad stole."

"Those guns are only for self-defense."

"Does Xavier know all this, too?"

"No. They only told me. Xavier's nonviolent. He didn't even have bullets in his gun the night you saw him."

"That's why you were layin' up in Strong's bed?" I asked. "Because you needed a man who could resort to violence?"

"You don't know a thing about me," she said from the spleen. "I do what I have to do."

"Did your friends kill Aldridge Brown?" I asked.

"For all I know, you and your cop friends killed him, too."

We were down around Ninetieth Street. A futile plan was all I had. My old house was on 116th. I still owned it. My friend Primo lived there for free.

"Where are we going?" I asked.

"Keep driving," she said.

Two green lights and four red ones later we came to the signal at 116th. It was turning amber when I was maybe three feet from the crosswalk. I gunned the engine to make the light and then suddenly cut across traffic to make a left turn. I used my left hand to steer and with my right I hit Tina in the head much harder than a man should ever strike a woman. Her head hit the window and made a small cracking sound. I hoped that it was glass I was hearing as I sped past the blasting horns toward the deep driveway and front yard of my old house.

Primo was sitting on the porch with his ebony-colored Panamanian wife, Flower. Around them were babies and children, some theirs, some their children's children.

"Easy," my old friend shouted.

"Come on over here, man," I cried.

*W*E CARRIED THE UNCONSCIOUS WOMAN into the house while Spanish-speaking babies and infants capered around us, wanting to be a part of the game. Tina's skull had broken the glass, but she didn't seem all that damaged. While Flower set her in the bed, I rummaged through her purse.

She was the same kind of liar that I had always been — she lied by telling the truth about something distracting while coming to her own conclusion. The only problem was that her conclusions about me were wrong.

Still, she had the receipt for the house she rented on 136th. The landlord, Jaguar Realty, had offices on Crenshaw.

*O*UTSIDE THE HOUSE Primo and I stood by my car. I was smoking a cigarette while he puffed on a slender cigar.

Primo was shorter than I was and broad in both the shoulders and hips. He was a thick man, but the only fat on him was around his belly. He had a full mane of black hair that hid a portion of his forehead and true-black eyes that were usually filled with mirth — but I had seen them when they were honed down to a killing glint.

He was serious that day, but his eyes still smiled.

"She tried to kill you?" he asked me.

"Kidnap me is more like it," I said. "Take me to some men who would like to do me in."

"What men?"

"Revolutionaries," I said. "Like Zapata."

"Oh," Primo said. "Good men for storybooks but you don't want to be around them when they're alive."

I chuckled and then I laughed. Primo laughed with me for a while.

"Can you keep her here a day or two?" I asked him. "Sleeping?"

"Sure," he said with no conflict, consideration, or question as to why. "I'll call you if I need to."

We shook hands and said good-bye.

42 / *THE HOUSE THAT* Christina Montes rented from Jaguar Realty was in the center of the block of a very residential street. There was no nearby nook where a spy could hide and survey them.

There was an alley at the end of the block. I backed in there, partially hidden by a stand of miniature evergreens that the last house had put in to hide the alley from view. I watched the white and blue two-story house and smoked cigarettes.

I'd been at my post for over an hour when Conrad cruised up in his Cadillac. Brawly was with him and so was BobbiAnne. Another man got out of the car, but I didn't recognize him.

I tried to imagine what was going on inside. Not the mischief they were planning, but the surroundings they were planning it in. There was no indication on the rental receipt that the house was furnished. So they must be in a big empty room, sitting on the floor, surrounded by food containers and bottles. Maybe the guns were stacked in a corner. Their plan was probably tacked up on the wall so they could all see it while they drilled the operation, whatever that was, over and over.

Because the rooms were empty, their voices would make a slight echo, lending to the fervor of their convictions. There was no phone or television but there was probably a radio. Would they be listening to music? I doubted it. The dial was probably turned to a news-oriented station. They were worried about being found out and also wondering where Tina was. Did they know that she was going to bring me to them the same way that Strong brought me to the construction site in Compton? Was she involved with the killing of Strong? No. There was love for him in her voice. She loved both the older and younger leaders.

"What you doin' here, man?" a voice said from behind.

I wasn't worried. If it was one of the revolutionaries, I would have already been either dead or unconscious.

The man who spoke was short and wore matching ochre pants and shirt. He had a protruding belly and small hands with stubby fingers. Only his voice held any kind of threat.

"Hey," I said, sticking out my hand. "I'm Troy. This your house?"

"Yes, it is," the little man replied. He took my hand out of reflex but let it go before I could complete the perfunctory shake.

"You must be wonderin' what I'm doin' out here," I said.

"Yes," the little man said.

"It's 'cause'a my girl — Royetta."

"I don't know any Royetta."

"She's my girl," I said again. "At least that's what she tells me. But I heard from Lucas that she been seein' a man on this block. Yeah, every day, Lucas said, she drive down to this block to see some man. He didn't have the address, so I decided to come down and use these here nice trees of yours so that she didn't see me or my car when she come down to meet her sidetrack."

It felt good to be lying again. It was as if I disappeared behind a cloud of black ink like the squid or cuttlefish.

The man I spoke to was muddy brown with many folds in his face. His head widened as it went toward his neck; with the folds, his head and face resembled a brown candle slowly melting down toward his shoulders.

"I don't want no trouble," the man told me. "This here is my property."

The alley was a public throughway and not his property, but I didn't say that.

"I don't want no trouble, either," I said. "But you see, Royetta got a sister named Cindy, and me and Cindy been messin' around ourselves. Now if I can prove to Royetta that I know about her man, then when I leave her and take up with Cindy she cain't get all that mad."

"Can't you just get your friend that . . . that —"

"Lucas," I said. "Lucas."

Out of the corner of my eye I saw a gold-colored Ford Galaxy drive past. I turned to my right to see where the car was headed.

"Can't Lucas just say that he saw her with this man and that'll be it?" the little man was saying.

But I was watching as Mercury Hall climbed out of his car and walked up to the revolutionaries' house.

"No," I said, returning to my fiction. "Lucas don't wanna get in between us where he's got to be there in the skin. No. I got to see for myself."

"Well," the little man said. "I don't want you here."

"I tell you what," I said. "What's your name?"

"Foreman."

"I'll tell you what, Foreman" — I reached into my pocket and came out with a twenty-dollar bill — "I'll give this here double saw-buck for the right to stand around in this public alley and look for my girlfriend to pass."

If he had turned me down, I would have driven down to the other end of the block, but Henry Strong's money was good. Foreman grabbed the twenty-dollar bill and shoved it in his pocket.

"How much longer you gonna be out here?" he asked.

"Two hours, tops," I said.

We talked a moment or two more and he retreated with his reward.

I WAS THERE for more than three hours when the tribe finally showed their faces again. Mercury took BobbiAnne in his Ford while Conrad climbed in the Cadillac with Brawly and the man I did not recognize. They drove right past me and off toward Central.

With them gone, I should have called John. I should have called the cops. I should have gone home and started Jesus's lessons and made it to bed early so the next morning I could get to work on time.

Instead, I walked straight to the hideout. I walked down the driveway and into the backyard. The back side of the home had a large porch that was walled in and had its own door. This door was unlocked. The porch contained a washing machine and dryer, modern luxuries down in the ghetto. There was a radio playing loud, too loud, so the sound of me forcing the lock might not have been heard if there had been anybody home to hear it.

The back entrance of the home was a slender hallway that was also the kitchen, small stove on one side, sink on the other.

I'd been right about the circumstances of the revolutionaries. The big living room was empty, except for white food cartons and paper plates used for ashtrays. There was a piece of blue-lined notebook paper tacked to the wall. Drawn in pencil was a square that stood for a building with a truck approaching and a car parked across the street from the door. Here and there X's were in position to over-power the guards.

It was a frightening document mainly because it looked like the notations of a grade-schooler playing cops and robbers on paper.

There were army duffel bags in the entranceway closet. There were toothbrushes and towels in the bathroom. And a stack of smut magazines hidden under the sink.

One of the canvas bags belonged to Brawly. He had a pair of black and white tennis shoes and a pocketknife along with two shirts, a copy of Hesse's *Steppenwolf*, and a small spiral-bound notebook. Just flipping through those pages told me more about Brawly than anyone else seemed to know.

It wasn't, strictly speaking, a diary, but every once in a while there was a journal-like entry with a date at the top of the page. The first such entry, which appeared on the third page of the two-hundred-sheet notebook, was dated January 19, 1958 — more than six years earlier.

He wrote about BobbiAnne and how he could see her only at school because he had to return to Sunrise House, the halfway home, by four P.M. He also wrote, *I miss Aunt Isolda but I know it's better if I don't see her. She only gets mad when I tell her how I feel. . . .*

The first thirty pages were in very dark blue ink from the same thick ballpoint pen. The next forty pages or so were in black. After that, he went back to blue pen. I was amazed that the young man could hold on to that one small notebook, each page covered with his tiny scrawl.

Along with his sporadic journal entries he had made small draw-ings of buildings, notes on school assignments, lists of resolutions on how to be a better man (a few of those were on how to be *friends* with Isolda), and sometimes there were simple reminders of where to go, what to buy, and what to say.

Less than six months earlier he had penned an entry separated halfway down the page. The top half was a list of requirements for service in the paratroopers. He had an ideal weight, number of pushups he should be able to do, and the reading level expected of new recruits. The bottom half seemed to be a comparison between superheroes. On the left side he'd listed Superman, Plastic Man, and Batman. On the right he had Thor, Mister Fantastic, and Spider-Man.

Three months later he was writing about the black revolution in America. Henry Strong had been giving him private instruction, telling him that his strength and intelligence had put a heavy weight of responsibility on his shoulders.

"It's up to us young men," Brawly wrote. "To lead the rest to freedom. We must be strong and willing to die for what's right."

A little later on he had received orders to "make contact with friends who could aid in the procurement of revolutionary funds and the maintenance of emergency refuge."

Brawly came from a very different generation than mine. He was intelligent and ambitious, where I had been crafty and happy if I made it through the day. I never questioned the white man's authority — that was a given.

But what really separated us was a need for love and his trust in people. He believed that there was a place for him and his in the world. I knew, from reading his words, that the only way to truly save him was to shatter this belief.

In one of the bedrooms there was a canvas cot with sheets and a pillow strewn across it. I imagined Conrad and BobbiAnne slipping away now and then to have sex on that cot. For some reason it reminded me of Isolda and her bedroom pictures. It was in that moment that I realized where those photographs had been taken.

I slipped out of the back door and walked across the street to my car.

43 / JESUS WAS SITTING on the front porch waiting for me when I got home. He'd already set up a place in the living room for me to sit while he stood and read.

"You could sit down, Juice," I said. "Forty-five minutes is a long time and I want you concentrating on the words, not your feet."

Jesus grinned. I had missed that grin. It was a brief thing, like sighting a rare scarlet bird in the deep woods. A flit of the wing and it was gone again.

I had gotten a large hardcover copy of *Moby-Dick* from the Robertson library for our first reading. While Feather and Bonnie puttered and played in the kitchen, Jesus read to me about Ishmael and his ill-fated voyage.

The reading was difficult. For many of the words he had to stop and use the *Webster's Dictionary* we kept under the coffee table. But when it was over I was surprised at Jesus's understanding of the story and its implications. We were twelve pages into his education and already we were a success.

Jackson called a few minutes after dinner. Jesus and Feather were working on the dishes while Bonnie hovered over them, making sure they didn't miss any spots.

"How's it goin', Easy?" he asked. Before I could answer he said, "I been workin' my butt off earnin' that two-fifty."

"All I need to know is about the payroll."

"Manelli pays his men once a month. It's always a Saturday payroll," Jackson said. He paused and then added, "Except for this week."

"What's that mean?"

"I went in to the assistant secretary, in the office bungalow, and made friends. She said that she was studyin' for her bookkeeper's two-year degree and I showed her how she could make a couple'a shortcuts in a year-end tax application with deductions."

I wasn't surprised that Jackson had studied accounting. Since he was both brilliant and a thief, it stood to reason that he'd study stealing from the inside out.

"After I was so helpful," Jackson continued, "I asked her if I could get a partial paycheck tomorrow because my rent was due and the landlord needed at least a li'l taste. She told me that maybe she could process it for Monday because they had heard that tomorrow's payday was going to have to be put off until Monday. She asked me not to tell nobody 'cause it was a secret. She was upset because she knew the men needed the money, especially since they had to balance everything on a once-a-month nut. I asked her why the delay, but she didn't know. I got an idea, though."

"What?"

"Well, Easy," he said, "I don't know what you into, but if the pay-

roll is switched secretly at the last minute, then it's got to be something big. You know them construction workers like to riot if they
don't get tomorrow's cash. I think it's a setup and I think you know
why."

"Thank you, Jackson," I said. "I'll bring your money by in a
couple'a days."

"What you into, Easy?" he asked. "You gonna start hittin' payrolls?"

"Jackson, how could you be so smart and so stupid at the same
time?"

I DROVE PAST the gang's hideout later that evening, but it looked
empty. I went in through the back porch. Everything but the food
containers had been cleared out — even the girly magazines were
gone.

BUT ISOLDA WAS AT HOME. She was still in her bathrobe, but
her hair was done and she had put on her makeup. I was carrying a small satchel that was open so I could get to my pistol quickly.

"Mr. Rawlins?" she said, looking down at the brown leather bag.
"What is it?"

"Can I come in?"

Her pouting lips curled back into a smile, but I felt nothing.
Young men respond to women purely by animal instinct. But in ma-
turity our minds are sometimes able to short-circuit those impulses.

We went to her window. Even though the sun was down, there
was a bright light shining in from a street sign. She poured me an
iced tea, which I put down on the jury-rigged, sheet-covered table.

"I'm surprised you came by again," she said.

"Why?" I asked. I was surveying the corners of the room. There didn't seem to be any place where a grown man could hide.

"You were so angry — you know, about me and Brawly."

"Yeah," I said, "Brawly. That's why I'm here."

"What about him?"

"Where is he?"

"I'm sure I don't know," she said, revealing from her choice of words that she was a daughter of the South.

"Oh yeah, baby," I said. "You know damn well where he is, or at least you know who knows. So let's not fuck around."

"Mr. Rawlins," she protested.

"I said, don't fuck with me, Issy. This is not the time to be coy. This is the time to talk turkey."

"What are you saying?"

"I'm sayin' that you are the one that holds it all together."

"Holds what together?"

"You're the one who knows everybody. Brawly," I said, holding up one finger, "Mercury —"

"I told you I only met him in passing."

"— Henry Strong," I said, putting up the third digit. "And you been with Aldridge on and off for years."

"Aldridge, yes," she said. "But I don't have anything to do with the other men."

"No," I said. "You were with Henry Strong. You met him through Brawly and you let him stay over a night or two. But he didn't know that Brawly told you everything. He didn't know that Brawly told you that he was planning a robbery just like his old man."

"You're crazy," Isolda said, and then she moved to stand.

"I already knocked out one woman today," I said. "And I liked her."

Hearing that, Isolda settled back down.

"Like I said," I continued, "Brawly told you what he was doin'
and I'll bet dollars to doughnuts that you found out that Henry was a
spy. He was going to run with you on the day before the robbery."

"That's crazy talk," Isolda said. She wouldn't even look in my direction.

"Your bikini says different."

She turned to me, the question in her eyes.

"I saw the pictures," I said. "You in a tan bikini on a bed that I
didn't come across for a few days. It didn't strike me at first, but then
I was in another bedroom and I remembered."

"What the hell are you saying?"

"Strong took pictures of you in his bedroom," I said. "I bet you
were modeling for him, practicing for how it was gonna be down in
the islands."

"Who told you that?" Issy's neck twitched.

"The same little bird who told me about Aldridge being Brawly's
uncle's partner in that robbery."

"What do you mean that Hank was a spy?" she asked.

"You didn't know?" I asked. And then, "Of course you didn't. If
you did, they'd've called off the robbery by now."

"What are you talking about?" Isolda said. By then they were just
words. She knew she was caught. Now she was just looking for the
way out.

"He fell for you and all," I said. "He was plannin' to run with
you, to get away forever down on the beach. But he didn't tell you
that he was a rat. No. Proud man like old Hank wouldn't do that."

"I don't know what you're talking about, Mr. Rawlins."

"No. But you got the idea. I can see that in your eyes," I said.
"Strong told you that you were leaving on the boat the day before the

job. For all he knew, you didn't know about the plans he'd made with Brawly and Conrad. He didn't have to tell you that he was a stool pigeon the whole time. He didn't have to tell you that he set up members of the First Men to hit a payroll, get caught in the act, and so discredit the whole organization."

My little speech made Isolda restless. I might not have been one hundred percent correct, but I had too much for her to dismiss me. She clasped her hands and turned her head from side to side. Then suddenly she hit a serious calm.

"What do you want?" she asked.

"I got the outline," I said. "What I need from you is to fill it in with names and addresses."

"And what do I get out of it?"

"First of all, I don't call up Hank's police masters and tell them that you're in on the plan. Second, I don't call John and tell him that you tried to frame Brawly for killing his father."

"I'm not afraid of that," she lied. "I'm innocent."

"No," I said. "You haven't been innocent since you were a schoolgirl. What you think is that you can run away. But that's wrong. If you don't tell me what I wanna know, I'ma hit you upside your head, tie you up like a hog, and drive you down to police headquarters in the trunk'a my car."

I wasn't lying and Isolda knew it. I didn't want to have to get so violent, but then again, this was the only chance I had to find out what was going on.

I must have impressed Isolda because she said, "And if you hear what you want, you gonna leave me be?"

"Let's hear what you got to say," I said.

Watching her was the most astonishing thing. The beauty just drained right out of her face. It was like a facade, a mask. Suddenly she was hard and angry — close to downright ugly.

"You were right about me an' Hank," she said. "The minute I saw him I knew that he was the man for me. He had that voice and knew how to dress. You know most'a the Negroes 'round here are country boys with holes in their jeans and shit on their shoes. They like it like that."

"But not Henry," I prodded.

"Brawly brought him by —"

"So you and Brawly still talked?"

"Of course we did. I was close as a mother to that boy. He'd get jealous when I had a man around. That's why him and Aldridge fought —"

"So that did happen?"

"Yeah," Isolda said. "Only it was just a push-fight. They were gettin' close again already. It was just the whiskey that made them mad."

"So what happened with Henry?"

"He said that he was tired of tryin' to fight for equal rights, that he'd been active in politics all these years and nuthin' was changin', not really. He said that he was gonna make a big deal and then go to a country where black men knew how to be bankers and presidents. He said he wanted me to be with him."

"He didn't tell you that his money was really comin' from the cops?"

"He didn't say nuthin' but that he was gonna make a deal. But now that you say it, it makes sense. You're right, I knew what was happenin' 'cause Brawly told me about it. Brawly tells me everything."

"What's Aldridge got to do with all this?"

"Brawly told him, too," Isolda whispered. "He knew that it was Aldridge with his uncle in that robbery all them years ago. That's why him and his daddy fought back then. He was mad at Aldridge 'cause he knew that Alva went crazy 'cause her brother died. For a long time he was mad but then he told Aldridge that he was gonna do the same thing. He was gonna rob a payroll."

There was a lull in the conversation then. Isolda was getting on thin ice and I was afraid to find out who might fall in with her.

Finally I asked, "So did Brawly do it?"

"No."

I couldn't help the smile on my face. Even if Isolda was lying, at least she was protecting Brawly.

"Who did?" I asked.

"Mercury."

I wasn't surprised. Mercury had the build for the kind of violence that was visited upon Aldridge.

I wasn't surprised but I asked, "How the hell did Mercury get in on it?"

"He was hangin' out with all of us. And one day I found cotton panties with that little bitch Tina Montes's name written in 'em — in Hank's bottom drawer."

"Oh."

"He didn't put no ring on my finger, so when he'd tell me he was too busy or he was tired, I'd call Mercury and get him to come by."

"So you told Mercury about the robbery?"

"Naw. He was already in it. Brawly told Hank about Mercury and he asked him to help us plan it. Then Merc found out that Aldridge was makin' noise that he wouldn't let Brawly be part of any robbery. He told me to ask him to my house so they could talk, alone."

"So you were in on the plan to kill him," I accused.

"No. I wasn't even in town. I was in Riverside, like I said. I didn't know what Merc was gonna do."

"What you think he was gonna do?"

"Talk," she complained. "Like he said. But after . . . after he told me that Aldridge attacked him. It was self-defense."

"And was Henry Strong self-defense, too?"

"I told Merc that Henry planned to run. I had to. Henry wouldn't let me in on what they was doin'. He wanted to take me away but he didn't wanna get married. What would I do if he left me high and dry in Jamaica?"

"So what was I doin' there?" I asked her.

"Mercury told Henry that you were followin' Brawly and Conrad. He said that he wanted to beat you up bad enough that you'd lay off until the job was over. Then he told Conrad that Henry and you was gonna throw 'em ovah."

"So they planned to kill me, too?"

Isolda looked away.

44 / *"WHERE'S BRAWLY?"* I asked, just to see what she would say.

"I don't know."

"If you in on the plan, then why wouldn't you know?"

"They were all shaken up with the bust and you nosin' around. With all that heat, they went into hiding," she said. "Mercury said that he was gonna come to me after it was all over. He said that we'd go down to Texas and split his share."

The fact that she could say those words amazed me. I just stared at her, wondering how she could get so deep into evil and not seem to have any remorse at all.

"What?" she asked. "What?"

"Why did Strong want to get in with Mercury in the first place?" I asked. "I mean, he's no race man."

"Henry didn't talk to me about that. He didn't even know that I knew anything," Isolda said. "But Brawly told me that he was inter-ested in the construction business from the beginning. He talked to him about payrolls and the police. And when he heard that Mercury and Chapman specialized in payrolls, Hank said that he wanted to meet them."

I just shook my head.

"It's not like you think," she said. "I'm just tryin' to make it."

"By turnin' Brawly in?"

"I was tryin' to save him."

"Save him how? By blamin' him for murder?"

"I only said that. I knew he had a alibi. He was with me. He the one drove me up to Riverside. All kindsa people saw us. I thought that if I told John and Alva that he might'a killed Aldridge, that they would have taken him away or somethin'. I didn't want him messed up with Merc an' them. I knew that it'd be dangerous."

"Why was Brawly with them in the first place?"

"He thought that they were raising money for the First Men," she said. "That they were going to use it to build their school."

"Where's Brawly?" I asked again.

"I don't know. They in hidin', like I told you. They was in a house down Watts but they got scared because that bitch Tina was supposed to show up but she never did. They thought that you must'a grabbed her or somethin'."

"Then they called off the robbery?"

"They never told her about what they were doin'," Isolda said. "They asked me to rent 'em a house, but I said no. I didn't want to be tied to no robbery. So they got her to do it, but she didn't know why."

"If you know where they ain't, then why don't you know where they are?" I asked.

"I don't," she whined. "They broke up and went into hidin'. All they told me was that they was gonna take refuge, that was somethin'

Strong used to talk about. They only gonna come out when it's time to do the job."

For some time I had wanted to slap Isolda Moore across her face. The desire became stronger as the minutes went by. Finally I stood up. The suddenness of my motion scared her enough that she pushed back and fell over in her chair.

I didn't help her to her feet.

"You better run, woman," I said. "Because I'm not gonna let that robbery take place. And when they catch your boy Mercury, you better believe he's gonna turn over on you."

*D*OWN ON THE STREET and in my car I didn't know what to do. I had solved a crime that nobody asked me to solve. It wasn't my job to catch murderers or foil robberies. All I had to do was keep Brawly out of trouble. But that was impossible because he was in trouble before I was called in.

I drove in circles, wondering what I should do. I was afraid to go to John because he might have put his own life on the line trying to save the boy. Lakeland was planning to catch them in the commission of the crime, I was sure of that. He would clean out the problem by setting them up.

Tina wouldn't have talked to me; neither would Xavier.

*C*LARISSA WAS AT SAM'S HOUSE but she refused to come to the phone.

I finally decided to go over to John's lots. Him and Chapman were working on the support for the front porch of a faux-adobe house. It struck me as senseless to be working while so much wrong was going on. How could those men still lift their hammers, knowing that their best friends and loved ones had gone so far astray?

"Easy," Chapman said, seeing me first.

"Ken, John."

"What you want, Easy?" John's tone was exasperated, as if he were Job in one more conflict with the Deity.

"What's wrong with you?" I said.

"Alva's in the hospital."

"What's happened?"

"Nerves. They got her under sedation, she so worried about Brawly and upset over Aldridge."

"I'm sorry, John. I just tried to do what you asked me to do."

That got me a hard look. John's fists clenched, his shoulders hunched. Chapman took a step backward. But John wasn't going to hit me. He knew I was right.

"I came by to ask you men some questions," I said.

"What?" Chapman asked.

"I'm lookin' for Brawly. I think he might'a run to ground somewhere for the day and part of the night. You got any idea where he could be?"

"If I knew, I'd be there," John said.

Chapman looked at the ground.

"Yeah?" I asked.

"I don't know nuthin' 'bout Brawly, Ease," he said. "I'd tell you if I did."

I had no idea if Chapman was lying to me or not. For all I knew, he and Mercury were in the heist together. They'd been partners for years, since they were children.

I had no idea what their childhood was like, so an image from my own early years crossed my mind. My mother was dead and my father was gone. My older half sister and half brother had been taken away to live with cousins on their mother's side in El Paso. I had been passed on to a man named Skyles. He had been married to one of my mother's sisters and owned a farm. He took me on to be his slave.

Skyles worked me from sunup to sundown and then fed me only the scraps from his nightly supper. After three weeks I decided to run away. I made up my mind on a Tuesday, but the train I had to jump didn't go by till Thursday night. I stole a full sack of Skyles's food and hid in an abandoned barn across the road from his house.

Those two nights I watched him through the loose boards yellin' and smashin' his own things — he was that mad that I stole from him and ran.

"Walk with me, John," I said to my friend.

We went out to my car in the street.

"Lemme have the keys to your apartment," I said.

"Why?"

"Don't ask me, man. Just trust me."

He hesitated for a moment and then produced a steel ring that held dozens of keys. He removed a brass Sergeant and handed it over.

I took the key to my car and drove it over to John's.

I FOUND THE NUMBER in John's little phone book in the top drawer of their bureau. I dialed it. He answered on the second ring.

"Hello?" The voice was breathy but brooding. I could almost see the taciturn young man's face in the words.

"Rita there?" I asked in a voice that, I hoped, sounded nothing like mine.

"Wrong number," he said, and then slammed down the phone.

I HADN'T BEEN to Odell's house in over a year. His wife, Maudria, had passed sixteen months earlier. I had gone to the funeral and then to their house to eat salami sandwiches and sit with Odell.

He was near seventy but didn't look much older than he had twenty years before. He was just softer and a little shorter — his ears were larger, too.

"Easy," he said through the brittle screen door. "How you doin'?"

"Fine."

He studied me for a moment and then said, "Come on in."

The house had become a mausoleum. The heavy brown drapes were drawn. The furniture was neat and for the most part unused. There was the smell of mothballs and scotch whiskey in the air.

He escorted me to a pitted maple table next to the sink in the kitchen. The unwashed windows allowed only a small amount of sunlight in, but it was enough. He poured me a glass of lemonade made from frozen concentrate and took out a bottle of scotch for himself.

"How you doin'?" I asked my oldest living friend.

"Oh, okay," he said. "Not too much. Like Maudria used to say, no news is good news."

"You goin' out?" I asked. "Seein' anybody?"

"No. Ain't nobody to see. You know when you get to be my age everybody's dyin'. Dyin' or dead. If I walk out that door wearing jeans and with bus money in my pocket, it means I'm goin' to the hospital to visit a friend. If I'm in a suit, it means a funeral."

We talked like that for a while. Odell kept quoting his dead wife or talking about funerals and disease. I was sad to see my old friend so broken-down. I wondered about Brawly while we talked. If I saved the boy, would he end up like my friend? Sad and broken-down at the end of his life?

"Well, you didn't come by to hear me complain," Odell said. "What can I do for you, Easy?"

"I need a pair of your thin cotton huntin' gloves and that rabbit gun," I said.

"What for?"

"Somethin' Mouse told me," I said. "In a dream."

He nodded as if my answer were perfectly reasonable.

I explained about John and Alva and the wayward Brawly Brown.

"Brawly's big as a grizzly bear," I was saying, "and at least as strong. There's no way I can stop him or force him. I don't believe that John and I together could hold him down. So I need you to do one more thing for me."

Odell took one more shot of scotch while I sipped on my lemonade. After our drink he got my gloves and rifle. The gun was all broken down in a leather case. I gave him the phone number with a little speech I wanted him to recite at seven-thirty.

I PARKED OUT BACK in an alley behind the empty office building next to the used-car lot and across the street from John's building. I jimmied open the back door and then forced my way into an office on the third floor. That was 6:35.

I opened the window and sat there in the twilight thinking that Mouse was advising me even after he was gone.

I thought about him and Etta, about their crazy life. There was no rancor or condemnation in my thoughts. We had all made it by sheer dumb luck. Any poor black child of the South who woke up in the morning was lucky if he lived to make it to bed that night. You were bound to be beaten, stabbed, and shot at least once or twice. The question wasn't if you were going to get killed, it was, were you going to get killed on that particular day?

"Easy," Mouse would say to me. "You know you just too sensi-tive. You think that you can keep somethin' bad from happenin' here or there. But that kinda power ain't in your reach. It was all settled a long time ago. What happens with you — when you get borned, when you die, who you kill, who kills you — that was all writ down in your shoes and your blood. Shit. You be walkin' down the road outside'a Pariah, hopin' that New Orleans is just beyond that yonder stand of live oaks. But it ain't. No, baby, you want it, you want it bad, but there's just more swamp after them trees, and more swamp after that."

My respect for Raymond was intense because he never worried about or second-guessed the world around him. He might have got-ten tired now and then, but he never gave up. When I thought about that, I knew I had to go search out his grave.

*A*T 7:15 *I PUT MY WATCH* on the windowsill and opened Odell's gun case. That .25-caliber rabbit gun was his pride and joy. I screwed in the barrel and fit the cherrywood stock into place. The best part of his rifle was its telescopic sight. Back when I first came to L.A., Odell would go out hunting and come back with enough rab-bits to feed Maudria, him, and me — and two or three others be-sides.

I filled the magazine and pointed the muzzle through the win-dow at the front door. I held that pose, glancing at the Gruen now and then. At 7:30 I knew that Odell was making the call.

"The cops!" Odell would have yelled. "The cops comin'!" And then he'd hang up.

At 7:32 the door swung open. Brawly came lumbering out with a large paper bag in his arms. When he turned back to the open door, I fired the first shot. He yelled in pain and fell to the ground. I fired

again. From the open door Conrad emerged. He screamed something and made to grab Brawly by his arm. I fired again. That bullet
missed Conrad. He was so scared that he dropped the bag he was carrying and fled down the street.

I raised my sight to the upper floor. John came out. When he saw
the prostrate boy, he ran for the stairs. I had never seen John run before.

I turned over on my back, broke down the rifle, packed it away,
and headed for the stairs. Within minutes I was in my car and driving back to my own home and my own children.

45 / JESUS READ TO ME from *Moby-Dick* and Feather bragged on her good math test. Bonnie served me reheated lamb shank in a cognac gravy, and I started on chores that I'd ignored for days.

No one called. There was going to be a robbery in the morning, but there was nothing I could do about that.

Before I went to bed I called Primo.

"Hey, Easy. How you doing?"

"How's the girl?" I asked.

"Still a little dizzy," he replied. "Flower been giving her a special tea that makes her sleep."

"You can stop that in the morning," I said.

———

*E*ASY?" *BONNIE ASKED*, lying there next to me. I was staring at the ceiling, wondering if I'd get a wink.

"Yeah?"

"Did you finish with that business about Alva's son?"

"Yeah. Finished."

"Is he in trouble?"

"Not no more he ain't."

"John is really lucky to have a friend like you."

"Yeah," I said. "Lucky as a prize pig after the county fair."

I HEARD IT on the radio at ten-thirty. Three black men and one white woman had gotten into a shootout with the city police and county sheriffs in Compton. The unidentified men were attempting to rob a payroll delivery for the Manelli Construction Company. They tried to run the armored car off the road, but little did they know that the authorities had been tipped off and the car was filled with armed officers. The would-be robbers had all died while still in their vehicle. The officers had opened fire when it became obvious that they were threatened by the sideswiping car.

I remembered the plans tacked to the wall in the thieves' temporary hideout. They hadn't planned to ram the payroll car. They were going to overpower the guards on their way to the office.

*A*T WORK THAT AFTERNOON I sat down to an Underwood typewriter and composed a letter to Teaford Lorne, captain of a special anticrime unit. In my unsigned letter I told him about Lakeland and Knorr and the extra-special police unit set up to take down the Urban Revolutionary Party. I sent copies of that letter to the regional office of the NAACP, the *Los Angeles Examiner*, and the mayor's office.

I never read about it in the newspaper, but three weeks after I sent those letters I drove by Lakeland's onetime headquarters. The building was up for lease. Maybe they had planned to close up shop after the killing of Mercury and his gang. Maybe I should have done more to bring their crime to the public eye, but I couldn't think of a thing that wouldn't have put my own family in danger.

*T*WO MONTHS LATER I took my little brood over to John's new house in Compton. He had invited us for a late-afternoon Sunday supper. Everybody on John's side of the table was convalescing. He had wrenched his back from falling off the roof of the very house we were eating in. He had been putting up the last touch, the television antenna, when he lost his balance and fell.

Alva was just two weeks out of the mental ward in the hospital. When we'd gotten to the house she was still in her bathrobe, with her hair going all over the place. Bonnie and Feather took her into the bedroom and when they came out she was dressed and brushed and made up. The only wear you could see was in her pained gaze.

Brawly still had a limp from where he'd been shot in the thigh and buttock. John had rushed him to the hospital and stayed with him for two days.

"How's L.A.C.C.?" I asked the boy.

"Good," he said. "They got me finishin' my high school courses. I'ma start college history classes next semester."

It was a simple meal, made by Sam Houston and delivered by Clarissa, who couldn't stay because she was due to work for her cousin that afternoon. Chicken and dumplings with a cranberry-orange relish and country salad.

Jesus told John all about his boat and his plans to travel up and down the Pacific Coast. He said that he was going to live off the ocean, eating fish and seaweed the way his friend Taki Takahashi's father said they did when their grandparents first came to America. It was more than he had ever told me.

"The minister says that prayer erodes the grip of sin in the world," Alva said at one point. She'd been reading her Bible every day while John and Chapman finished off his lot.

*A*FTER DINNER JOHN AND I went outside for a smoke. For a long time we just stared out at the sky. He was leaning against the front wall because of the injury and I was sitting on the stair.

"Nice house," I said after a few minutes of silence.

"Yep."

"You say you still workin' with Chapman?" I asked.

John looked at me then. "Yeah. Why?"

"Oh. I don't know. I mean with Mercury all messed up in that robbery attempt . . . I don't know . . . I thought you might wanna let him loose."

"He didn't have nuthin' to do with it."

"He tell you that?"

"Brawly told me," John said.

"Oh." It was the first time John had hinted that he knew anything about Brawly's dealings with Mercury and the crew.

"He was in on it," John continued. "Alva was right about them people he was runnin' with."

"I guess the man who shot him that day saved his life."

"They could'a killed him," John said. "As it is, he's gonna limp for the rest of his life. Doctor said that that bullet in his buttock came within half a inch from his main nerve."

"Better lame than dead," I said.

A harsh note escaped John's lips. Someone who didn't know him might have mistaken it for a cry of derision, but I recognized coarse humor in his tone.

"What about Isolda?" I asked.

"What about her?"

"Brawly still in touch?"

"He said she left L.A. The police were lookin' to talk to her about Aldridge, and she asked him for bus money for down South."

John pushed himself into a standing position and lurched up past me. He stopped at the door.

"You a good friend, Easy Rawlins," he said. "But if I had my druthers, I'd never have to call on you again."

He went into the house and I stayed outside, smoking in the desert twilight.

ABOUT THE AUTHOR

Walter Mosley is the author of the acclaimed Easy Rawlins series of mysteries, including national bestsellers *Cinnamon Kiss*, *Little Scarlet*, and *Bad Boy Brawly Brown*; the Fearless Jones series, including *Fearless Jones* and *Fear Itself*; the novels *Blue Light* and *RL's Dream*; and two collections of stories featuring Socrates Fortlow, *Always Outnumbered, Always Outgunned*, for which he received the Anisfield-Wolf Book Award, and *Walkin' the Dog*. He was born in Los Angeles and lives in New York.